# DEADLY
## COINCIDENCE

# DEADLY
# COINCIDENCE

An Adam Grant Novel

## GENE HELVESTON

MARLI BAR PRESS | INDIANAPOLIS

**MarLi Bar Press**
Indianapolis, Indiana

Names:   Helveston, Eugene M., 1934– author.
Title:   Deadly Coincidence / an Adam Grant novel / Gene Helveston.
Description:   First edition. | Indianapolis : MarLi Bar Press, [2019] | Book 3 in the Adam Grant series. |
Identifiers:   ISBN: 978-0-9972230-4-0 | LCCN: 2019906536
Subjects:     LCSH: Murder—Cuba_Fiction. | Cuba—Fiction. | Criminal investigation—Cuba—Fiction. | Homicide investigation—Cuba—Fiction. | Criminal investigation—International cooperation—Fiction. | Hydrocodone—Fiction. | Opioid abuse—United States—Fiction. | United States—Politics and government—Fiction. | BISAC: FICTION / Crime.
Classification:    LCC: PS3608.E39252 O65 2019 | DDC: 813/.6—dc23

Printed in the United States of America
First Printing

Cover and text design by Mary Jo Zazueta
tothepointsolutions.com

*To my grandchildren:*
*Henry, Charlie, Caroline, and Fred*

# DEADLY

## COINCIDENCE

# ONE

**J**im Cappelletti and Brad Pletcher left the FBI's Detroit field office almost an hour ago. Cappelletti drove while Pletcher, the senior agent with ten years on the job, navigated. They were in a quiet residential neighborhood when Pletcher announced that, according to Google Maps, the address they were looking for was in the next block. As they drove past well-maintained homes, Pletcher thought about the difficult job they had to do, one that never got any easier.

Five minutes later, Pletcher and his partner mounted the steps at 1432 Heather Way in Ann Arbor. With the kind of dread that never lessened, Brad pressed the doorbell. In less than a minute, they heard agitation on the other side of a solid, vibrant-red, wood door. With no window or peephole, it was a bastion of safety—although not for long.

The door swung open to reveal a pleasant woman who looked to be just shy of retirement age. Her happy countenance instantly shifted to a look of puzzlement and concern when she saw two official-looking men on her doorstep in the middle of the afternoon when her husband was out of town.

The FBI agents stood on the porch, just outside the threshold. The one who was clearly senior said, "Mrs. Jane Rodriguez?"

"Yes."

"My name is Brad Pletcher. And this is Agent Cappelletti. May we come in?" So far, he had never had anyone say no. There would be a time, but it was not today.

The slight, athletic-looking woman nodded, murmured a barely audible assent, and bid them to enter. Once inside, Agent Pletcher asked, "Is there a place where we can sit for a moment?" The news Brad was going to deliver should not be offered with the recipient standing. Even though requesting they sit did nothing but portend trouble, there was no other way when devastating news was to be delivered. The only uncertainty now was how bad the encounter would be.

They sat. The two men were side by side on a settee, their shoulders almost touching. They were positioned slightly forward on the cushioned seats, in anticipation. The woman sat in a chair opposite in a similar posture. Agent Pletcher spoke. "Mrs. Rodriguez, we have sad news about your husband, Dr. Michael Rodriguez. He was found dead in his hotel room this morning, by his friend Dr. Alejandro Rivera. The initial report from the FBI, who responded after Dr. Rivera contacted the American Consular Office, is that Dr. Rodriguez was found in the bathroom, where he sustained a head injury. We don't know if your husband's death preceded the fall or if he fell from another cause and then hit his head. The answer can be determined only after further examination."

You mean *autopsy*, was the woman's unspoken reply, as her face turned ashen. Stifling a sob, she moaned in disbelief. "My husband had successful heart surgery two years ago, but he took good care of himself, and his doctor said he was now a healthy man. How could this have happened? I don't understand. Oh, my God. Why did this happen? What can I do? I told him not to go." She put her face in her hands and began to cry with great, heaving sobs.

There was nothing else the men could do except remain seated while the doctor's wife regained some measure of control. Protocol in a case like this was to assist Mrs. Rodriguez in marshalling her immediate support system and to stay with her until she had withstood the initial shock and arranged for someone responsible to be with her. The men knew there were two married children who lived in other cities, and that both the doctor and Mrs. Rodriguez had siblings, but none lived nearby. Pletcher and Cappelletti could only assume there was a friend or neighbor who could help.

"Is there someone you would like us to call?" asked Jim Cappelletti.

"Yes," said Jane Rodriguez. Cautiously making her first decision as a widow, she stood on shaking legs and walked over to a small desk to retrieve her cell phone. She handed it to Agent Cappelletti and said, "Please, call Dottie Plaice. Her name is in the contacts. Ask her if she can come over. I will call my children and the rest of the family when I get myself together, or I might ask Dottie to do it. I will feel better with her here." This was followed by a stream-of-consciousness recitation of the pedestrian concerns of a person overwhelmed and totally unprepared for the responsibility she now faced. "How will I get him home? Who should I call for arrangements? What about his patients?"

"All of this will be taken care of, Ma'am; and we will be here to help you in any way we can," reassured Brad Pletcher.

The men knew that the couple's son and his family lived in Chicago and their daughter and her family lived in Kansas City. From what the agents had learned in the few hours they had to gather information after they received this assignment, it seemed there were no other immediate and regular responsibilities Mrs. Rodriguez faced beyond being a wife and homemaker along with several volunteer activities. The two FBI agents would remain with Mrs. Rodriguez until her friend arrived and the essential telephone calls were made to her children.

After Dottie arrived, the situation stabilized. The men offered to leave, saying they would return in the morning with more details. In response, Jane said that wouldn't be necessary. "I would like you to tell me everything you know now. It will be hard, but it won't get any easier. I never wanted him to go there. I'm sorry, that's not your concern. I appreciate what you are doing. Please, tell me all that you can."

Brad Pletcher spoke. "Mrs. Rodriguez, the only solid information given to us is that your husband was in Havana as part of a teaching program at Raul Mesa Carreras Eye Hospital. He had been there nine days, completed his duties, and was scheduled to return home on Saturday. This information was supplied by Dr. Alejandro Rivera, who discovered your husband and was the person who contacted the authorities. Dr. Rivera said he was a longtime friend of your husband's. I suspect he is a person you know and trust." The wife nodded assent.

"Good. We were told this was your husband's fourth trip to Havana, where he taught and provided care as a volunteer. Dr. Rivera said your husband worked with several doctors there, who he had remained close to since his first visit; especially three young women he was mentoring. With his obligation at the hospital fulfilled, your husband planned to remain in Cuba three additional days to learn more about the country's medical-education programs and its export health care industry. He was eager to visit clinics used for medical tourism, that offered a variety of questionable methods to treat patients, including people who were diagnosed with terminal illnesses and those interested in low-cost elective surgeries, especially for cosmetic purposes."

Now steadier, Jane Rodriguez said, "I knew Michael's plans for the last part of the trip, and that was what worried me most. Michael had an unpleasant experience with a group of government officials during his last visit. It dealt with something as simple as internet connections for telemedicine. He got nowhere with these discussions. He told me the people he dealt with all wore uniforms, but he was not sure what they represented. He said they were unbending in their views and were 'masters at deflection.' I remember those were his words. He told me he made no progress with the telemedicine project he was proposing. I can't think of anything else he told me that might be important for you to know."

"We know your husband was staying at the Hotel Sevilla, which you probably already knew," Pletcher continued. "We obtained most of the information about Dr. Rodriguez from the international NGO he was representing. We understand that Doctors for a Better World sends teams in a variety of specialties, including family medicine, to assist people in medically underserved countries. They considered your husband to be one of the best."

Before visiting the Rodriguez home, Brad Pletcher had called the offices of Doctors for a Better World to deliver the devastating news. The organization, which was headquartered in New York City, said they had not been contacted by anyone from the Cuba team, and the call from Agent Pletcher was the first they had heard of the doctor's death. The director asked Pletcher how they should handle this and whether they should make a public announcement. The FBI man told the director it would be in the best interests of the ongoing investigation to hold off on saying anything and to refrain from contacting the Cuban authorities or the hospital where Dr. Rodriguez had been volunteering until it was cleared by the FBI. Pletcher explained they did not want to raise any alarm before there were more facts.

The current flap about bizarre health complaints from several U.S. Embassy personnel, well covered in the media, had resulted in the withdrawal of many Embassy staff and a temporary travel ban was put in place for American tourists. The FBI and government wanted to manage this issue with extra care.

Jane Rodriguez said, "Of course, I knew where he was staying. That was always the first thing he did when he went on a trip like this—tell me about his hotel and how to contact him. After the first night, he would call me if there was something important. It turned out he called most days but not every day. I was not alarmed when he missed a day because I always received at least one text message from him."

"When did you last speak with your husband?" asked Jim Cappelletti, who knew that anyone could have used the doctor's cell phone to send a text message.

"He called me yesterday afternoon before dinner. It was about four o'clock. He mentioned the team dinner he had attended the night before. He said he stayed out later than he wanted because the group was traveling together. My husband was not a night owl. He believed it was important to get proper rest when he was working hard, like he did on these trips. Michael was funny about that—no, not funny—conscientious is more like it. He thought a surgeon should enter the operating room rested and ready to perform at his very best. He compared this to an airline pilot who he expected would behave the same way. My guess is that he would have turned in early last night, as he prepared for his visits to the health facilities with Alejandro."

"Did your husband say where he ate the night before, or who he was with?"

"Not really. He made it sound like he was with a large group, including both the volunteer team members and doctors and staff from the host hospital. He said the meal was family-style with lots of chicken and rice ... that was all he said about the evening."

"Did he say where he intended to have dinner last night?" asked Brad. "Or did he say anything else about his immediate plans?"

"Nothing special. He had called me as soon as he returned to his hotel after finishing at the hospital. He told me he would be ordering room service and turning in early. Well, maybe there was something. I could hear his room phone ringing as we were talking. Michael said he would say goodbye and get the call. If it was important, he would call me back. That's it. He said, 'I love you, goodbye.'"

"Nothing more?"

"Nope. That's it. He said, 'I'll get this call. I love you. Sleep well, I'll be home soon.' That is how it ended ... our life together ... after thirty-four years and two beautiful children ..."

Jane Rodriguez slumped in a chair while Dottie stood over her and stroked her friend's head. Dottie told Jane she would stay with her as long as necessary; the woman knew that meant for the night and maybe longer. She would make the necessary calls and, most important, just be there for her friend. Dottie told the agents she expected that at least one of the children would arrive tomorrow.

# TWO

**W**hen the man entered, Eduardo Sanchez hung the closed sign in the window of his shop in Old Town Havana. It was nearly 9:00 p.m. Eduardo looked at Luis, who stood just inside the entry of the partially darkened shop. Luis was a large man whose aspect was now clouded by a look of concern. An observer making a snap judgment would be correct in recognizing the man was distressed. To those who knew him, he was strong; willing; and, for the most part, could be trusted to follow orders. But he was not a person you expected to be in on the planning or to demonstrate initiative. He was broad-shouldered and stood over six feet tall. His physical presence and menacing countenance were assets when it came to carrying out certain unpleasant tasks for Eduardo. Based on what Luis had just done, Eduardo decided his reckless act must be dealt with immediately. Eduardo frequently employed the man for jobs that were unpleasant, potentially dangerous, and until, now closely supervised.

What Luis had done today was stupid; there was no conceivable way to justify his actions. It was an error that would threaten both men unless dealt with in a timely way. And when Luis announced over the phone to Eduardo what he had done, that was just another example of the man's poor judgment.

Luis's immediate goal was to convince Eduardo that what he had done hours earlier was unavoidable. His justification for his actions, as he explained the events to Eduardo, did not even make sense to Luis himself. But he tried. "There was nothing I could do," whined the big man, who seemed so much smaller and diminished in the role of a remorseful supplicant, even when standing near his physically smaller boss. "I saw him in the basement. He was looking at the bottle. It was sitting on top of the box that came from the boat person. The bottle was clearly labeled hydrocodone 10/325 and was half full. The box it sat on was closed and there was no label. It had some bottles that looked like the one on top, but they were empty. The rest of the pills were in plastic bags in the same box. I was just about to bring all the stuff to you when he saw them. The guy, I think he was a doctor from a different hospital, asked me how often this kind of pain medication was used in an eye hospital. I didn't say anything, but I know he read the label. He had a phone in his hand. I didn't see him take a picture, but he could have. I didn't like the way he was acting. And besides, even though the name on his lab coat said Rodriguez, he sounded like an American. What else could I do?"

"You could have called me, you idiot. There is always a way to explain something. And if that doesn't work, a situation like this can be taken care of in a much better way than murdering a man in his hotel room! Tell me what you did, *exactly*. I want to know what happened in that room—and don't give me any crap that you make up so that what you did sounds like it was the right thing."

Luis fidgeted and then he began, "After the doctor left the storage area, I guessed he would be heading upstairs to the lobby of the hospital. I wanted to keep him in sight, so I could find out where he was staying. He wasn't in the lobby when I got there, so I looked outside. He was in the parking lot and looked like he was expecting to be picked up. He was just standing and waiting. I didn't go up to him. I just watched. In a few minutes, a hospital security car drove up, he got in, and it was gone before I had a chance to figure out a way to follow. I waited for a half hour and when I saw the same driver come back, I stopped him and asked how a person like me gets a job like his." Luis assumed a satisfied look at his clever ploy and continued. "He wasn't very helpful, but when I asked him what kind of driving, he does, he said he had just taken a fellow to the Hotel Sevilla—and that was all I needed."

"Then what did you do?"

"I called the hotel and asked for the doctor's room number. They said they could ring his room, but they could not give out the room number. I said never mind and hung up. Then I went to the Hotel Sevilla and used a house phone in the lobby to call the front desk. When I was connected to the doctor's room, I asked him if I could come up to his room and deliver a package from one of the doctors at the eye clinic. He told me his room number and I went up. When I got there, I knocked, and he let me in. When he saw that I had no package, he looked surprised and not very happy to see me. I was sure he remembered me from the basement. This was confirmed when he asked me if I was here about the pills."

"And?" questioned Eduardo.

"He said I had better leave and that he was going to call hotel security. Before he got to the phone, I grabbed him and threw him on the floor. His head hit the corner of the desk. Lying on the floor, he looked dazed but conscious. His head was bleeding. He began struggling to get up, so I grabbed a pillow from the bed and put it over his face and held it there. That was it. He kicked for a few minutes; I suppose he tried to scream but the pillow blocked all of that."

"You killed him, you moron."

"Yes. But I didn't intend to. I'm sorry. He didn't do anything to me, but we were going to make so much ...

Not letting Luis finish, Eduardo asked, "What did you do then?"

"I dragged him into the bathroom, broke one of the hinges on the toilet seat, and put some of his blood on the edge of the rim. It is supposed to look like he fell in the bathroom, hit his head on the seat, and died there."

"Did you smear the blood with your fingers?"

"No. I used my handkerchief so there would be no fingerprints, and then I threw it away."

"Where?"

"In a trash container on the street."

*Good, finally something smart*, thought Eduardo. "What about the room?"

"I took the pillowcase with the blood on it, the one I held over his face, and straightened up the room. After that, I left by the back stairs."

"What did you do with the pillowcase?"

"I wrapped it in newspaper, so no one could tell what it was, and put it in the same trash can."

Now in control, the shop owner asked, "Did anyone see you enter the doctor's room, and how did you know his name?"

"I told you, I saw his name on his lab coat in the basement. I used it when I called the hotel the first time, to get his room number, and I used the doctor's name again when I called on the house phone in the hotel lobby and told him I was from the eye clinic. He sounded friendly when I talked to him. He told me his room number and invited me to come right up."

Eduardo was reassured that Luis had taken some precautions and had not been totally inept. "Do you think there is any way you could be traced?"

"No."

**By local** standards, Eduardo was a successful businessman. He was not a criminal, although he was on the brink with the scheme he was about to launch. Eduardo was an entrepreneur in a society where people who were able, took advantage of any opportunity to make money. His big opportunity was now in jeopardy. His thoughts raced as he reviewed his predicament. *We have 6,250 hydrocodone 10/325 tablets—a controlled prescription drug with 10 milligrams of opioid and 325 milligrams of acetaminophen. Even though hundreds of millions, if not billions, of these pills are prescribed every year in the United States, I would be in big trouble if someone caught me with them. Making matters worse, I owe the woman from the boat a chunk of money that I can't repay until I sell the drugs.*

Eduardo had decided to participate in this get-rich-quick

scheme because he rationalized it was only semi-illegal. He knew that at least two million people in the United States used hydrocodone for purely recreational purposes. The opioid in the hydrocodone provides a feeling of relaxation leading to euphoria, in contrast to cocaine, which produces a frenetic, even manic, mood elevation that can be pleasurable to the user but in a high-energy way. Because hydrocodone was considered medicine, Eduardo had decided to have the shipment delivered to the receiving dock at Raul Mesa Carreras Eye Hospital.

Eduardo knew he had no way to pay his supplier $25,000 for the shipment, which amounted to $4.50 per pill, until he was able to sell the product. If he sold the pills for $5.50 each, he would make more than six thousand dollars profit in a month—and that was the minimum. He could make a lot more. He would be a rich man in Cuba, although Eduardo didn't want to stop there. He wanted to be a rich man when he traveled to Europe, and maybe even the United States. With more cruise ships visiting Havana, and the ships' crews sending customers to him on a regular basis, who knew how many of these pills Eduardo could sell, and how much higher a price he could charge? Payment in full, in American dollars, was expected by his supplier when the second order was delivered a month later. Thereafter, the prior shipment would be paid for every time a new shipment was delivered.

With today's unwelcome events, Eduardo knew he would have to tell his supplier that he needed an extension on the time of payment for this first delivery. He would be laying low; there would be no sales for a while. He could not do anything more tonight. Eduardo looked at Luis and said, "Be here in the morning, and bring the pills. I will keep them here, in the shop, until the issue at the hotel is dealt with. After that, we can begin selling."

# THREE

**A**dam Grant looked out the window of his corner office in the New Building. That was what the George H. W. Bush Center for Intelligence was called for short. A light blanket of snow covered a brown, dormant lawn dotted with a few conifers, some barren deciduous trees, and a handful of shrubs stubbornly holding on to last year's wilted leaves. He was looking northeast, away from the acres of parking. It was a perfect location for an office—then he checked himself. Not just an office—it was his office; home of the newly established Select Home for Operational Personnel—which had the ringing acronym SHOP. *There were now two conveniently named places associated with the CIA,* Adam mused. *The Farm at Camp Peary, where they "grew spies," and now SHOP, where they fixed things.*

As Director of SHOP, Adam would lead a team housed on the main campus at Langley, but not officially part of the CIA. SHOP's responsibility was to forge cooperation and provide support for agencies within the federal government that dealt with international relationships, regulations, and law enforcement inside and outside the country.

It was the end of January. The past year had been one of unbelievable consequence for Adam. In other years, he had experienced momentous events: happy, dangerous, and even tragic, but nothing could match the challenges he had faced in the last twelve months. Last February, while serving as the new Adjutant to the Chairman of the Joint Chiefs of Staff, he had been assigned to work undercover for the CIA, in close association with officials at the highest levels of government, where he led a team that took down the Supreme Leader of North Korea in a bloodless coup. Then, a few weeks later, working in an adjunct role with the CIA, he led a team that captured thirty-two Middle Eastern terrorists on U.S. soil. Momentous as these assignments were, on a personal level, they paled when he thought of meeting Erin O'Leary. He remembered his first glimpse of her as she stood on the other side of the Great Seal in the lobby of the Central Intelligence Agency Headquarters. This was where Adam had been told to meet his contact—an unconventional location, but Adam's endorsement from the Chairman of the Joint Chiefs, Bill Weiland, delivered directly to the head of the CIA, probably did much to cut through the customary red tape. After tentative looks across the Seal, Erin and Adam each concluded the person they were observing was who they were to meet. The purpose of the meeting was for Adam to be introduced to the CIA and, in fact, to be recruited.

Erin was smart, a quick study, and especially well-versed in the scope of the organization. Adam would soon learn she had both beauty and brains. The more time he spent with Erin, the stronger his feelings grew. It was a mutual attraction that became love with a promise of commitment. They planned to be married this coming spring.

Erin was a sensible woman. At her insistence, it was decided that each would keep their own apartment until the wedding. After that, they would set up housekeeping properly, as husband and wife. There was not much that the two couldn't, wouldn't, or hadn't already shared, but that was the way Erin wanted it until they were married. Adam said he would comply, though acquiescing reluctantly.

The Select Home for Operational Personnel was the brainchild of Bob Zinsky, Director of the CIA, and FBI Director Phil Stark. Both felt such a collaborative operation had been nascent for years and now was the time to act. With the concurrence of the President of the United States, Directors Zinsky and Stark tapped Adam Grant to both design and head the new interdepartmental agency. All three of these men, the President and the directors, had been impressed by the covert work Adam had done in the last year—and they all wanted to retain his services for the country and not lose this rising star.

The idea behind SHOP was straightforward. It recognized that in the United States bureaucracy there were services that were high-quality and effective but sometimes redundant and ill-used. Although effective in their own rights, organizations could face obstacles: they sometimes operated in areas outside of their expertise because they started the action and couldn't find a way to stop; and well-meaning agencies might operate at cross purposes—not intentionally, it just happened. When President Tripp gave the two directors the go-ahead to make plans to establish a new organization to ensure interagency cooperation, the men agreed there was one best person to undertake the task: Lt. Colonel Adam Grant.

The physical space assigned at the Langley campus was all that Adam could hope for. SHOP was assigned ten thousand square feet on the third floor of the New Building, and Adam appreciated that he was given a corner office. SHOP would start with fourteen people. Five were in place, with nine still to be recruited. The idea of having a full staff was a pleasant change for Adam. He was used to operating shorthanded. In Afghanistan, during the nearly five years of his service, it always seemed that he needed more manpower to fulfill an assignment.

One night, when their barracks was overrun by Taliban who killed three of his men, Adam had to fill the breach himself, which led to him killing four of the terrorists to save a fourth member of his team that had been seriously wounded in the skirmish. For this, Adam received a Silver Star, the second highest medal awarded to a soldier for valor in a foreign war. He accepted it gratefully, but in no way did the medal, which he had only worn the day he received it, assuage the feelings of loss he had experienced. He would have preferred that his men still lived.

Adam felt guilty because he was starting out with more people than he could keep busy—although he was confident this situation would change once they'd been in operation for a while. He had worked with three of the staff before. One was Marilyn Helm, a bright millennial with a generous helping of common sense, who was especially adept at everything related to computers and how to use them effectively. The second was Eddie Freeman, an electronics genius who had played a key role in both projects completed last year; and then there was Cissy Friend, his office manager, who would be indispensable and a godsend. Adam had first worked with Cissy when he was Adjutant to the Chairman of the Joint Chiefs of Staff. She had stayed on, to serve General Paul Lippmann after Adam's boss, Bill Weiland, was murdered in the Pentagon parking lot by an assassin hired by Kim Il-un using VX toxin. During the few months Cissy worked for the new General, her third Chairman of the Joint Chiefs, it became clear that his former assistant was available and eager to rejoin her old boss. In a smooth transition, with both parties being winners, this woman got her wish and Cissy jumped at the chance to again work with Adam. In addition, her new job was on the same side of the Potomac as Cissy's home, which was a huge plus when it came to commute time.

**Over the** next two weeks, with Cissy's help, Adam assembled the rest of the team. SHOP would be staffed by a talented and diverse group of people who exuded positive attitudes and created the impression they had the stuff to get things done. Adam made the executive decision that if he could get along with a person, the rest of the team would have to do the same. He didn't rule out a talented firebrand or a quiet thinker if each could contribute in his or her own way and work as a team player. Adam had also agreed to take on as his deputy a captain on loan from the Army, a man recommended by Chairman Lippmann, who Adam trusted implicitly.

Cissy, Eddie, and Marilyn were the only familiar faces, but everyone on the team had experience in government service; in most cases, working with one of the agencies that the Select Home for Operational Personnel would interact with. These included people from the FBI, Homeland Security, Drug Enforcement Administration, Transportation Security Administration, CIA, NSA, and the Joint Chiefs. There were only two members whose prior experience was limited to the CIA. One was a fresh face and the other was a seasoned veteran. Half of the team were women. Adam hoped this signaled that there would be no gender bias. All interaction would be respectful and professional, and teamwork would be the rule.

Of the CIA carryovers, Adam was pleased that Marilyn Helm had accepted his offer to transfer to SHOP. Her prior work with Adam was outstanding. For more than a month she had taken the lead in monitoring the movement of a ship transporting thirty-two terrorists to the U.S. across the Atlantic and into the Great Lakes. Their aim was to reign terror and death at the New World Trade Center using explosives and sarin gas. Marilyn had carried out her duties quietly and with dogged determination. She was thorough, dependable, and professional. And, she was a true millennial. When Adam had asked Marilyn to locate a carousel projector, she had no idea what he was talking about! Adam chuckled at the memory, but then reminded himself that few people her age, with the ubiquity of PowerPoint, digital photography, and modern projectors today, would be familiar with this "ancient" media form. It reminded Adam of his own reaction when one of his teachers at West Point had referred to making copies with a mimeograph. What goes around, comes around.

# FOUR

**February was** keeping its promise of being unpredictable. As Adam strode back to his office, he looked forward to shedding the monochromatic chill that accompanied his walk, a distance that seemed inversely related to the temperature. His thoughts were not on the drab landscape, or anything that might be occurring back in his office. He was thinking of Erin. Adam was relieved that his fiancée had received a clean bill of health from the cardiologist in Miami. The doctor's advice was that she cut down on caffeine and get an appropriate amount of rest. He also prescribed a medicine that reduced the heart's irritability, making it less likely to develop an arrhythmia, but this was just a preventive measure. Erin had experienced no other episodes of cardiac arrhythmia and was feeling fine. That was the good news. But there was also a not-so-good part. She was well enough that Robert Zinsky, the CIA Director and her boss, felt it was okay to send her back to Rome, where she would continue as Assistant Station Chief. She would remain there for three months to wrap up affairs in that office before she returned to Langley to assume her job as the CIA Chief's assistant.

As Adam stepped inside the SHOP office, he saw a look of urgency on Cissy's face and his thoughts hurtled back to the present. One of the many things he liked about this woman was that there was no deceit or obfuscation in her makeup. She remained in the moment, while being both honest and transparent. With a big smile, Cissy Friend said, "Colonel Grant, we may be getting our first honest-to-goodness business."

"Okay, Cissy. Let's have it."

Trying to sound professional, relaxed, and not overly excited at the first nibble that could develop into their initial project, Cissy said, "An agent from Consular Affairs in D.C. just called for you. He sounded like a man whose hair was on fire, telling me what he had to say was important, 'very important,' and he needed an answer immediately. I told him I expected you to return any minute. When the caller insisted that the message he had was of the highest priority, I promised to call him back in five minutes, one way or the other. That was four minutes ago. Can I dial now?"

"Of course," said Adam, who was also trying to remain calm but not so phony as to give the impression that he was not excited about the prospect of having something to do.

Before Cissy dialed the number, she told Adam, "The man who called said his name was Prem Rao. He said that if we didn't get back to him within five minutes, he would have to make another call elsewhere. He wasn't nasty or anything, but he did sound agitated, almost desperate. He said he needed to talk with somebody who could deal with the problem that had landed on him, and that the situation was acute."

"Okay, Cissy. Call him. I'll take it in my office."

Cissy dialed the number. Even after Adam was connected, she kept the receiver to her ear. She knew Adam would be sharing every word of the conversation with her, so she might as well listen firsthand and be on the same page, sparing her boss the need to repeat what he had just heard before decisions were made for the next step.

"Colonel Grant, this is Prem Rao from the Bureau of Consular Affairs. We have a potentially delicate and serious situation that I hope you can help with." Before Adam could respond, the man continued. "Jeff Rhoads from our office was very impressed with what he saw of your operation when he visited last week. Based on his enthusiasm and what he shared with us, when I got this call,

I decided to contact you first. I hope I am doing the right thing. If you can't help, maybe you can help me find somebody to deal with this problem without wasting any time."

Adam remembered meeting the man from Consular Affairs and was glad he had decided to hold several meetings to introduce people in the government to SHOP. The clock on Adam's desk showed 10:30. It was not digital. The small hand was between ten and eleven and the big hand was on six. Adam was an analog guy and this timepiece was both comforting and reassuring. The continual movement of the clock hands expressed for him the true nature of the march of time. It was February 9. This day could chronicle the first official mission for SHOP.

The man from the consular office continued, "We received a call from our representative in Havana telling us an American doctor was found dead in his hotel room, from what has been called an accidental fall. His body was discovered by a colleague, a Cuban doctor, who called our Consular Office in Havana, and they contacted us. It has only been a couple hours since the body was discovered. But we are told the doctor's death must have occurred at least twelve hours earlier. No one else has been notified, including Doctors for a Better World, the medical organization the doctor was representing. The doctor who found the body is Alejandro Rivera. He called from the American's hotel room and promised to remain there until we called him back. The clock is ticking, and we don't have much time. Dr. Rivera, a Cuban native, insists this death not be handled by Cuban authorities alone. He will remain with the body, but we need to get someone there fast. How should we do this?"

Believing he had only minutes, Adam told Rao to stay by his phone and do nothing until Adam called him back, within the hour. Adam assured Rao that there was a protocol in place for this situation and it would be put into operation immediately. Adam considered this reassurance to be an acceptable stretch of the truth. Then he asked, "Can you give me a phone number to contact Dr. Rivera?"

Prem Rao replied, "The best I can do is tell you it is the Hotel

Sevilla in Havana, and the room is under the name of Dr. Michael Rodriguez." Before Adam could hang up, Prem Rao added, "Colonel Grant, the Consular Office in Havana said that Dr. Rivera is concerned about the timing of his colleague's death. This morning he had planned to take Dr. Rodriguez to visit several medical facilities that make exorbitant claims about a variety of medical successes. They use this to lure people, mostly from Europe and the Middle East, and increasing numbers from the U.S. as well, to Cuba. Dr. Rodriguez had no specific agenda or cause, he just wanted to be more informed about something that was becoming urban legend at home in the U.S.; that is, the brilliance and success of Cuban medicine developed under the Castro regime. Dr. Rivera said their visit to these institutions could be interpreted as a threat to the government, and that somebody might have wanted to stop them. On top of this, but unrelated, he said Dr. Rodriguez told him he had seen something yesterday that particularly alarmed him. He didn't want to discuss it on the phone but would share it with Dr. Rivera when they met this morning. Dr. Rivera said he had no more details, but he felt the situation should be treated as a crime scene."

# FIVE

**The moment** he ended his phone call with Prem Rao, Adam saw that the light on his second line was blinking. Based on the information she had heard, Cissy had already called the Hotel Sevilla and was being connected to Dr. Michael Rodriguez's room. When Dr. Alejandro Rivera answered, she said she was calling from the Department of Personnel Operations in Washington, D.C. She didn't know why, but she decided under the circumstances it was a good idea to shorten the name. As she was speaking, she depressed the button on her phone to signal her boss's desk.

Because things would be moving fast, Cissy continued to stay on the line. The importance of weighing the balance between privacy and safety was on her mind. Cissy recalled an advisory she had read on a sign in the bathroom when she had helped her mother in the hospital a year ago. It said: Don't let observation of modesty lead to eventual harm.

"This is Colonel Adam Grant," was Adam's preemptive greeting the moment he heard the phone being picked up.

"Colonel Grant, thank God," Dr. Rivera said. There was agitation in his voice. "I need help—now. Something must be done. Can you help me?"

"I realize, doctor," Adam responded, "that you are in a difficult position. The Bureau of Consular Affairs in Washington just called to tell me you are at the Hotel Sevilla with an American colleague you found dead, and that you want help from U.S. authorities before anything is done with the body. Can I ask why you are requesting our help?"

"Colonel Grant, I have more than twenty years of experience in medicine. I knew Mike Rodriguez well, and I know he did not die by falling and hitting his head on a toilet. He was a healthy, gutsy, and competent person; definitely not someone who would just fall over and die."

"Do you have any reason to think that someone would want to harm Dr. Rodriguez?"

"The people who are in control in this country would do anything to anyone at any time if they wanted. For this reason, I wouldn't even know where to start."

"Was Dr. Rodriguez involved in anything that would call attention to him? Was he planning an activity that somebody would want to stop?"

"Today we were planning to visit what has been touted as the world's largest medical school. It was established by Fidel Castro and is located here, in Havana. After that, we were going to visit several clinics to evaluate them; not officially or professionally but from the perspective of a foreigner seeking help for a serious health problem, or as someone eager to receive elective cosmetic surgery at a bargain price. Neither of us shared this information in a way that could have ruffled the feathers of any officials," said the doctor, who was regaining control and was more at ease now that he believed something was being done.

"Can you think of anything else?" Adam asked.

"Only this. The last time I spoke with Mike Rodriguez was yesterday afternoon. He called from the hospital to confirm the time we were to meet this morning. He told me he had seen something that seemed to be out of the ordinary. Those were his words, 'out of the ordinary.' But he told me he wanted to wait until we met this morning before he said any more."

"What would you like us to do?"

"Sir, with the suspicions I have, I don't want the local police or anyone from the Cuban government coming here and simply carting off the body, and then saying his death was an accident—not without a proper investigation. Unless we do something now, their slipshod procedures will destroy evidence and the whole issue will be treated in the way they decide, and not on facts. I am certain this will happen unless you intervene. I believe Michael Rodriguez's death was a homicide. His room should be treated like a crime scene. I also believe that a thorough forensic autopsy should be performed to determine the true cause of death. None of this will happen without prompt and effective intervention by your government. Without your involvement, this will be swept under the rug and there will be no way to see that justice is done. Please, help with this, Colonel Grant."

Adam heard the strong words and believed they were spoken by a man who was fully aware of the situation. "Okay. But you must hold on for a while longer, Dr. Rivera. It will be several hours before we can get somebody to the hotel. If that is acceptable, I request that you not let anyone else in the room and that you remain with the body. If you need to notify anyone that Dr. Rodriguez might have planned to work with today, just stall them for now and don't say anything to cause alarm. I'll give you my cell phone number; you can call me anytime."

"Colonel Grant, Mike and I had intended to be on our own during his last three days in the country. Our plans were not secret, but they hadn't been shared with anybody either, so it is unlikely we will be missed. Mike was not planning to go home until Saturday. His responsibilities at Carreras are completed, and he already said his goodbyes."

"Please, do not call Mrs. Rodriguez," added Adam. "I will have an FBI team visit her this afternoon to break the news. But first, I will call the FBI's field office in Miami to alert them and to find out how they will respond. As soon as I know what we can expect from the FBI, I will call you back. I am sure they will do everything possible to support you." Then he repeated his earlier instruction, "Until help arrives this afternoon, do not leave the room. This is important. Nothing should be disturbed in the room, even though it might seem insignificant. I expect whoever is sent by the FBI will know how and when to alert the local authorities." As Adam said this, he knew he was flying by the seat of his pants while promising things that he only hoped he could deliver. He hoped the FBI would come through.

Looking at the clock on his desk, Adam saw the big hand was on the nine. Fifteen minutes had passed since the alert from Prem Rao. Adam had accomplished a lot and had promised even more. As soon as Adam hung up from speaking to Dr. Rivera, Cissy signaled him to pick up line 2. The timing was perfect. Adam heard a woman's voice, firm and official.

"FBI Miami field office. Evelyn Pease speaking. How can I help you?"

"Colonel Adam Grant here, from the Select Home for Operational Personnel in D.C." The name wasn't gliding off Adam's tongue yet, and he realized he was not consistent in his use of *operation* versus *operational*—that would come in time. He hoped the acronym SHOP would take over soon. "I have urgent business. Can I speak with the director?"

"I'm sorry, Colonel Grant. The director is not here. Would you like to speak with his deputy?"

"Yes, that would be fine."

"Please hold."

Within seconds, Adam heard: "John Bridges here, Colonel Grant. How can I help you?"

In the fewest words possible, Adam explained the situation to the Deputy Director.

"Colonel Grant, I can get two men to Havana inside of three hours. Both have experience dealing with Cubans, and they will be able to secure a crime scene. The Miami Office is aware that the Cubans are on tender hooks. The flap over our personnel experiencing neurological damage is front and center. The Cuban government dreads the re-institution of travel restrictions for United States citizens. They are just now starting to see the cash flow from the increased tourist activity and they don't want anything to happen that would cut down the number of tourists and the money they spend."

"Thanks, Director Bridges. Also, can you please contact the nearest FBI field office, I expect that would be in Detroit, and explain the situation so they can dispatch a team to the Rodriguez home to inform Mrs. Rodriguez of her husband's death? Their home is in Ann Arbor, about an hour away. You can brief them. Also, ask these men to contact me as soon as they are finished, and then I will call the woman myself. But first I will call Doctors for a Better World, to get the doctor's home address, and then let your office know."

"Will do, Colonel. Why don't you keep me informed from your end? And, you can expect I will do the same."

"Absolutely. If you don't hear from me directly, it will be from my associate Tom Hodges."

Adam hung up and asked Cissy to contact Doctors for a Better World's headquarters. When the connection was made, Adam identified himself and asked to speak with the director. He was connected in minutes, which for Adam seemed like hours. "Mr. Richardson, this is Adam Grant from Select Home for Operational Personnel in D.C. I am sorry to deliver tragic news about your volunteer Dr. Michael Rodriguez. He was found dead in his hotel room this morning by a colleague, Dr. Alejandro Rivera." Adam heard the Director moan and gave him a few seconds of silence. Then Adam explained what he knew thus far. "Mr. Richardson, I have shared all I know, and we are working fast to learn more. After I hear from the FBI, I will get back with you. In the meantime, all of us are withholding information until we learn more. I ask that you not share this information with anyone."

The director said that he understood the delicacy of the situation, but he could not keep it quiet indefinitely. Adam said he understood and promised to call the director by this evening.

Adam wasn't sure how easy or necessary it was for the CIA to have a presence at the scene. He would have to check that out. It was now time to get back to Prem Rao.

Cissy made the connection. Adam explained to Rao that although the situation was under control, there was still a lot more to be done; and that it was not necessary for Prem or the Consular

Affairs Office to take any action now. He said he would keep Prem updated on events as needed.

Only after these calls were completed did the significance of what had just happened sink in. SHOP had assumed the responsibility to coordinate a delicate situation in Cuba—a country whose relations with the United States were strained. In just minutes, communication had been established and events were underway. This happened much quicker than would have been possible without SHOP. Adam was quietly satisfied at how matters had progressed. SHOP had responded exactly as it should.

Although Adam would not make any further decisions until after hearing from the FBI team once they were in Havana, it was time to gather his team in the conference room. This included Maha, the receptionist, who could remain connected to her desk phone via a headset, making it possible for her to manage any incoming calls while still being a part of the meeting. This practice of inclusiveness was a leadership dictum to which Adam adhered. He believed that the people you left out of the loop automatically became a weak link because they were made to feel that what they knew was not important; and since they did not know the details, neither they nor their job was important.

In Adam's mind, SHOP, its mission, and the team were inseparable. Everybody had an important role and if they all had the necessary information, then they could do their part. There would be no weak links.

Adam felt the excitement as people assembled in the conference room. After just a few weeks, SHOP was in operation! Adam thanked everybody for the work they had done so far to help get ready for this moment—and then he told the group what he knew about their first assignment, which was not much at this point. After sharing the information, Adam assigned specific tasks to several of the team members. Being their first case, he went into detail about how they would function individually and as a unit. Adam expected his team to tell him what had progressed smoothly and what hadn't. SHOP was a work in progress.

The first assignment was for Donna Fisher to call Mrs.

Rodriguez later that afternoon, to assure her there was an open phone line to SHOP any time she had a question or thought of something she wanted to share. In turn, she would hear from this office with any news.

Ted Lear was assigned to contact the FBI field office in Detroit as soon as the meeting ended, to suggest in the most diplomatic way possible, that the agents check the doctor's and Mrs. Rodriguez's computers. It was likely they would do this without a reminder, but Adam wanted to be sure. Angie Fortune was the point person to answer questions from Doctors for a Better World, although she was not to initiate any calls unless told to do so. Cissy Friend would relay any directives from Adam that he couldn't deliver personally, and these instructions should be considered official and from Adam. Captain Tom Hodges was assigned the task of obtaining background material on anything Cuban that could possibly impact the case, and also to run complete background checks on Dr. Rodriguez and Dr. Rivera.

After the meeting ended and people started to exit the conference room, Adam motioned to Eddie Freeman. "Eddie, I didn't assign anything specific to you. Instead I want you to be my eyes and ears in the office and help the eager, young people we have on our team. Your experience and steady hand will be invaluable to them."

Smiling and happy to have this special role Eddie said, "Thanks boss. Will do."

Turning to his Deputy, Adam said, "Tom, would you come into my office?" Once there, Adam motioned for Tom to have a seat. They faced each other; both sat in front of the desk. Adam began, "In the process of dealing with the learning curve I faced taking on this job, I haven't spent as much time with you as you deserve."

"Colonel, to be honest, I think you have been more than fair, and doing me a favor by allowing me to settle into this job at my own speed. If you think you are facing a learning curve, I feel like I am at the base of the Matterhorn looking up."

"Thanks, Tom. As you and I get to know each other better, I'm sure we will find ourselves on the same page. This is something I believe will come naturally. If you have any concerns, let me know right away. If you don't have an answer to something, just let me know and we can work it out, as a team. I won't have all the answers either. When that happens, the best thing for us to do will be to put our heads together. And, I want you to know that I authorize you to speak to the staff as you see fit."

Tom Hodges left the room confident this would be good duty.

# SIX

**FBI Agent** Matt Hull heard the muted buzz from his phone and saw the yellow light come on at its base. It was Wednesday morning. He was at his desk, finishing routine paperwork while wondering why he'd joined the FBI if all he was going to do was sit in a vinyl desk chair in a not very well air-conditioned office in a hot and humid city and spend all day wrinkling the seat of his pants. When he picked up the phone he heard, "Matt, this is John Bridges. I need you in my office right away.

Happy for the break, Agent Hull said, "Sure, be there in a sec."

As Agent Hull entered the Deputy Director's office, he saw Peter Seldon already seated.

"Gentlemen," said Bridges, "I have a job for you. It's short notice, but I want you both in Havana by two o'clock this afternoon. Will this be a problem for either of you?"

Matt looked at Peter and detected the faintest trace of a smile. "I'm game," said Matt.

"Me, too," said Peter. "What's the gig?"

"Before I tell you what this is all about, let me make a call to arrange for a plane. We've used these guys before and I know they can deliver on short notice." The two agents listened while the Deputy Director called General Aviation at Miami Dade International Airport. He asked to be connected to Aviation Solutions, a small operation on the government's approved contract list. When he was connected, John Bridges quickly described his needs. He was told that they could count on a wheels-up time as early as 12:00 p.m. The flight to Havana would take less than an hour, and the man said the José Marti International Airport was only nine miles from the Hotel Sevilla in Old Havana. The weather was good and, barring any unexpected problems, it would be possible to meet the deadline, but just.

With this accomplished, Deputy Director Bridges explained the importance and the delicate nature of the task the two men faced. He said their first job would be to reassure and calm Dr. Rivera, who was keeping vigil over a dead American. After that, they would proceed, following protocol. While the two agents remained seated, digesting what they had just heard, John Bridges picked up a book from his desk, one that was familiar to both men. It was the FBI field manual for operations.

"I won't read it all to you, but there is justification for what you will be doing in Havana." Paraphrasing from the manual, the Deputy Director explained the extraordinary role of the FBI in situations like this. Then he read aloud from the manual: "'When operating outside of the United States in cases involving a U.S. citizen, the FBI can be responsible for evacuations, obtaining official death certificates, arranging crisis intervention, and carrying out investigative interviews.'" Seeing both men shift slightly forward in their chairs, he knew he had their attention. The Deputy Director continued. "Even though you will be functioning under established guidelines, these are our rules and not necessarily theirs. For that reason, it is essential that you do all you need to at the crime scene before contacting the local authorities. Even if the locals agree to cooperate and say they welcome our help, it may take them so long to get their act together that it will be impossible for you to do your work in a timely fashion. We all know that what we get in the first forty-eight hours is crucial.

"After the necessary contact with the Cuban authorities has been established, it will be up to you to figure out the best way to handle ongoing relations with them. I know we will piss them off by calling them in so late, but we could also wreck the case if they get involved too soon. We're damned both ways! To take at least some of the heat off you guys, the first call to the Havana Police will be when you say the time is right. I will then let you know what the locals tell me. That way, you will be in the clear and not get blamed for the delay."

Bridges reinforced the extraordinary sensitivity of this case. He told them they should emphasize to the Cubans that this death involves a prominent doctor who was volunteering as part of a health care project at the country's leading eye hospital. "Use your judgment and deal with whatever comes up the best way you can. You're both good agents and able to think on your feet. I am confident you can handle the situation."

The men promised that after they had surveyed the scene and collected all the evidence to be had, they would report to Bridges and provide him enough information to set the stage for contacting the Cubans.

For emphasis, Bridges repeated, "The minute you have told me the situation is under control, the local police will be informed. Do not call until you have done everything you can. After that, we will have a conference call with the Director of the Select Home for Operational Personnel, that new agency in D.C., that alerted us. I don't know much about them, but the guy I spoke with seemed to know what he was doing and gave the impression he was representing a credible, no-nonsense outfit."

When the two agents left the Deputy Director's office, it was with a new sense of purpose. They had been placed at the heart of the kind of adventure, maybe even danger, that had attracted them to the job in the first place. Matt Hull would call his wife and tell her he would not be home tonight. He would check in with her when he knew more, but not to expect a call before tomorrow afternoon. She would not ask where he was going. This level of uncertainty came with the job, one that was not Matt's alone. Pete Seldon was a bachelor and had nobody to call. Sometimes he wished he did.

Before heading to the airport, each man stopped at their locker in the breakroom at the office and retrieved a small carry-on suitably packed for just such an emergency. Exchanging their dress shirts and ties for short-sleeved polos, they now looked like the tourists they intended to represent as they began their job in Havana.

# SEVEN

**T**he Cessna 425 turboprop landed at José Martí International Airport seventy minutes after wheels-up in Miami. Just for the fun of it, Matt Hull had put his iPhone on stopwatch mode to record the exact time. Even at that, he realized that almost fifteen minutes of the flight was consumed by take-off and landing maneuvers for the 228-mile trip. This included being required to take off to the northwest because of the wind, the opposite of the direction they were going. The much ballyhooed ninety-mile separation between the U.S. and Cuba, Matt reminded himself, was from Key West to Havana, not from Miami.

The charter discharged the two passengers at Terminal 2, the designated location for U.S. charter flights. This terminal was built in 1988, ten years before Terminal 1, which now served as the airport's main passenger facility, handling international flights that now included Delta, American, and Jet Blue from the U.S.

This was the fourth trip to Cuba for Matt, who was raised in South Florida. The first three were fishing trips, and each included a short stop at Hemingway Bay Marina and a quick trip to the old downtown, which only allowed for a superficial look around. This first business trip caused Matt to regret not making more of an effort to learn Spanish. He knew a few words and phrases, but that was it. He would be depending on the Cubans to translate.

Born and raised in Massachusetts, this was Peter Seldon's first visit to Cuba; although during the year he had worked in the Miami field office, he had had many dealings with Cubans who had fled the island. Pete felt he had a pretty good handle on the place, but it was all secondhand and biased. He was glad to finally be seeing the country for himself.

Their main cargo was the wheeled Pelican case that contained assorted equipment for acquiring and cataloging evidence at a crime scene. Customs and Immigration clearance went smoothly. When their Pelican case was opened for inspection, the two explained that they were in Cuba to make a commercial demonstration. To cover for this, a brochure was included in the case to support their story. The visitors explained that the contents were for demonstration purposes only. They were samples of products their company, the Zelda Corporation, sold and supplied on a lease basis. *The FBI man who came up with this name was an F. Scott Fitzgerald fan*, thought Pete Seldon. The men added to the story by saying that they would also be inquiring about the possibility of having local fabricators become involved in the manufacture of some of the products they sold.

Standing at the curb outside the terminal, the men noticed the eclectic array of garishly painted and pimped-out vintage vehicles that had started life as Fords, Chevrolets, Plymouths, Buicks, Studebakers, and other U.S.-built automobiles produced in the 1950s; including some that hadn't been manufactured for decades. Matt Hull knew that many were now powered by smaller Hyundai engines instead of the original engines that had worn out long ago. The skill and ingenuity of the Cuban auto fabricators was mind boggling. Necessity is, indeed, the mother of invention. Most cars used in the business of transporting people for hire were newer KIAs, Hyundais, and Toyotas, which in the milieu of vintage vehicles, made them look like Rolls Royces. The men hopped in a yellow KIA for the ride to the hotel.

According to the information that had been provided to the agents before they departed, the Hotel Sevilla was built in 1908. Owned and maintained by foreign investors, it presented an impressive façade in the Moorish style and carried out a successful business in the center of Old Havana. The hotel was located just minutes from the old presidential palace, which now served as a museum that highlighted the events beginning in 1953 that had led to the ouster of Fulgencio Battista by Fidel Castro in 1959.

The Revolution Museum was surrounded by rusted trucks, vintage aircraft, and even the boat named *Granma* that had delivered eighty-two revolutionaries from Mexico. It was a symbol of the recent past. Other buildings in the area, like the old Opera House, which had just undergone renovations, remained suspended between two dictatorial regimes.

The streets around the hotel were narrow, and many were dressed in pavers. They were plied by an array of serviceable vehicles that included two-seat rickshaws adapted as bicycle conveyances; vividly painted cars from the mid-twentieth century; and a few shiny, late-model European and Japanese cars mostly for hire. Along with the vehicles, throngs of people walked on the sidewalks and in the streets in a seemingly aimless parade. The crowd consisted of locals wearing old but serviceable clothes and better dressed eager and finger-pointing tourists.

In the lobby of the Hotel Sevilla, the agents approached a wide service desk that was adorned with attractive and colorful Moorish tiles up to the level of the heavy marble countertop. They asked for Dr. Michael Rodriguez's room. The phone connection was made by a pleasant young woman in a crisp, white blouse and a colorful scarf around her neck.

When the connection was made, she handed the phone to Matt Hull. "Hullo," was all that issued forth from the instrument.

Confident that the voice he heard was that of the doctor who had remained with the dead man, Matt Hull said, "Dr. Rivera, we are the people you are expecting. If you give us the room number, we will come up immediately."

"I'm in room 514." Alejandro had nothing more to say. This had been the longest day of his life. Things would now change, but he knew the torment would not end soon. He was glad this part of the nightmare would be over, but he was sure there would be more to come based on something he had discovered during his vigil, something that could change his life.

# EIGHT

**R**oom 514 was situated at the end of a hall. After Pete Seldon's gentle knock, the door was opened cautiously, just a crack. Seeing men that looked like those he was expecting; the occupant opened the door. The portal revealed a small man with slicked over dark hair. He was wearing a light-colored short-sleeved shirt with an open collar, dark slacks, and scuffed shoes that had once been dark brown. He wore gold-rimmed glasses and a worried look.

"Hello, gentlemen," said Dr. Alejandro Rivera in excellent English. "Thank you for coming." His look revealed the obvious strain inflicted by the vigil he had kept under the most unpleasant of circumstances, and from something else he alone knew.

Peter Seldon pushed the wheeled Pelican case into the room and saw a look of alarm on the doctor's face. The FBI man offered an explanation. "Dr. Rivera, because of the concerns that you expressed when you called the Consulate, our office decided we should treat this room no differently than we would any crime scene. We are doing this only because you expressed concern; it is just to be sure. I don't want you to be alarmed by the size of the container. It includes extra equipment that could be described as 'just in case.'"

"I am sure you will want to see my friend first," said the doctor.

With a nod and a spoken yes, the two FBI agents followed Dr. Rivera to face a dark-stained wooden door that accessed the bathroom. It had ornate brass hardware that could have been original.

As Dr. Rivera opened the door, the Americans saw a body sprawled face-down on the floor. The man's arms were outstretched slightly above his head and his face was turned to the right. The body was closer to the sink than the tub and about at the level of the toilet, which was of special interest because the liftable ring seat was askew. The bolt at the back, on the right-hand side of the toilet seat had snapped and the seat was shifted at a twenty-five-degree angle away from the body. A blood smear was on the seat and there was a trail of blood on the floor between the dead man's head and the toilet. There was a bluish swelling the size of a plum on the right side of his forehead at the hairline. Coagulated blood over the swelling suggested a laceration beneath.

Matt Hull observed and processed these details quickly. He was an experienced crime-scene investigator, good but not even close to the skill level of the Miami homicide detectives he had worked with who dealt with scenes like this on an almost daily basis. They had it all over him when it came to speed. However, Matt and the others like him in the Bureau, who were experienced in this kind of thing, had a broad background in all aspects of criminal behavior, making them the total package of quality.

Agent Hull uttered none of what he saw. He was compiling raw data that would need processing and confirmation before being revealed. This would come later, maybe much later. "Dr. Rivera, we know you have had a long, stressful, and tragic day, and we don't want to do anything to make it worse. If we could impose on you for just a few more minutes, then you will be free to go. We know that the loss of a friend and colleague, especially under these circumstances, must be very difficult. You have done an amazing job alerting the authorities and stabilizing the situation. This makes it possible for us to obtain the information we need before we involve the local police which, of course, we must do. But, before you go, could we ask you a few questions?"

"Of course, Agent Hull. I don't have much to say, but I will do my very best to help."

"What was your relationship with Dr. Rodriguez? What were you planning to do with your friend today, and how did you come to find him here, in his hotel room?"

"I met Mike Rodriguez twenty years ago, when we were both training at Johns Hopkins Hospital in Baltimore. He was completing a post-residency fellowship in ophthalmology and I was just beginning a year of study in internal medicine and public health. At that time, it was very unusual for a Cuban citizen to be afforded this kind of opportunity. My special goal which, of course, had to be done with the blessing of the government, was to learn as much as I could about public health. This was in keeping with Castro's plan to provide free medical care to all the citizens of Cuba.

"Mike Rodriguez and I kept in touch over the years, mostly with Christmas and birthday cards, until our friendship was rekindled three years ago when he began visiting Cuba with the organization called Doctors for a Better World. This was his fourth visit here, and on each of the three prior occasions, we got together, mostly socially, but this time he wanted to do something professional and outside of ophthalmology. If I might add, gentlemen, we both shared the irony of his mission work here, to help Cuban doctors learn advanced techniques while the Cuban government touts its excellence in health care as a major industry and source of income. This country operates what is said to be the largest medical school in the world and offers medical tourism to patients from nearly every country, and Cuba exports thousands of doctors to Third World countries, but still needs the help of foreign doctors like Dr. Rodriguez."

"What was Dr. Rodriguez hoping to learn while working with you?" asked Peter Seldon.

"Mike wanted to visit the medical schools and the facilities and doctors that provide care to medical tourists. He also wanted to know more about the doctors and services involved in overseas activities, like those in Venezuela, Central America, Africa, and some parts of the Middle East. From his four visits to Cuba, including the last nine days, Mike felt he had a pretty good idea of the kind of care ordinary Cubans received. He wanted to learn more about the kind of health care Cuba was exporting. Our plans for these three days were completely outside the remit of his duties on behalf of Doctors for a Better World. He was not bent on muckraking. Mike just wanted to be informed about what was really going on here with medicine and to do anything he could, in a positive way, based on what he learned—nothing more."

"What was your schedule for today?" asked Matt Hull.

"We were planning to visit the Latin American Medical School, which is said to have two thousand students enrolled. After that, we were going to visit a private eye clinic that specialized in retinal disease. They employ catchy-sounding methods like ozone therapy, Vitamin B12 infusion and stem cells for the treatment of retinitis pigmentosa and age-related macular degeneration. The catch with conditions like this is that surefire successful treatment is rarely, if ever, accomplished and it is never achieved with this kind of hit-and-run care. Patients seeking this care are desperate, the doctors are convincing, and the patients they attract come here because they want to believe.

"For the most part, the treatments are provided with a flourish and with a promise of results but only after a time delay that involves the patient returning home. Payment is at the time of service, and whatever is accomplished by the treatment is determined later. Disappointed patients, and that is nearly all of them, rarely complain—no, make that *never*. The doctors and other personnel who provide these services are adept at acting professional and know how to appear to be caring at the point of service."

"Were other visits planned?" asked Pete.

"Yes, but we were going to decide as we went along. He wanted to start with eye care because he was familiar with this area of medicine. People come here from halfway around the world for treatment for a variety of conditions, like intractable pain, arthritis, skin diseases, cancer, and more. Maybe they are uplifted, if only briefly, because they think something is being done. People who argue for this practice are quick to point out that the sick still make the pilgrimage to Lourdes, which offers nothing when it comes to scientific credibility. Mike was a fair guy and I believe his aim was to be a positive force and not just a critic." After a pause that reflected a real sense of loss, Dr. Rivera said, "What a waste. Mike was a good man."

"Dr. Rivera, you have performed above and beyond. We thank you for the courage and diligence you have shown. We have just a few more questions."

In answer to their questions, Dr. Rivera told the agents he decided to come to the hotel when Dr. Rodriguez failed to show up at the medical school where they had planned to begin. He arrived at the Hotel Sevilla a little after 9:00 a.m. and was admitted to the room by a maid on instructions from the desk. The woman did not enter the room. When he saw the body and confirmed that his friend was dead, Dr. Rivera said he simply sat on the edge of the bed for fifteen minutes, thinking of what he should do. He decided that the best plan would be to call the United States Consular Office in Havana, which he did. The person he spoke with told him to wait with the body and do nothing until he received a call back. "Then, after spending the longest thirty minutes of my life, I received a call on the hotel phone from a Colonel Adam Grant. He told me to stay with the body and continue what I was doing, which turned out to be nothing but to talk on the phone twice and then wait for the FBI to arrive."

"Okay, Dr. Rivera," said Matt Hull. "Again, thank you. Here is my card. You can call us any time. Of course, we will keep you informed. I'm sure we'll talk more before our investigation is done."

In exchange, Alejandro gave each of the men his card, apologizing for it being in Spanish, but he pointed out the numbers were the same in English. As he headed for the door, almost reluctantly giving up his vigil, the doctor turned and said, "I expect an autopsy will be required. I don't trust the judgment or the motives of the Cuban authorities in this situation. I hope you are successful in insisting that the autopsy be done by a qualified and honest person. I know of one, and I hope my recommendation will be heeded."

With this, the tired and now stooped man left the room.

# NINE

**The two** FBI agents stood at the foot of the bed, facing each other and waiting to see who spoke first. "Whadya think, Pete?" said Agent Matt Hull.

"I think someone knocked the guy off. How about you?"

"The same."

"Why?" asked Pete.

"I dunno," said Matt Hull, the senior agent. "But that's why we're here; so, let's get at it."

Without touching anything, the men surveyed the scene and took more than a hundred pictures with a high-end digital camera. In the main room, the bed was slightly rumpled, which was explained by Dr. Rivera sitting on it after he discovered the body. "It looks like the desk was moved," said Agent Seldon. "See the dents in the carpet? Someone or something pushed it to one side by at least an inch."

The men continued their study. A bentwood oak chair with a wicker seat was in place by one of the windows in the corner of the room. Between the windows, which were in adjacent walls of this corner room, a small rectangular table was placed at an angle. An old tube TV sat on top. The heavy drapes were open and sheers on the windows were closed, hanging in place. The desk chair was pushed all the way into the knee hole of the desk with the back of the chair against the front edge of the desk top. Nothing else looked out of place. A small suitcase was on the floor of the closet and a man's clothes were on hangers; with underwear, socks, and shirts on the shelf above. A black-leather briefcase that had seen much use was also on the floor of the closet. A laptop computer, a small notebook, and an iPhone were on the desk, which also held the hotel's standard ivory-colored telephone.

In the bathroom, as they had already noticed, a trail of blood extended from the head facing to the right of the body toward the toilet and the tub. A closer look at the blue lump revealed nothing new. Matt Hull couldn't put his finger on it, but things didn't look right. Everything in the bathroom was precisely in place except for the toilet ring and the body.

Pete took photos of the body before rolling it over to look for anything new; there was nothing more. When they were finished cataloging the observable contents of the scene, they dusted any non-porous surfaces in the room that would likely have been touched and have latent fingerprints. With this accomplished, the scene was stabilized. Now the agents could move objects as necessary without destroying any evidence.

"Take a look at the corner of the desk," said Seldon. "The molding is cracked. It looks like there could be dried blood and even some hair. Is that why the desk looks like it was moved?"

"Good eye, Pete. Get an evidence bag and see what you can get off the corner. It looks like something might have happened out here first." With this, Matt Hull got on his hands and knees to study the carpet. "Pete, look at these two parallel grooves. They start about five feet from the desk and go right to the door of the bathroom."

"Matt, that guy was hit here and then dragged into the bathroom. Immediately after death, the body would be flaccid. The killer could have turned the head and positioned the arm and hand however he wanted."

"I think you're right. There is no question in my mind that he was killed in here and then dragged to where he is now."

It was time to thoroughly check the body. Rigor mortis had set in, which meant the body had been there for at least twelve hours, and maybe longer, before it was discovered by Dr. Rivera. Both agents believed that death likely occurred soon after Dr. Rodriguez returned to his room from the hospital because no towels had been used, the point on the toilet-paper roll always left by the maid was still in place, and there were no watermarks in the sink. This indicated he had most likely died shortly after he last spoke with his wife.

Pete Seldon emptied the doctor's pockets. He wore gloves to avoid adding to or smearing any prints on the items. He pulled out a wallet, a comb, a handkerchief, and several convertible pesos. That was all. The driver's license, health insurance cards, and identification found in his wallet were important but would not provide information about what had happened prior to the doctor's death. There were no business cards or recent receipts to shed any light on what Dr. Rodriguez had done or where he had been yesterday.

The object that would reveal most about the dead man's last hours was an iPhone, presumably his, that lay undisturbed on the small desk next to a closed laptop. Peter Seldon was careful to grasp the phone by the edge, while wearing nitrile gloves. He laid it flat on a clean piece of white paper and, with a brush that contained black fingerprint powder, lightly coated the screen side of the doctor's iPhone. With the same brush, he gently whisked away the excess powder, expecting to see fine black swirls representing the fingerprints of the last person who had touched the phone. There were none!

"Matt, I want you to do something for me."

"What?"

"I want you to brush the other side of this phone to see if you can pick up any prints."

Matt Hull, using the same technique, confirmed that no fingerprints were on the back.

"Something's wrong, Pete. This phone's been wiped clean."

Pete Seldon then dusted the hotel phone on the desk. As expected, it produced a crowded collection of fingerprints. "Matt, we've got a crime scene here. A guy is killed a few minutes after he returns to his room, but he dies in one place and is found in another, and his phone has been wiped clean. Let's take one more look and call Bridges."

They found nothing out of the ordinary in the pockets of the doctor's clothes that were neatly hung in the closet. The doctor's compartmented pill case had only three pills in each section. The smallest was probably a baby aspirin; a large dark-blue capsule could have been a vitamin; and the third, a white, oblong pill, was most likely a statin. Nothing unusual for an adult male who had a well-healed midline scar that could be seen when he was rolled over and his shirt unbuttoned.

The doctor's computer was turned off and password protected. Any information it might provide would only be uncovered in the lab. Smudged and partially wiped surfaces did not reveal any clean prints from doorknobs and other surfaces that might have been touched by the perpetrator, and since the iPhone had been wiped, the agents didn't know if these prints would shed any light on the person who had murdered the doctor.

Several loose items were placed in evidence bags, including a note for the lab that explained careful dusting of the iPhone at the scene had revealed no fingerprints. The agents wanted to be sure that they wouldn't be accused of inadvertently wiping the phone clean themselves.

Turning his attention to the bed, Pete Seldon pulled down the bedspread and said, "Take a look here, Matt. One of the pillow-cases is missing."

"Pete, that pillowcase didn't walk away on its own. It's missing for a reason. Let's take the pillow as evidence. And, we will need to speak with the maid who cleaned this room last."

"I have an idea. Let's check his shoes for fibers that might have stuck to them when he was dragged across the carpet. We should get fibers from the rug too. And, if I can suggest one more thing, we should ask the person doing the autopsy to look for skin under his fingernails. There may have been a struggle."

"Pete, you are starting to act like a cop, and that's a good thing."

While the two agents remained in the hotel room with the deceased, they called John Bridges in the Miami office. With his agents still on the line, the Deputy Director patched them through to Adam Grant in Washington, D.C. After introductions were made, John Bridges asked his agents in Havana to provide an update.

As the senior agent, Matt offered a concise twenty-minute narrative of their findings. When the recitation of facts was completed, both the FBI Deputy Director and Adam congratulated the agents on what appeared to be a thorough job. Adam said, "Matt and Pete, thank you for the facts. Now, I'd like to know your initial thoughts for our next actions."

"We believe Dr. Rodriguez died after he hit his head on the corner of the desk, but not necessarily from the blow. Our best guess is he was murdered in the main room and then dragged into the bathroom where his death was staged to look like he died from hitting his head on the toilet. Questions that remain to be answered are why is one pillowcase missing and why was his cell phone free of any fingerprints?

"Moving forward, we need to interview the hotel's desk clerk, maids, and other staff to get any information on who visited his room; then we'll need to access the contents of his phone, and laptop; and we need to interview the last people he talked with at the hospital yesterday; find out the source of the fingerprints we did collect in the room; and, of course, await the autopsy results."

"Do you have anything to add, Peter?" asked John Bridges.

"No. I think Matt nailed it."

"Okay, then," continued Bridges. "I know you guys are probably dreading this, but it's time to alert the Cuban police."

Adam spoke before Matt or Pete could reply. "If I may, I will initiate that call from our office, to smooth things over in advance and to take some of the heat off Matt and Pete. I will insist that the FBI continue as an integral part of the process, but we will leave it to the Cubans to handle the investigation however they choose."

"That's fine with us," said Deputy Director Bridges. "A call coming from D.C. is probably more effective than one coming from Miami. And, the FBI's involvement in a case like this is justified until the body is returned home. After that, it will be up to the Cubans to decide how much help they want from us."

"It's probably going to be a late night for you fellows," said Adam. "I will call the Cubans immediately and ask that the locals meet with you tonight, in the hotel room. This should help avoid any friction, and maybe even lead to cooperation. I know being stuck in Havana is not great, but your presence there is essential. I will do all I can to see that you guys can get started with the locals as soon as possible. Do your best to wrap up the initial phase tonight and then get a fresh start in the morning. You guys need some rest."

"Okay, Colonel," said Matt and Pete in unison. "We will wait here for the police."

# TEN

**A** quick review of the events led Adam to consider two widely different explanations for Dr. Rodriguez's death. One, a healthy man died due to a fall or a cardiac event; or he was murdered, and the scene was staged to suggest otherwise. Adam knew determination of the cause of death would have to wait for the autopsy results, which could only be trusted if the autopsy was done properly.

Adam decided to phone the U.S. Consular in Havana first because they would be prepared to mitigate any tensions that might arise. Plus, Adam was sure they would be eager to receive a follow-up report and would be willing to offer their assistance.

Cissy had agreed to stay late. When she connected with the U.S. Consular Office in Havana, she said, "Adam, I have the Consul on the line for you." Informality like this in private moments felt natural to Adam, who considered Cissy the big sister he never had. She was a friend and an indispensable part of his professional life.

Adam realized he didn't know the Consul's name. "Mr. Consul, this is Adam Grant from the Select Home for Operational Personnel in Washington. I hope I didn't keep you waiting too long."

"That is not a problem," said a female voice. "My name is Amanda Boncoski—Ms. Consul—but how would you know? I get that a lot."

Doing a quick re-think, Adam recalled Cissy had said she was going to call Amanda Boncoski. He had missed it. *Pay attention,* thought Adam.

"I think I know why you are calling, Colonel Grant. Tell me, what can I do? And, you can call me Amanda."

"Thank you, Amanda—you can call me Adam. I called to update you on the situation at the Hotel Sevilla. The Miami office dispatched two FBI agents to the hotel; they arrived about three this afternoon. They stabilized the scene and interviewed Dr. Alejandro Rivera, the man who called your office this morning. He's since left the hotel. Right now, we are calling this a death of undetermined cause, just to be on the safe side, but the agents are considering it to be a crime scene. The Cuban authorities need to be notified, and it will be necessary for us to do some explaining about our delay in contacting them. Dr. Rivera has some strong feelings about how arrangements for the autopsy should be made, and we will be doing everything in our power to see that it is done properly. How should we proceed when it comes to notifying the local police?"

"Good question, Adam. I can help with that. This kind of situation is handled by the National Revolutionary Police Force and, as you can imagine, there is a difference in the competence and intentions of the people who work in that outfit. There are some people in the police force who we have dealt with in the past that we trust. The person I will be recommending is a good guy. If it is okay with you, I will make the call and ask that Inspector Jorge Lopez be sent to the hotel immediately. He will probably have another officer with him, but knowing Jorge, he will pick a good one."

"That would be great, Amanda. Anything you can do will be light years better than what I can do from here."

"Great, Adam. When I make the contact and have more information, I will let your office know."

"Thanks, Amanda."

As Adam ended his conversation, Cissy connected with John Bridges, who then patched the call through to Matt Hull and Peter Seldon, still in room 514. Cissy buzzed Adam's phone to connect him on the line.

"Adam Grant here, with some good news. Consular Amanda Boncoski in Havana will notify Inspector Jorge Lopez, a local police officer she knows and trusts, to request that he take the lead on the Cuban side of the investigation. Lopez, probably with a colleague, will meet you at the hotel within the hour."

"Matt and Pete," said Deputy Director Bridges, "you will be on your own when it comes to dealing with the locals. Some non-negotiable issues are that we maintain control of the evidence you collected and do the evaluations in our lab here, stateside. We will share all the results with the Cubans. Next, the autopsy will be done according to the wishes of the family, and those directions will come from the dead man's friend Dr. Rivera. When the autopsy is completed, the body will be returned to the family in the U.S. for internment. Am I leaving anything out?"

"How do we conduct the questioning of possible witnesses?" asked Matt.

"Good point," said John Bridges. "You should conduct your interviews along with the Cuban police—but be sure you have an interpreter with you at all times. If you have any trouble with that, I will put in a request with the Consular Office in Havana. Anything else?"

Adam heard the director's comment about contacting Amanda Boncoski with a pang but suppressed it successfully. He already had a connection with Amanda and could deliver this message himself, but the role of SHOP was to be a facilitator not the leader. Adam was sure there would be times when he and his team should take the lead, but this would be determined by circumstances; until then, nothing should be done by SHOP that would diminish the role of the people and agencies they worked with. Adam chalked this up as a learning moment and continued to listen.

"How long do you want us to stay here?" asked Matt.

"At least until the body is shipped home."

"What about our clothes? Neither of us brought much."

"Buy what you need and put it on your expenses, but don't come back with a wardrobe like Desi Arnez! Seriously, we appreciate you two going the extra mile."

"When do you want to hear from us again?" asked Matt.

"Your call. We'll be here."

"Will do," said Matt. The men in Cuba clicked off the cell phone which had been on speaker.

With only John Bridges on the line, Adam asked, "Do you think there is more to this than an accidental death?"

"Honestly, right now I have a hunch. But on the record, I'm not leaning either way. Although, I am sure of one thing. After we get the results from the lab and the autopsy report is available, we should know if it was a homicide or not. If no conclusive findings come from these tests, there could still be a question. We just have to wait." Then he added, "This homicide business—like paternity testing, is much easier to confirm than rule out."

**Matt and** Pete were hungry. After the second call with Bridges and Adam, they had nothing to do but wait. Each had their own thoughts, but both harbored a degree of dread at the anticipated arrival of the Cuban police. Just to add some novelty to the scene, they flipped a coin to see who would go out for food. They had toyed with the idea of calling room service, but that didn't seem right. Matt lost the coin toss.

After thirty minutes, he was back in room 514 with a large, greasy bag that smelled like hamburgers and French fries, which is exactly what it contained. The hamburgers were alike, a thick mass of ingredients in a fat sesame-seed bun. There were two meat patties, tomatoes, lettuce, onion, cheese, and bacon. The concoction, which Matt said was the house specialty, was more than three inches tall. It took a combination of compression and wide opening for the men to get the behemoths into their mouths. There was no ketchup for the French fries, but the condiments plastered between the multiple ingredients of the burger made up for this deficiency. Washed down with large regular Pepsis, Diet Pepsi was not available, neither man left a scrap, and both were satisfied.

With the acrid smell of their repast hanging in the air to accost the olfactory system of anyone who entered the room, they heard a firm knock. Sprinting to the door, Peter Seldon opened it to see two men in tan uniforms with epaulets that were different. He suspected the one with the most stripes was the senior officer. That was probably a correct assumption because this man was the first to speak. In excellent English, he said, "My name is Jorge Lopez, from the National Police Force."

Pete stuck out his hand and said, "Peter Seldon." The agent noticed Jorge Lopez had left out "Revolutionary" and hoped this was a good omen.

"We received a call requesting that we join you to assist in the investigation of the death of a visiting U.S. doctor."

*Another good sign,* thought Peter, when he heard the word *assist.* "Yes. This is my partner, Matt Hull."

The second Cuban policeman, who was still outside the door, extended his hand and, in less-polished English, said, "I am Ricardo Ortiz."

There were only two chairs in the room, which were offered to the Cubans while Matt and Pete sat on the edge of the bed. The Cuban officers listened attentively as the FBI agents related the facts and their impression of what had taken place over the past twenty-four hours.

The Cuban officers registered satisfaction with the work the FBI agents had done so far and had nothing to add when it came to the investigation of the scene. They agreed it was unusual that the cell phone had no fingerprints on it and thought it was significant that a pillowcase was missing. They agreed it was a good idea to examine the pillow as well. They acknowledged the two long indentations in the carpet that had been left undisturbed by the agents and agreed the lab results comparing the material on the shoes and the fibers in the carpet would confirm what they already suspected.

Jorge Lopez spoke. "I will call for a vehicle to take the body to the morgue. With any luck, we can do the autopsy tomorrow."

"Officer Lopez," said Matt Hull, who was eager to maintain the progress they were making, "the dead man's colleague, a Cuban doctor by the name of Dr. Alejandro Rivera, has made a specific request that the autopsy be observed by a qualified pathologist known to him and the deceased. Would it be possible to arrange for that?"

"That should be no problem, Agent Hull, if the doctor is licensed and accredited," said Jorge Lopez. After phoning for an ambulance, Officer Lopez said they would interview the hotel staff tomorrow, and from there others whose names would come up as the investigation progressed, adding that the FBI agents were welcome to join them.

Matt Hull volunteered, "We will go to the airport now and arrange for the evidence we collected to be flown to FBI headquarters, where the lab will get to work first thing in the morning. Pete and I will stay here, at the Hotel Sevilla, in another room. We will call Dr. Rivera and ask him to contact you about the name of the pathologist he recommends. If you will contact us when a time is set for the interviews, we will be available. I suspect that by the end of the day tomorrow we will have partial results from the lab and at least preliminaries from the autopsy."

Ricardo Ortiz suggested he drive Peter to the airport and bring him back to the hotel, allowing Agent Hull and Officer Lopez to finish up with anything more they needed to discuss. This made sense to everyone. When the men left, Jorge Lopez said, "Agent Hull, from what I have read about your organization, there is much to admire. I am looking forward to working with you and expect that I will learn a lot."

"Jorge, we will be working together for a while and there is no reason for more formality than necessary. Please, call me Matt. I also want to say that I didn't know what to expect when Peter and I arrived. We know we are interlopers and that our two countries still operate pretty much at arm's length. The fact that you have been so professional and cooperative makes me feel ashamed that I was worried. So, thank you."

Jorge chuckled. "Well, Matt, I was concerned that you might treat us as bumpkins and be condescending and disrespectful. That sounds strong, I know, and they are just my personal feelings;

so please, don't quote me. Thank you for accepting us as colleagues. By tomorrow night, we will be closing the case if the death
is ruled natural or accidental. If it looks like it was murder, we will
have a longer investigation. And, if that is the case, I will look upon
working with you as a chance for me to maybe learn some forensic
science."

# ELEVEN

**H**avana had not aged well—not like Detroit and East St. Louis, cities cursed by urban blight, where decrepit buildings and dangerous neighborhoods in the center city were simply abandoned in favor of urban flight. Instead, ravaged structures in Havana, regardless of condition, remained havens for a population that had no alternative. There was no place to flee, and revitalization of the city had not happened. Most Cubans had little or no choice but to accept what was available.

In contrast, tourists in Cuba enjoyed upscale hotels, restaurants, bars, and specialty medical clinics that exclusively catered to them. These amenities were made possible by foreign investors who erected new structures, like the so-called cigar hotels that prominently overlooked Havana Harbor. Catering to tourists looking for an exotic destination and a chance to regale the folks at home with their visit to a recently forbidden destination, meant Cuban tourism was on the rise and prospering from an influx of cash provided by stylish spenders. The easing of U.S. sanctions brought a new rush of American tourists to join what had mostly been European visitors.

Some classic buildings had been spruced up on the outside and the old buildings in central Havana remained appealing because they represented, for the most part, what Havana once was. Structures that had no potential to turn a profit and private residences remained subject to the ravages of time. These dilapidated structures were cast in a monotonous, rundown sameness and were home to more than two million people who had no alternative housing.

**In this** milieu, Eduardo Sanchez was a businessman. His shop was old but profitable; aided by its appearance that faithfully represented the appeal of Old Havana to his customers, who were exclusively tourists. In his establishment, he sold souvenirs and curios in an authentic old-world pre-revolutionary atmosphere. Strategically located only two blocks from the Museum of the Revolution, his shop was well within comfortable walking distance for tourists who radiated out from the City Plaza. It was nestled on a picturesque street that was bedecked with a constant parade of sixty-year-old automobiles. These cars were meticulously cared for by their owners, and usually had quirky modifications and frequently sported bright pink or purple paint jobs. They were a boon as an attraction. These unique vehicles were nowhere else in the world and represented a mobile museum that only added to the appeal of shops like Eduardo's.

Most of the small items he sold were readily identified as having been purchased in Havana. The trade embargo all but guaranteed they were also made in Cuba, which meant they were genuine souvenirs. These everyday objects ranged from T-shirts to bottle openers, and included placemats, coasters, fans, baseball caps, and just about every gadget in between that would catch the eye of tourists with money to spend on a trinket emblematic of their visit to the city.

The store also contained a few impressive items. Eduardo Sanchez's establishment proudly displayed a collection of above-average oil and water-color paintings by local artists. Eduardo took a measure of pride in displaying these and other quality works created by his talented countrymen. This art, when framed, commanded as much as thirty dollars each, but no prices were displayed. Eduardo had a keen sense of the possible when it came to his business. His practice was to put no price tags on his higher-end merchandise, instead he preferred to set the price at the time of the sale based on his gut feeling from the appearance and level of interest on the part of the customer.

One special object available only in his shop were decorative model helicopters. About ten inches long, they were clad entirely with material salvaged from aluminum beer cans. The proprietor called them his "Crystal Cerveza" air force. They were testament not only to his countrymen's artistic sense but also to their resourcefulness. Eduardo sold so many of these small treasures that he purchased the artist's full output and remained the sole distributor.

The shop's prize offering was a two-foot-tall wood carving—a sculpture fashioned from a single tree trunk that weighed more than fifteen pounds. Eduardo did not know the kind of wood, but he had counted the number of rings at the base of the tree trunk, and there were more than sixty. Secretly he wondered if it had been planted by Batista. The carving showed two upward-reaching hands holding a crucifix while the wrists were shackled. This might have been inspired by one of the Pope's visits, but he hadn't asked the artist if that was the inspiration. This work was frequently admired by customers, and he suspected especially by Christians, but also by anyone who took umbrage to the Castro regime for any reason. Either way, this was a conversation piece and good for sales. He was not eager to part with it, but he would do so if the price was right.

Eduardo was a practical man. For a Cuban, he was doing well, certainly better than most. The income from his store was above the national average of 720 Cuban pesos per month, which was equivalent to about $29.50 in U.S. currency. He knew that medical doctors, even those who were specialists, earned pitifully little, only two dollars a day. This was not much reward for a higher education and a responsible job. When these doctors were sent overseas as contract health care providers in Venezuela and other countries, the Cuban government charged the host countries $5,000 a year per doctor. Of this money, the doctors were paid slightly over a dollar a day. They were provided room and board, transportation, and their families at home received a small stipend.

Eduardo suspected these doctors derived a certain satisfaction from fleeing the bleakness of their island home, a place that for some differed little from a prison. He also knew that his friends that were cab drivers and tour guides, and others in a variety of jobs that offered them the opportunity to have direct contact with visitors, were likely to be the highest paid workers in the country. A bizarre fact about the labor force in Cuba was that garbage collectors made as much as those working in financial institutions, even supervisors; and more than double those who worked in restaurant kitchens and other backroom occupations. This crazy system made Eduardo's head swim, but it was the only life he knew.

Eduardo Sanchez was thirty-seven, single, and had an off-and-on relationship with his family, except for one brother, with whom he was close. Born in 1980, Eduardo's childhood coincided with the start of an unwelcome economic adjustment in Cuba called the Special Period in Time of Peace. The resulting privatization and austerity spawned by this event continued to influence Eduardo, and everyone else in the country. It began with the fall of the Soviet Union and withdrawal of the comforting cloak of money and trade that came with Russian sponsorship. Financial security and implied military support were abruptly ripped from Cuba, which meant the country and its people were on their own.

The enduring feature of living in Cuba today, for Eduardo, was the need to survive despite the United States' wide-ranging sanctions. The richest and most powerful country in the world not only blocked tourism and boycotted trade for its own people, but also used its influence to keep other countries from trading with Cuba. The U.S. told its allies, "You trade with us or them, not with both."

The brief respite for Cuba, offered by the Venezuelan dictator Hugo Chavez, lasted only a few years. This second loss of economic support for Cuba was another example of collateral damage inflicted by a failed state that had propped up his country's economy. Eduardo realized that if the bomb killed you, you are dead, whether it was aimed at you or not. Eduardo was realistic and knew the economic problems besetting Cuba would only be slightly mollified by the recent U.S. administration's lifting of some sanctions against his country, including lifting the ban on tourism and restoring normal diplomatic relations. Things were a bit better, but there were rumblings that a new administration could restore some, if not all, of the onerous sanctions Cuba had so long endured. Based on his assessment of what it would take to have any hope of reaching his financial goals, Eduardo Sanchez had concluded he must do whatever it took to succeed—and that was the path he had chosen.

**The closed** sign still hung on the door. It was 9:00 a.m. and too early for tourists to purchase souvenirs. They were concentrating on breakfast and not willing to shop early only to have to carry their spoils around all day.

Eduardo watched Luis approach the shop. He was carrying a cardboard box that looked like it could hold a pair of work boots. Eduardo was expecting him, and immediately opened the door. "Luis," he said coldly, "yesterday afternoon you killed the doctor. Now, I must clean up the mess you created."

The harsh words stung Luis. He was not a cold-blooded killer. He had simply lost control and acted impulsively.

Eduardo asked, "Did you say anything to your girlfriend?" He knew her name was Isabelle, but Eduardo refused to dignify the relationship by referring to her by name. Luis's longtime live-in girlfriend was a waitress and supported herself. She and Luis lived together but led independent lives. "Does she know anything about yesterday? Does she know you were here?"

"I swear to you, I said nothing. She has no idea I was here. I have never spoken with her about our plans. When she came home last night, she was tired and went right to bed. We barely spoke. She was still asleep when I left this morning."

"Good," said Eduardo. "What did you do yesterday, before you came here and told me what you had done?"

"I told you last night. After I left the Hotel Sevilla, I went back to the hospital. I put the loose bottle that had been on top, the one that was seen by the doctor, inside the box. I then closed the box and put it at the bottom of another stack and out of sight. When I finished that, I walked around for a while, got some dinner, and came to see you, here. This morning, I went to the hospital and picked up the pills. That is what I have here," he said as he held out the box.

"Did anyone see you at the hospital, last night or this morning?"

A little more confident now, Luis answered, "No. Nobody saw me after the doctor died. When I was in the storeroom, earlier in the afternoon, when the doctor walked in, nobody else was there. I had just opened the box and taken the bottle out, so I am sure nobody saw it except the doctor. He was the only one in the room during that time. We were alone."

With an exasperated look, Eduardo, who was suspicious of anyone who said the same thing three times as though to convince themselves, asked, "Why was a bottle out in the open, where the doctor could see it?"

Sulking at having his foolish mistake brought up again but knowing it would only be made worse if he lied, Luis truthfully explained, "I was planning on selling one bottle, with only fifty pills, to a man who said he had a customer on a private fishing boat in Hemingway Harbor Marina. I told him the pills were six dollars each and that I would need three hundred dollars for fifty. He said he would pay it, and I should bring the pills to the marina at nine. That would have been last night. He is probably wondering why I never showed up. I would have given the money to you and taken my cut according to what you said." Then, as an afterthought, Luis continued, "Of course, this was arranged in the morning, before the doctor saw the pills."

Both men knew it was a lie about the money and that Luis would have kept all of it, but this point remained unchallenged by Eduardo. He had to make plans about how to deal with things as they were now, not how they should have been. It was a time for action. Luis would get his due, but in time. One thing that Eduardo was sure of, the situation would only get worse with Luis around. He would have to go.

Eduardo said, "Luis, if you had gone to the marina with the bottle last night, the best thing that could have happened to you would be a wrap on the head and empty pockets. More likely, those men would have done that and then dumped you in the water to drown." Finished with the lecture, Eduardo asked, "What do you know about the FBI at the hotel?"

"The news that I have so far is good, Eduardo. I know several people who know people who work at the hotel and the word is that the doctor died as the result of an accident or from a heart attack. The FBI came only because the doctor's friend called the U.S. Consulate first. They said there will be an autopsy—but except for the bump on his head, there will be no signs on the body."

"I hope you are right, Luis. But I do know one thing for sure, and that is we will have to sit on this merchandise for a while, until things settle down. Killing the doctor was bad, but you must have thought it was necessary if seeing the bottle would have led him to us. The thing that never should have happened was to have the pills out in the open."

To his surprise, Luis then heard Eduardo say, "Luis, here is a ticket on Copa Airlines to Caracas. The plane leaves in two hours. Here is two hundred dollars to get you started—but don't spend it all. Save enough to buy a ticket to get back here when I call. Don't call me; I will call you in two days. You are to lay low. I know you have friends there, so you can find a place to stay, especially if they know you have money. If you need more, I can help, but only so much. I am going to trust you that all the pills from the delivery, including the bottle of fifty, are in the box. I will keep them hidden in the shop. They will remain out of sight and I will make no attempt to sell any of them until things quiet down. We can only hope the investigation ends with the police saying his death was accidental or from natural causes, like a heart attack or a stroke."

Luis left the shop, surprised and happy to have survived this encounter. When the door closed, Eduardo took the cardboard box of plastic medicine bottles and pills in two plastic bags and placed it in the middle of a large container that held colorful scarves that were handmade by a local woman in her home. She sold them on the street and to shops like Eduardo's. He then placed the large box in the middle of a stack of similar boxes in the small storeroom. Hidden in plain sight, the drugs would remain there until this matter was settled—except, Eduardo admitted only to himself, a few might be sold to the right people.

Luis was gone. It was time for the next step in damage control, which meant Eduardo had to go back to the beginning.

**A month** ago, Arturo introduced Eduardo to Greta Schmidt, the dining room director of the *Princess Court*, part of the Regal Seas Cruise Ship line that served the Caribbean and now visited Havana on a regular basis. Having these cruise ships in port was a new and exciting change, made possible when the President of the United States lifted the travel ban. Eduardo was not surprised when Arturo, who was into many ventures, thought of Eduardo when Greta told him she was eager to meet a local businessman with a retail store that catered to tourists and was within easy walking distance of the docks.

At the fateful meeting, Arturo had said, "Eduardo, this is my friend Greta Schmidt. I told Greta you had a very nice shop and she was interested in meeting you. Now, I'll let you talk about whatever you want. I hope it turns out well for both of you." As Arturo left, he gave Eduardo a look that said, "Buddy, you owe me."

The downtown plaza was only three blocks from the docks. The outline of the mammoth ship that Greta Schmidt worked on framed the mannish-looking woman as she faced Eduardo. When Arturo left, the two sat on a sun-bleached, teak park bench as tourists passed by, almost touching them—but paradoxically, there were so many people and they were so intent on the sights around them, that the two on the bench felt like they were alone. "Arturo tells me you have a very nice shop near here."

"Yes, my shop is not far." He was going to elaborate but then thought better of it. He wanted to let her do the talking at first.

"What do you sell?" questioned Greta.

"All sorts of things, costing from a few pesos to a few thousand, depending on what people want."

Greta asked, "How much do these customers have to spend?"

Eduardo did not answer. It was none of her concern. How was she going to use this information? Was she from the government and checking up on how he ran his business? He wondered if she was German; she was not American. Eduardo found her questions disturbing.

Seeing the concern on his face, Greta Schmidt decided she should quit sparring and get to the point. "I apologize if I am asking too many questions. Let me tell you why I am here. I asked Arturo to introduce me to a businessman who had a successful shop near the harbor. He told me about you. He said you had an impressive array of nice items that would attract tourists, but also some cheaper things so as not to scare people away. He said your policy was that even high-rollers liked a bargain, but once they saw something of value, they would be willing to part with their money."

Now more relaxed, Eduardo said, "To be perfectly honest, Greta, you have pretty much hit on my business philosophy. Before I started, a man who had been in the business for a long time told me that I should have at least one item in the store that was very expensive, large, and impressive. It could be something on the order of a museum piece, at least in relative terms. People will come in just to look at it. It's not important that they buy it. Even if they make an offer, I can make the price so high they will never make the purchase. Or, if they offer what I ask, I can sell it at a huge profit. What happens on a day-to-day basis is that people admire the object but end up buying something else, maybe several items. The relative value of the cheaper things they purchase is increased simply by them being in a shop that also contains something so valuable. Make sense?"

Excited by Eduardo's explanation, Greta said, "Eduardo, I am convinced you are just the person I should be talking to. I want to propose a business deal. It is this: I will supply a product at a distributor's price. It will be small and suitable for packaging in units of one hundred, but it also can be sold in whatever amount you wish, even singly. The mark-up to the customer would be established by you, the seller, and could be adjusted depending on what you think the buyer is willing to pay but always at a profit. The merchandise would be handed off personally by me or my representative and replenished each time the ship visits Havana, which is about once a month. Each transaction would be between us personally, or by my agent, and this would happen only if arranged ahead of time by mutual agreement. I will supply the initial order on consignment but will expect full payment in one month. Thereafter, you would pay for the product upon delivery. The profit for you for the first month's supply could be six thousand dollars, and possibly more, that depends on you."

Eduardo took a deep breath after hearing the potential profit. He was certain it could not be legal merchandise.

Greta continued, "You haven't asked what it is I am offering for sale. Does that mean you are not interested?"

"On the contrary, Greta. I am very interested. Please, tell me what it is you want me to sell in my shop."

Still dangling the carrot, the woman continued, "It is a very portable, high-profit item that is sold legally by the millions—but when I sell it to you, and you in turn to the public, it is slightly outside of the law—but I find no guilt in doing this because people will use it anyway. What I am offering is of high quality and safe when used properly."

Eduardo looked Greta in the eyes. "I have a pretty good idea what will come next, but you tell me what it is we are talking about."


**Eduardo wondered** how he had let an idiot like Luis screw things up so badly—before he had made even one sale of a high-quality, medical-grade opioid that could make him rich. It was a helluva way to start a new business.

# TWELVE

**A**gents Hull and Seldon were in 520, a double room just down the hallway from room 514. At the request of the Cuban police, the hotel had closed off the entire wing, ostensibly for maintenance, to avoid the negative reaction of guests if they had discovered a death had occurred. Occupancy at the hotel was just over fifty percent, so this action did not represent a loss of revenue for the management.

Getting up at a leisurely 8:00 a.m., Matt and Pete planned to spend a full day conducting interviews of the staff with Jorge and Ricardo. During any free time, they would rely on the advice of their colleagues and find a store where they could augment their meager clothing supplies. Peter, a stylish bachelor, said he would buy two shirts if he found some he liked.

**When the** interviews started, Ricardo did most of the questioning, while Jorge translated for the two FBI agents. First, they talked with the hotel clerk who had given Dr. Rodriguez his room key Tuesday afternoon when he returned from the hospital. She had noticed nothing out of the ordinary. As far as she and her colleague, who was also on duty could recall, the doctor did not return to the lobby after he went up to his room. They said he left the desk and headed directly toward the elevators, although neither of them actually saw him enter.

The hotel operator remembered receiving a phone call that came from outside the hotel around four o'clock, from a man asking for Dr. Rodriguez's room number. She told the caller she could not give him the room number but she could ring the room for him. The man said that was not necessary and he would call back later. At approximately four thirty, a call from inside the hotel was received. It was a man who sounded like the previous caller; this time he asked to be connected to Dr. Rodriguez's room. The man spoke Spanish like a native. This was useful information for the investigators because it indicated that someone was eager to speak with the doctor around the time he was killed.

There was nothing to learn from the doorman, who had only seen Dr. Rodriguez briefly when he exited the car and walked into the hotel. The maid had nothing of consequence to offer. She had cleaned the room at one thirty that afternoon. When asked if there was any chance she could have neglected to put a pillowcase on one of the pillows, the woman became indignant at the suggestion she might not have done her job properly. Ricardo quickly reassured her that was not what they were implying; eventually the woman was mollified.

Next, the four men drove to Raul Mesa Carreras Eye Hospital, where they spoke with the driver who had delivered Dr. Rodriguez to the Hotel Sevilla. At first, the driver had nothing to add beyond, "Dr. Rodriguez was pleasant and spoke in rusty Spanish. Nothing seemed out of the ordinary in the doctor's behavior." But after a pause, the driver added, "However, when I returned to the hospital, after dropping off the doctor, a man walked up to me in the parking lot and asked about how he could get a job driving for the hospital. He also asked what kind of trips I made. I told him I had just taken a doctor to the Hotel Sevilla."

"Do you know the man?"

"Not his name, but I have seen him around. I think he works at the hospital, but I don't know what he does. I thought it was odd that he would ask me about this job and not just go to the hospital's employment office to inquire."

"Would you recognize the man if you saw him again?"

"Yes, I think so."

"Thank you. We may have more questions later."

"Okay."

The men also spoke with a dozen people at the hospital who had interacted with Dr. Michael Rodriguez on Tuesday, his last day there. The information obtained from all of them was much the same: Dr. Rodriguez was pleasant, hardworking, open, and smart. He was a pleasure to work with and his visit had been very productive—a total success. When he said goodbye, Dr. Rodriguez had told everyone he was looking forward to returning next year. He also said he would be sightseeing with an old friend, a Cuban physician and longtime colleague, for a few days before he returned to the States. He didn't tell them where they would be going or the purpose of the activity.

An assistant in the Administrator's Office, who seemed to have been the last person the doctor had spoken with at the hospital, said she and Dr. Rodriguez had discussed the possibility of his being able to arrange for some supplies to be donated to the hospital. These included several specialty surgical instruments he had introduced to the team and a variety of eye medications that were currently in short supply or unavailable in Cuba. He also said he would try to find a way to purchase some high-quality, but low-priced intraocular lenses for use in cataract surgery. They were produced in India, and he had some connections in Chennai at the Aravind Eye Hospital, where the production facility was located. He had asked her where the lenses would be stored and who would be receiving them if arrangements could be made to have these items shipped. The assistant said she directed Dr. Rodriguez to Shipping and Receiving and told him to look for the supervisor, Luis Espinosa.

By the time the four men made it to Shipping and Receiving, it was four o'clock and the area was deserted. Since no one was around, they took the opportunity to examine the boxes that were stored in what looked like an orderly fashion. A few were opened, but most were sealed and labeled in Spanish; only a few labels were in English.

According to Jorge, the boxes consisted of janitorial cleaning and maintenance supplies; and items you would use in a hospital, including IV fluids, catheters, dressings, several kinds of medicines, and several boxes labeled anesthesia. After searching for about fifteen minutes, looking for anything suspicious and that might have caused Dr. Rodriguez to be alarmed, the four officers conceded that they had found nothing.

With the obvious need to review and discuss what they had learned during the long day, Jorge invited Agents Hull and Seldon to his office at the headquarters of the National Revolutionary Police Force. They all rode together in an old, white, dingy Lada, barely large enough to hold them. It was no doubt left over from the salad days with the Soviet Union.

On the way to police headquarters, they stopped by the Hotel Sevilla to retrieve the preliminary results from the FBI Crime Lab's analysis of the evidence they had collected. It had been delivered to the desk in a sealed envelope addressed to Agent Matthew Hull, with the notation that it would be turned over only with his signature. Under normal circumstances, the delivery service would only give the envelope to Matt, but in this case, protocol had not been followed. Matt examined the envelope. It was a little rumpled but still tightly sealed, which meant the contents had likely remained undisturbed.

Matt thought the police headquarters building looked substantial and in good order. It had straight lines and a grey stucco exterior. It was in no way reminiscent of the ornate, rundown buildings in Old Havana. The structure was likely post-revolutionary and no doubt its design had been influenced by the architectural tastes, or lack of taste, typical in Communist Russia.

They parked in an expansive but nearly empty parking lot. Several newer cars were in evidence; some were familiar brands, like Volkswagen and Hyundai, but none were American-made.

On closer look, the building looked substantial but was not

well maintained, which aligned with it being a necessary building although not a revenue producer. Jorge led the three men up a flight of stairs, turned left at the landing, and after proceeding down a hallway, opened the third door on the right. The room was small. It was not an office. It was an interrogation room.

Once they were all inside, Jorge spoke. "I picked this room because we can spread out and we won't be bothered. We have a lot of stuff to go through and it will take a couple hours. Would you guys like something to eat?"

"No, thanks," said Matt and Pete almost in unison. Then Matt added, "That lunch at the hospital was very good and filling. We're doing great; but there is nothing that a cup of coffee can't fix."

"You beat me to it," said Jorge as he nodded at Ricardo.

Ricardo asked, "Cream and sugar?" Hearing that black was preferred by both guests, he left to get four cups of coffee. He knew Jorge would expect cream and sugar in his.


**On Thursday** morning, Adam Grant was happy to hear from John Bridges that things were moving along well in Havana. Most of the interviews would be completed; the contents of the evidence bags were being examined at the FBI's lab in Miami, and preliminary results would be sent to the team by the afternoon. And the autopsy was underway. The Deputy Director clarified, "At this point in the investigation, we are making no official statement. We are treating it as an accidental death or a death from natural causes until we have reason to conclude otherwise. Either way, our investigation will continue until we determine with certainty the cause of death. We will avoid even hinting we suspect foul play until we are sure."

"That makes sense, John. But just between us, which way are you leaning?"

"All I can say is, if this man was murdered, I believe the evidence will come up quickly. If that is the direction we are headed, then our work will be to determine the motive and find the culprit.

Not easy, but doable. If convincing evidence is lacking, but we continue to believe this death is a murder, then we have our work cut out for us. But, in my experience, when the possibility of murder is even in the mix, in most cases, it turns out that's what it is. That's a roundabout way of saying what I don't want to say definitively and out loud."

"I get it, John; and I think you said it very well."

"Adam, I will call you the minute I hear something. Are there any time constraints on your end?"

"None. I just want to hear the results as soon as possible. If this is a homicide, there will be important diplomatic issues that will need tending to."

"I agree."

"One more thing, John. What did we tell Mrs. Rodriguez?"

The Deputy Director responded, "Our agents implied that she would hear something from us today. And, we know that Dr. Rivera called Mrs. Rodriguez early this morning to tell her an autopsy was being done with a doctor of his choice participating. Adam, since you have already spoken with the Consul in Cuba, and are privy to everything in this case, would you be willing to be the next official person to speak with the doctor's wife?"

Adam paused for a second to reflect on the pain he experienced when he had to speak with the devastated families of the three soldiers on his team who had lost their lives in Afghanistan. "John, I am kind of new at the 'Official Washington' thing, but I have done this before and I am willing to do it now. Yes, I can be the one to talk next with Mrs. Rodriguez."

# THIRTEEN

**The men** sat two on a side, facing each other across a sturdy, brown-plastic folding table; a heavy white coffee mug sat in front of each. Jorge Lopez began. "This has been a big day, gentlemen, but we have more loose ends to tie up before we move ahead. What we accomplish now will help us stay on track when we are back at it tomorrow." Ricardo understood English much better than he spoke it, so he would not miss much. If he didn't understand something, he could ask his partner to repeat it in Spanish. Directing his gaze across the table, Jorge said, "Let's start with the evidence you collected from the hotel room."

Peter Seldon spoke first. "The blood found on the bathroom floor, the toilet seat, the corner of the desk, and the pillow are all the same blood type and likely from the same person. We will wait for the blood typing from the autopsy report to see if it's a match with Dr. Rodriguez. A bonus, at least for the investigation, is that the bloodstain on the pillow is the same type as the blood found elsewhere in the room."

"If I may interrupt, the autopsy report indicates the doctor's blood was type B," said Jorge.

"That is the same as the blood we found in the room," confirmed Peter. "So, all the blood could be from the deceased." The word *victim* was still being avoided. "We'll know more in a day or so, when the DNA matching with tissue from the autopsy is completed. It is possible that the blood on the pillow was already there. It will take a DNA match to tie it to the doctor; and if it does, suffocation is a possible cause of death, but I won't go there now."

"Excellent work," said Ricardo. This comment indicated he wasn't being shut out by the language barrier he faced.

Peter continued. "The fibers from the carpet and those wedged between the sole and the uppers of the doc's shoes are the same. This means the body was dragged into the bathroom where the death was staged. Since this would not have any chance of being an ante mortem event; we can now refer to the deceased as 'the victim.' He was murdered. The man died in the room, either from hitting his head on the corner of the desk or from something else. Then, the body was moved."

"Is there any reason to believe that hitting the desk corner caused his death?" asked Jorge.

Matt Hull fielded this question. "Jorge, we believe the desk, which is pretty flimsy, was moved, about an inch. Dents in the rug indicate it had been there for a long time before it was moved. From the swelling and laceration on the doctor's head and the blood on the broken edge of the desk corner, our best guess is that the doctor's head hit the desk. It could have stunned him, but it did not kill him."

"Thanks," chimed the Cubans.

Then Peter spoke, "Although we are not yet finished with the analysis of the fingerprints we collected, we don't expect the findings to add anything. Any surfaces the perpetrator would have touched were wiped clean. When it comes to fingerprints, we are more interested in those we don't find." This was said with a bit of a flourish. In the few seconds before he moved on with this disclosure, Peter observed the expectancy of his colleagues across the table, before reminding them of a finding he had shared the night before but had not emphasized. "Dr. Rodriguez's cell phone was found on the desk. It was an iPhone 7 and it had no fingerprints—not even his! We concluded that the only way this could possibly have happened is that after he called his wife in Michigan, at about 4:15, his phone was carefully wiped clean of fingerprints and replaced on the desk where we found it. It is possible he did this himself, but the likelihood is too remote to even consider. Once it was confirmed that the phone was clean of fingerprints, the lab checked the phone's contents. The only outgoing and incoming calls for the entire time the doctor was in Cuba were to or from his home telephone number."

"Not much help there," said Jorge.

Agent Seldon continued, "The lab looked at the pictures stored on the phone. The last hundred or so are from the time Dr. Rodriguez spent at the eye hospital. They were mostly taken in the clinic and the operating room; and are of patients and equipment. Other photos are of the doctors, nurses, and other staff. There were also a few from after-work social occasions, including the dinner when the group was together the last evening of his official visit. The last picture on his phone was taken at 3:00 p.m. on the day he was killed. It is a group picture in the administrator's office. It had to be taken by someone other than Dr. Rodriguez because he is in it and the subjects are too far away for it to be a selfie."

"I agree that the most unusual finding so far is that there are no fingerprints on his phone. Who would have wiped it clean?" Then, answering his own question, Ricardo offered, "The murderer?"

This astute conclusion made it clear that the second man on the Cuban team, as Peter was on his own team, was fully engaged and contributing.

Matt Hull dropped the bombshell. "That's only part of it. The lab looked at the doctor's iPhone pictures and then at the text messages on his phone. The last text message he sent was at 4:10 p.m., immediately after he returned to his hotel room and just minutes before he called his wife. There were two photos attached to a text message to his wife, but these photos are not in the photo gallery; they had to have been erased. They show a medicine bottle sitting on top of what looks like a large shoe box. Different from the other boxes around it. These photos were taken in the Shipping and Receiving area of the hospital, where we were today. The lab thought this was valuable information, so they sent it to us immediately by courier."

The Cubans viewed the close-up of a small medicine bottle. Its label indicated the bottle contained hydrocodone 10/325 and was dispensed by Ametz Pharmacy in Albuquerque, New Mexico.

"The lab said they scoured the internet but could not find a pharmacy with this name in Albuquerque, or anywhere," said Matt. "They found nearly a dozen companies that produce this drug combination, including in a generic form, but none of the names are on the label of this bottle. Since the box is no longer in the store room, or at least where it was when the picture was taken, it is possible that these pills are not for the hospital but for some other purpose. My guess is that whoever put the bottle of pills there intends to sell them and was not happy that Dr. Rodriguez stumbled onto them and was curious enough to take a picture."

"No offense, gentlemen," said Peter, "but it's unlikely there are many ordinary people in Cuba who have enough money to spend on stuff like this. So, the question is: why were the pills sent here?"

"You're right," said Jorge. "I'd like to say that Cubans are too smart to use this stuff, but we all know consumption is more likely to depend on an inverse relationship between how much money a person has to spend and their level of common sense. In our country, the average worker would be able to buy five or six pills a month with hard currency—and that would be the person's entire income. Nobody should be that dumb!"

"If the market for this stuff is just tourists," said Matt, "I am guessing that the number of drugs the doctor discovered is just the tip of the iceberg. This could be a mom-and-pop operation, or it could be something big, especially if someone was willing to kill over it. From the size of the box, I suspect the cache could contain several hundred or even thousands of loose pills, and about half that many if they were in bottles like the one in the picture."

"What would be the street value?" asked Ricardo.

"Hard to say," Pete responded. "It depends how hungry the seller is and what the market will bear. Five bucks a pill would be at the low end. In some cases, the price could go as high as ten or twenty dollars a pill, depending on the willingness of the customer to pay. At the very least, one of these pills would cost the same as a six-pack of beer in the U.S. That could be a lot of money if Matt's guess about the number is correct. Even if that were the only box with pills, and the markup was at the lower end, an enterprising dealer could do quite well. The real problem is not this one stash. It means that there is, for the lack of a better term, a wholesale source for this stuff, and we are likely to be seeing only the beginning. In our experience, big operations can eventually be taken down starting with mistakes made at the street level. We may be dealing with just this kind of thing here."

"I agree with what you are saying, Pete," said Matt. "It looks like a fairly sophisticated player has figured out a way to wholesale the merchandise to a small dealer here, in Havana, and possibly other places like this in the Caribbean. I would bet the stuff is not produced here or anywhere in Latin America. With the easing of the travel restrictions and the increased number of American tourists, this stuff could be coming from the States. A label from a fictitious American pharmacy is slapped on to add authenticity—and I suspect inside the pills are the real thing. The dispensing information on the bottle is fake and just for show. The pills could be counterfeit too, although with billions of these available from reliable manufacturers, it is more likely that this is a high-quality drug that has been diverted for illegal street sale.

"What this may boil down to is that someone in Havana is selling this stuff to the ever-increasing number of tourists now visiting the island. This person or persons could pick up a pretty good paycheck for a small effort. The fact that Dr. Rodriguez saw the pills was bad news for the local sellers and, as it turned out, even worse news for the doc."

"Matt and Pete, your theory could very well be true," offered Jorge. "An enterprising Cuban could be interested in selling this stuff, even in small amounts, to tourists who arrive weekly on cruise ships or fly in with a tour. My guess is the sale of the contents of just the bottle we saw in the photo would net the seller an amount close to the average yearly income of the typical Cuban. Selling a boxful would make the person rich here. If that is the case, and this turns out to be a significant drug bust, that would be a big deal. But based on what we have seen, the discovery of a small stash of drugs is of little importance compared to the murder of a fine man. Life is a priceless thing. Regardless of the quantity of drugs involved, what deserves to be called a 'big bust' is catching the murderer."

Matt Hull and Peter Seldon listened in silence, impressed with both the forceful language and the compassion expressed by their companion. "Jorge, what you said makes a helluva lot of sense and puts this whole thing in perspective," said Matt. "I want to stop this drug enterprise, but more importantly, I want to get the murderer."

"Let's hear more about the autopsy findings," said Pete.

Jorge picked up a sheaf of papers and said, "I'll read directly from the report, with a little paraphrasing. 'The lips and gums show bruising and the nasal cartilage is displaced laterally twenty degrees. The head and face show cyanosis and there are numerous petechial hemorrhages in the face and conjunctiva. Frothy blood-staining is present in the air passages and the back of the mouth. There is acute emphysema and edema of the lungs. All of the major internal organs are deeply congested and show small hemorrhages.' Jorge looked up when he had finished and, as expected, saw expressions that were noncommittal but expectant.

Putting words to what each of the listeners was thinking, Matt Hull asked, "What in the heck does that mean?"

Jorge answered, "The report concludes by saying that the 'finding in this body is consistent with the deceased succumbing from suffocation-smothering.' The report ends with this: 'Homicidal smothering is difficult to detect. These pathologic changes must be interpreted while keeping in view the medical history of the deceased and the specific circumstances surrounding the death.' Anybody want to say where all of this leads us?"

Matt Hull looked satisfied by what he had just heard. "To me, that says it all! Now we know the guy died from suffocation. He didn't do it himself or however you want to figure out a bizarre suicide. Someone else did it. This means, we have a murder on our hands. We know that, at some point, Dr. Rivera was in the hotel room with Dr. Rodriguez, since he was the one who made the call that eventually alerted us to the death of the doctor. He made the call Wednesday morning, when Dr. Rodriguez had been dead for at least twelve hours. I suspect Dr. Rivera's whereabouts since Tuesday afternoon will be accounted for. That means we have every reason to believe that another person, probably a strong man capable of subduing his victim, and likely the same person who attempted to contact the doctor twice, finally succeeded in confronting Dr. Rodriguez in his hotel room. We don't know for sure, but it is reasonable to assume that the perpetrator confronted the doctor. When it was confirmed he had seen the pills, he killed him. And, when it comes to motive, it's clear the doctor's death was linked to his knowledge of a cache of drugs he discovered in the basement of Raul Mesa Carreras Eye Hospital." Looking at Jorge, Matt continued, "And Jorge, your conclusion that even if this is a small-scale drug operation that has resulted in a murder, it has become an offense that is no longer scalable."

Jorge nodded in agreement. "That's a very convincing scenario. Where do we go from here?"

"If you guys are agreeable, I think we should quietly get the word out that we are tying up the loose ends of an accidental death. We don't have to be outright liars, but we should not say anything that will tip off the perpetrator to what we know or think we know. Whoever did this is likely to be skittish, and I bet a dollar to a donut that the reason we didn't find the drugs in the storeroom is that they were removed. For starters, let's meet with Dr. Alejandro Rivera again, and then follow up with the hospital."

"Good idea," said Jorge. "I will go with you. Ricardo, you get the word out on the street that we are looking for some drugs that might be for sale in amounts suitable for personal use. We will not say anything about the doctor's death being connected, even with those here in the building. You can say we are concerned about some possible drug action related to tourists from the cruise ships—or whatever sounds convincing. This has been a long day, but a productive one. Ricardo will take you back to the hotel and I will pick you up tomorrow about nine. Is that good?"

"Perfect," said Matt.

As they were leaving, Jorge said, "Oh, there's something that's bothering me. Before we pick you up at the hotel tomorrow, I want to talk with the maid who cleaned the doctor's room." With that, Jorge watched Ricardo and the two FBI men depart. He had a little more work to do before going home. For one thing, he needed to explain the suspected drug angle to his boss, Colonel Diaz. This news should make their efforts a priority and give Ricardo and him more leeway with the investigation.

# FOURTEEN

**A**lejandro was forty-seven years old, twelve years younger than his friend Michael Rodriguez. When they first met, Mike was a combination informal mentor and big brother. While both were studying at Johns Hopkins Hospital in Baltimore, the two met in the cafeteria and a friendship developed. The senior trainee, aware of their common heritage, had befriended the young Cuban. Their career stages were vastly different. Alejandro was an intern while Mike was completing a post-doctoral fellowship. At the end of that year, they parted, corresponding only sporadically, mostly with Christmas cards.

When Mike Rodriguez first visited Cuba three years ago, his first official act outside of specific duties at the hospital was to look up his friend. They reunited in a way that melted the years but fully exposed the gulf that existed between them. Both had carved out solid positions in their own professional communities and each was a success, but it was only when their friendship was renewed that Alejandro fully realized the differences between success in the United States and success in Cuba.

In 1965, Mike Rodriguez's father, at the age of forty-five, left Cuba by taking advantage of a program initiated by Castro that allowed Cuban dissidents to emigrate to the United States or another country of their choice. At that time, Mike Rodriguez was in primary school. Mike and his family were part of a group of as many as two hundred and fifty thousand Cubans who participated in Freedom Flights between 1965 and 1971. Castro was riding high in relative prosperity as a client state of the Soviet Union. His country was losing a group of educated and professional people in these Freedom Flights, but the Cubans that left didn't like him or the new regime and, as such, were an ongoing annoyance. By allowing these Cubans to leave the country, Castro was getting rid of potentially dangerous opponents. Another bonus was these wealthy and successful people could flee with only limited personal belongings, which meant the Cuban government was able to confiscate the hundreds of millions of dollars in property they had to leave behind.

After arriving in the United States, the Rodriguez family soon settled in Detroit, Michigan. Michael's father, who had been a surgeon in Cuba and spoke good English, began a family medicine practice on Detroit's east side. He maintained the practice for nearly twenty years until his death. Michael quickly learned English, eventually enrolling at the University of Michigan, where he remained for nine years; completing undergrad, medical school, and an internship. After that, he completed a residency in ophthalmology that was followed by two years of fellowship training at Johns Hopkins Hospital. Married and with two young children, Michael, in the final year of his fellowship, met Alejandro.

The crowning achievement for the Rodriguez family was Michael, who became a prominent physician with a brilliant career, a beautiful family, and an annual income that put him in the top ten percent of earners in the country. Mike worked hard, but the money he earned was not what motivated him. He spent the equivalent of one day each week and many nights and weekends, teaching, carrying out clinical research, and participating in unpaid overseas service programs.

In contrast, Alejandro's grandfather was born into poverty, uneducated, and worked as a farm laborer before moving the family to Havana, where he continued a hardscrabble life, with the only difference that it was now in a city. Alejandro's father was born in Havana and became the first family member to attend high school, but he never graduated. After Alejandro's father, Pedro Rivera, left school, he began working at a series of menial jobs before securing a position working at a casino. This was in the heyday of these lavish institutions that prospered with the support of corrupt government, culminating in the period of Batista's rule. Pedro's employment ended with the revolution in 1959, when Fidel Castro closed the casinos, which he considered emblematic of the corrupt regime his movement had overthrown.

Pedro Rivera, being both intelligent and a survivor, switched his allegiance from the trappings of the Batista regime to a new life as a revolutionary who supported Castro. Demonstrating his willingness to make the most of the new situation, Pedro landed a position in Castro's Revolutionary Police Force. He had no policing skills, but he solidified his position by supporting the new government and doing whatever he was asked to do. The family not only survived but prospered in the new Cuba and continued to live a life that was better than most.

By 1970, when Alejandro was born, his family had successfully completed the transition to the new way of life in Cuba. His parents were living a comfortable life in a country where the separation of classes continued, but in this case being aligned with the government put a person on the winning side. Alejandro's early life was during the salad years of a regime that promised to see workers directly participating in companies, working in self-governed agricultural cooperatives, and joining in a democratic society. These promises were bolstered by the support of Russia, who prized its client state, which was only ninety miles from U.S. soil. Despite the failed nuclear threat of '62 and the Bay of Pigs invasion a few years later, life in Cuba, at least on the surface, was good.

In December of 1988, when Alejandro was entering medical school and relying mainly on government largess, Angola, Cuba, and South Africa signed the Tripartite Accord. Cuba was now a global player! The complete goals of the revolution had not been fully realized, yet Cuba, having survived the loss of its benefactor

Soviet Russia, was inching its way toward reaching the goals of the dictator. The small country's only remaining major obstacle was the United States, and even that was changing.

The recent re-establishment of diplomatic relations and trade with the U.S. was accomplished by the U.S. President by fiat and it could be reversed by the same method at any time. The best thing about the new relationship, so far, was the influx of gawking tourists who behaved as though they were visiting a theme park and viewing a civilization that had been frozen in time. This event benefited the economy, but to Alejandro, it had not been uplifting for the spirit.

Alejandro Rivera was married and had one daughter. Nothing that he could do within the framework of the life he was leading allowed him to do anything to improve his own existence or that of his family, not even incrementally. He was a man in the middle of a large pool without the ability or privilege of swimming. He could only tread water, stay in the same place, endure life as it was, or he could stop kicking and flailing his arms and simply sink and drown. Alejandro was a Catholic in the best way he could be in a repressive society. He maintained a firm belief that his life was subsumed by a higher power, but he didn't always know how to connect.

# FIFTEEN

**W**ednesday was harrowing for Alejandro Rivera. He had lost a good friend and circumstances had forced him to make a hard decision. Although he answered the FBI's questions about what he had found in the room and what he and Mike Rodriguez had planned for the day, he had not told them everything.

Alejandro's day had started with mild annoyance when Mike was late for their appointed meeting, and it became concerning when after nearly an hour, his friend failed to show up at the Latin American School of Medicine. The frustration continued when he looked for his friend at his hotel; and it became excruciating when he confronted the indelible image of his good friend sprawled dead on the cold tile floor of a hotel bathroom, and Alejandro had to spend seven agonizing hours in the room before being joined by the FBI.

Alejandro explained to the agents the doubts he had about the authenticity of the medical training provided by the Latin American School of Medicine, which was why he was eager to visit the facility with Mike, who was well versed in medical education in the U.S. Alejandro told the agents he lived in the city and worked only a mile away, but had never visited the school, which had received mixed reviews locally among his peers.

The school was established in 1998 and was said to have more than two thousand students enrolled and over ten thousand graduates since its founding. The school accepted students who met stipulated undergraduate requirements and offered tuition-free education for a seven-year curriculum that included four years of hands-on training with students providing service to patients at one of twenty-one hospitals located throughout Cuba. In addition to paying no tuition, students were provided free room and board. Most of the students represented minorities, including those from Third World countries, and preference was given to applicants from low-income families. All courses were conducted in Spanish, and a semester of Spanish-language training was available for students who needed it. Alejandro and his American colleague believed the institution was creating nothing more than cheap medical help of dubious quality for Cubans and others who would pay.

Additionally, when they graduated, most students were assigned to overseas duty as part of a Cuban-government program that offered medical care to underserved countries on a for-profit, contract basis. The Cuban government was paid a substantial amount and the doctor a pittance. The duration of this indentured service was not clearly stipulated.

Now, two days after the death of Michael Rodriguez, Alejandro Rivera awaited a visit from the police. He expected it would not only be the local police but also the FBI agents he had met in the hotel room. How much would he tell them? He had heard nothing official about the results of the autopsy, but he had a pretty good idea of what he would hear.

# SIXTEEN

**Friday morning**, Jorge Lopez and Matt Hull left the Hotel Sevilla moments after Ricardo and Peter departed for their assigned duty, which was to make inquiries on the street about any new illegal drug activity, especially high-quality prescription drugs. While this was happening, the two senior officers would visit Dr. Alejandro Rivera at his home. Matt had no idea what to expect, Jorge did.

As they drove through the narrow streets of Old Havana, Jorge did his best to explain something that he was not sure even he understood. "Matt, you may be a bit surprised when you see the home of a prominent physician in this country. Housing, and for that matter life in general, in Cuba, is not something that will be easy for you to understand, especially coming from the society you live in."

"You're right, Jorge. I don't know what to expect. I must admit, most people in the U.S. are pretty ignorant about your country's past, and for that matter, its current situation."

"Well, when you see Dr. Rivera's house, it might surprise you."

"How so?" responded Matt.

"First of all, especially now with freer travel from the U.S., some houses in Cuba can cost up to two million U.S. and more, and most decent houses—and I mean ones that are small but livable—would be seventy-five thousand dollars on the open market. When you realize that a doctor in Cuba makes under seventy dollars a month ..." He paused. "Well, go figure."

"I got it, Jorge."

"But that's not the whole story. In 1959, with the revolution and Castro, everything changed. Most people were simply given the houses they already lived in. They could pay rent or purchase the home by taking out a loan from the government, which had taken it in the first place. With this scheme, people paid nothing or a small percentage of their income as a form of rent or a loan payment. Since that time, there have been lots of minor changes and adjustments, but for the most part, people live in what they had or what they found. It may not be much more than a simple roof over their head, with a chance for running water, electricity, and sanitation services. Shelter from the elements in this climate doesn't include the cold. In Cuba, the house you live in makes no statement about who you are, what you were, or who you will be, just that you are here now. The only property in Cuba that is newly built or that is existing and well-maintained is something that can be used to make money, and that is mostly from the tourist trade. And now, Matt, before we get to the house, let me tell you what I started to say yesterday."

"Shoot."

"I think all of us just naturally assumed that a room with a man who had died alone wouldn't be serviced by the maid until an investigation had been completed," said Jorge.

"Agree."

"But how would the maid know? I asked the woman who was assigned to clean room 514 on Wednesday, and she said that she checked the room at one thirty and again a little after two before she left for the day, and the do-not-disturb sign was displayed both times. She said it was hotel policy for the maid to check rooms for daily cleaning at least two times when they saw this sign, but they should never knock. She said that following the rules, she checked his room twice and, because the do-not-disturb sign was still there, she did not enter. Or knock on the door."

"That's interesting, Jorge. I can say for sure that the do-not-disturb sign was not there when Peter and I arrived later that afternoon. If what the maid said is accurate, I would assume the do-not-disturb sign was not displayed when she let Dr. Rivera into the room in the morning either. That means the sign was placed sometime after she let Dr. Rivera in, and was removed before we arrived about three. If Dr. Rivera never left the room, as he said, how or why was the do-not-disturb sign placed and then taken down?"

"I plan to ask around that question when we talk with Dr. Rivera, so don't push me. I don't think we should challenge him either way, at least not now. It is not likely we will get an answer unless he volunteers the information," said Jorge. "But if our conversation goes well and it seems appropriate, I might mention the sign."

"I agree," said Matt Hull. "And, we shouldn't mention anything to the doctor about the two photos that Dr. Rodriguez texted to his wife, the ones that must have been erased from the photo gallery on his phone, nor will we say anything about there being no fingerprints on the cell phone. It is important to the investigation that we hold back some key facts. And, there may be explanations for some things we can't figure out now; let's give him the benefit of the doubt."

"Okay," said Jorge. "And ... here we are." The newer white Hyundai sedan with *Policia* in white letters on a blue horizontal stripe that Jorge had been assigned this morning, stopped in front of a modest, freestanding structure on a street lined with similar buildings. It stood behind a three-foot-high, wrought-iron fence that was shedding white paint. The structure clearly had two front doors, no doubt serving two separate families. The house was not large but looked solid, well-built, and clearly pre-revolutionary. The left-hand side of the structure, as the two men approached, had three square pillars supporting a small roof over a front porch. The other side of the building had a door at its center that was flanked by two large windows. The glass of all the windows at the front of the building was protected by vertical metal bars reinforced with three cross pieces each. Like the fence, they were painted white, but not recently. Overall, the façade looked slightly better maintained than most of the older structures Matt had seen elsewhere in the city.

"I can guess right now," said Jorge. "Dr. Rivera's family must have had some money at the time of the revolution. They were probably able to keep the home the family lived in, or they were rewarded with different and slightly better-than-average housing. They might even have had something to do with the government. Not big, but something."

Matt noticed that Jorge was careful to apologize in advance for the expected shabbiness of the doctor's house, and now felt obliged to explain the above-average appearance by telling him that the doctor's family might have had some pull at the time of the government change. This mild contradiction was an example that humans have multi-layered and probably unconscious ways of adjusting to keep their sanity. Matt suspected the doctor had seen them arrive, because he was at the door to meet the two men as soon as they stepped onto the small front stoop.

"Come in, gentlemen. I have been expecting you," said Dr. Rivera.

"Thank you for taking the time to meet with us," said Jorge while Matt smiled with a nod. "We will not take up much of your time, Dr. Rivera. Actually, this is more of a courtesy call to catch you up on what we have found so far with the investigation."

"Thank you. I am eager to hear anything you know."

"Without going into all the details, Dr. Rivera," said Jorge, "we are now convinced that your friend was the victim of foul play. We believe that after a brief scuffle, the doctor's head hit the corner of the desk and he fell to the floor, stunned. He was then smothered with a pillow and his body was dragged into the bathroom where it was staged to appear that his death was accidental."

Looking at the men with sad eyes, Alejandro responded, "That is awful, but I suspected it. Now, the only thing that could make the death of my friend even more tragic would be for whoever did this to get away with murder by passing it off as an accident. I heard briefly from my colleague, Dr. Hernandez, saying he would be doing the autopsy. He is a competent, and above all, an honest forensic pathologist. I trust him completely. Did his work shed any light?" Then the doctor added apologetically, "I have not left my house since I returned from the hotel two days ago. This has been an ordeal."

Jorge hesitated for a moment, then with a look, indicated that Matt Hull should answer. "The autopsy findings, as we suspected from the blood on the pillow and from the missing pillowcase, were compatible with suffocation as the cause of Dr. Rodriguez's death. This, along with other findings at the scene, make it clear to us that your friend's death was a homicide. Our challenge now is to determine motive and find the killer."

"If there is anything I can do, gentlemen, I will do it gladly, if you will just tell me what it is you need," said the doctor.

Appreciating this small opening, Jorge said, "Doctor, I have one question. It is about the do-not-disturb sign on the door. Was it there when you went to the doctor's room in the morning, and discovered the body?"

Slightly taken aback, Dr. Rivera thought for a moment and said, "Not that I noticed."

"Did you leave the room at any time during the day while you were waiting for help to arrive?"

After another pause, a little longer this time, the doctor said, "Now that you mention it, I did put the sign on the door after I had been there an hour, and I took it down before it was time for Agent Hull and his partner to arrive." The two men looked at him impassively, leading the doctor to further explain. "Yes, the reason I put it out was to keep the maid from coming in on a scene that I was watching over and didn't want anybody to know about." Then the doctor abruptly stood and said, "I don't know where my manners are. Could I offer you some refreshment?"

Matt didn't want anything, and he suspected Jorge didn't either, so he was surprised when Jorge said yes. After some back and forth, it was decided each would have coffee. It was also agreed that all would have the same, and Jorge did not ask for his usual cream and sugar. With the orders taken, Dr. Rivera left the room. This gave Matt his first chance to look around. The floor of the main room consisted of off-white tile in large squares. A small fireplace was on one wall, but it didn't look active. There were two chairs, much like lawn furniture, that the two men sat in, and a small upholstered chair across from them that Dr. Rivera had just vacated. A couch with several white doilies and a glass-topped coffee table in front was on the side of the room opposite the dormant fireplace, which had a three-foot-tall mirror above it. Three small pictures, probably prints, were on the wall opposite the two officers. They were hung a little higher than needed. Everything in the room looked well-used and serviceable.

The room that the doctor had entered, which appeared to be a kitchen, could be closed off by a curtain, but was partially open now. The room where the men remained was clean but spartan. A quick calculation on Matt's part determined that the living quarters could not be much more than two thousand square feet, including the upstairs with bedrooms, and most likely where the doctor's wife was now. Dr. Rivera returned after a short interval and the conversation continued with nothing of consequence being said. The doctor, now seeming more at ease, conversed in serious tones but seemed comfortable. After the three finished their coffees, Jorge stood, both men thanked the doctor, said their goodbyes, and promised to keep him informed.

When they were in the car, Matt said, "Jorge, what do you think?"

"The doctor didn't do it. I am certain of that, but he is not telling us everything. I am sure he is holding something back."

# SEVENTEEN

**A**lejandro pulled the window shade back ever so slightly and watched the men get into the white police car and drive off. He wondered what would happen next, and he hoped his explanation of the do-not-disturb sign satisfied the two officers. He had not expected the question, but he thought what he had said was a plausible explanation and that it would not be mentioned again.

Thinking about the sequence of events that followed his placing the sign on the hotel room door, it was feasible that he would have done exactly what he said he had to avoid having the maid come in. She would have been shocked at the sight and there would be no way to stop her from calling for help. He was only doing what he had been told by the man in Washington. If he had allowed her to enter the room with her key, it could have been difficult to send her away, even if she didn't have a chance to look in the bathroom. The problem Alejandro was dealing with now was that the reason he gave for placing the sign was not for the purpose he described. Yes, the sign was put on the door to keep the maid out—but to also cover up the fact that he had left the room.

**Three days** earlier, after discovering his friend sprawled on the bathroom floor, Alejandro touched the man's neck just long enough to confirm there was no carotid pulse. He was dead. Shaken, he moved to the bed and sat in stunned silence until a rush of adrenaline initiated a reflexive response. Dr. Alejandro Rivera grabbed the room phone on the desk and told the hotel operator to connect him with the U.S. Embassy in Havana. When he was connected, he asked for the Consular Office and told the person who answered that he had found a U.S. citizen dead under suspicious circumstances, and that he needed help. The person from the Consular Office told him to stay with the body, contact nobody, and help would arrive shortly. With nothing left to do but wait, Alejandro Rivera returned to the spot where he had been sitting on the edge of the bed. The call from Washington, D.C. came in less than thirty minutes and put a time frame on his ordeal. He was told help would come with the arrival of agents from the U.S. Federal Bureau of Investigation. He was to do nothing but wait until the men arrived, in about five hours.

Knowing he had time on his hands, Alejandro took a deep breath and started to carefully look around the room. Nothing seemed odd or out of place. Mike's phone and computer were on the small desk on the wall opposite the foot of the bed. Without thinking, Alejandro picked up the phone and pressed the green phone icon at the bottom. When he pressed "Recents," he saw the only calls made from the phone were to the Rodriguez's home. The last call was placed yesterday at 4:15 p.m., no doubt to his wife. This meant that the call Alejandro received from his friend yesterday, to confirm their meeting at the medical school this morning, had been made on a landline. It was in this brief conversation when Mike told Alejandro he wanted to discuss something important, but he couldn't talk about it over the phone.

His friend had not sent an email in 24 hours. That left photos as the most likely potential source of current information. When he opened the Picture Gallery, Alejandro noted something that he thought was curious. The last two photos were taken at 3:30 p.m. and were of a medicine bottle sitting on top of a stack of boxes in what appeared to be a storeroom. Scrolling back to the last picture taken before the medicine bottle revealed a group of doctors, including Mike, and several others at the eye hospital, most likely taken in the administrator's office. Going back to the pictures of the medicine bottle and recreating the time frame, the pictures had to have been taken in the storeroom of the eye hospital just before Mike left and shortly before the last time Alejandro had spoken with his friend.

Alejandro was alarmed when he read the label on the bottle—Hydrocodone 10/325—a strong opioid that was not used at the eye hospital. It was little used outside of the United States, for a variety of reasons, not the least of which was because of its addictive potential. Alejandro had recently read that deaths from opioid overdose in the United States now exceeded those from automobile accidents and gun violence.

Alejandro's mind went into the cerebral equivalent of overdrive. This odd discovery in the storeroom must have been what his friend wanted to speak with him about but didn't want to discuss over the phone. Had Michael Rodriguez stumbled onto an illegal drug situation? Was Alejandro over-thinking or was this something important? Then, revving his mental function to the maximum, he decided that this question could be put to a tie-breaker, and to accomplish this he needed to look no farther than the bathroom where his friend lay dead.

There must be a reason for his unexpected death. Was his friend killed because of what he knew or suspected? The agitated doctor now became an analytical machine, thinking clearly and with precision as time seemed to slow. He put the cell phone in his pocket and looked at his watch. It was 11:45. He grabbed the do-not-disturb sign, hung it on the doorknob and left, heading for the Raul Mesa Carreras Eye Hospital. He had no firm plan except to go into the storeroom. Knowing that speed trumped frugality, he took a cab that deposited him at the hospital in fifteen minutes. He asked the information clerk in the lobby for directions to the medical storeroom and was directed to a stairway in a back hall.

In the storeroom, when he confirmed that he was alone, he

took the phone out and looked at the pictures of the bottle. It appeared to have been taken from the spot where he was standing, which was several feet from a stack of boxes. The box that the medicine bottle had been sitting on, was not there. He recognized several other features of the room that were identical to when the pictures were taken. This was where Michael Rodriguez had seen the bottle containing opioids, but the bottle and the box were gone.

Alejandro began to look in the hall outside the storeroom. He came to an office with a window that revealed a desk where a woman was seated. "Are you in charge here?" he asked.

The young woman, whose bored look betrayed her indifference, said, "No, Luis is."

"Is he here?"

"No, he didn't come in today."

"Do you know how to contact him?"

"Just a minute," said the woman. "I have the name of his girlfriend and a number to call him, but only in an emergency."

"This is an emergency."

Noting that the man making the request looked important, she scratched out a phone number on a scrap of paper and handed it to Alejandro, who hovered over her desk. "Thank you," he said. "You did the right thing. Luis will be glad to hear from me. Oh, what is his last name?"

The woman immediately wondered how much of a friend this man was, but it was too late now, so she said, "Espinosa."

With nothing further said, Alejandro turned and left. Once in the lobby, he started to dial the number he had been given using his own cell phone but realized there were too many people around. With more privacy outside, on a long porch with a ramp going to the parking area, he dialed the number. On the fourth ring, a woman answered. Nervously holding the handpiece near his mouth to guard against prying ears, Alejandro spoke. "Is Luis there?"

"Who is this?"

"A friend from the hospital."

"He's not here."

"Do you know where I can contact him? It's important."

"No. He was out late last night, and he left early this morning. He said he didn't know when he would be back."

"Is there anyone who might know how to contact him?"

"You could try Eduardo."

"Eduardo who?"

"I don't know his last name."

"How can I find him?"

"He has a fancy gift shop near the Revolution Museum. I don't know the name or address, but it has a big statue of a crucifix in the window that he is very proud of and won't sell unless he gets a bundle. If you see the bastard, tell him to get the hell home. He owes me."

"Which one?" Alejandro asked before he could stop himself.

"Luis. I don't give a shit about Eduardo."

He hung up, thankful for the information but even more thankful to be done speaking with a woman he wanted to get no nearer to than he had with the phone connection. It was now twelve thirty. He had some time left to find Eduardo's store; so, he got another cab and decided the Revolution Museum would be a good place to start.

After the cab discharged him at the museum, Alejandro headed down the most likely street in the direction where most of the stores looked like the kind of shop she had described. He walked for three blocks until the stores began to thin out. He crossed the street and retraced his steps, walking back to his starting point on the other side of the street. No luck. Back at the museum, he went down the next most likely street but didn't find what he was looking for there either. Walking down the third street, after forty-five minutes on the hunt, he considered giving up and returning to the Hotel Sevilla. Then he saw it: a two-foot-tall wooden carving of two hands holding up a crucifix. It could be seen through the window but was perched on a shelf inside a shop that was crowded with a cacophony of merchandise. The sign over the store said Regalos.

Entering the shop, Alejandro saw a man a little less than medium height and with no remarkable features. The proprietor didn't seem to be interested in a person who was obviously Cuban and, therefore, not likely to be a paying customer. This all changed, however, when Alejandro said he admired the crucifix held aloft in shackled hands and asked how much it was. The proprietor, with a touch of ambivalence, told him the price was one thousand pesos, not CUC but the tourist kind that was equal to U.S. dollars. Eduardo was pleased that his customer didn't seem fazed and wished he had said more. The man could be Mexican or from the U.S.

"That seems like a fair price" said Alejandro. "But I will think about it. May I have your card, so I can get back with you?"

"Yes," said Eduardo, as he handed his business card to a person, he hoped would eventually be a cash customer. If this sale worked out, he would contact the carver with a request for an even larger piece, maybe even two, when the money from the drugs started rolling in.

Having completed a productive outing, Alejandro returned to the hotel to resume his vigil, in anticipation of the U.S. agents' arrival. At the door to room 514, he retrieved the do-not-disturb sign and entered. Barely recognizing his motives, or admitting exactly what he was doing, he erased the last two pictures on Mike's iPhone, took out his handkerchief, and thoroughly wiped all surfaces of the phone. Holding the instrument with the cloth, he replaced it on the desk where it had been lying next to the computer. Alejandro had checked the laptop earlier but couldn't open it because it was password protected. With this done, he sat in the small desk chair and waited.

# EIGHTEEN

On the drive back to the police station, Jorge and Matt both weighed what they had just heard; trying to arrive at their own conclusions without saying anything that might sway the other. They pursued small talk and speculated about what Ricardo and Pete might have learned. The twenty-minute drive ended without the bubble of anticipation being violated.

They had agreed to meet in the same room they used last night. Jorge and Matt mounted the stairs, headed down the hall, and turned into the now familiar room. Ricardo and Pete were already seated. "Any news?" asked Jorge.

Ricardo answered. "We talked to about a dozen people on the street and we learned a little."

"As for me, I learned a lot," said Peter. "Ricardo, why don't you tell Matt some of the stuff you told me? I bet he'll learn something too."

"Okay," said Ricardo. "Even though Cuba officially has a zero tolerance for drugs, marijuana is available; and there are even some premium brands, like Creole and Yuma Herb, but most is locally produced by small-time operators. Locals can buy a joint for about five CUC. These convertible pesos are worth, give or take, one U.S. dollar. Tourists can change dollars for CUCs if they pay a fee that is usually around ten percent."

"Is there enough local money to support a market for drugs?" asked Matt.

Jorge spoke. "The answer to that has to be a qualified yes. Cuba controls its economy using a dual-monetary system, one of which is nonconvertible and used only in-country. It is referred to as CUP. This peso, used by locals, is also called the *Moneda Nacional* or MN. This money is used to purchase food, clothing, and other essentials in government stores that accept this currency. It takes about thirty CUP to equal one CUC. Anyway, a country that has a dual-monetary system must face the reality of dealing with the outside world. The CUC, which floats with the American dollar, controls a large part of the economy that depends on tourism. Tourists come to our country with their own dollar-based money and are more likely to spend it on things that carry a recognizable price, and these prices are usually a bargain compared to those at home.

"Having convertible currency with a published exchange rate encourages tourist spending and is a plus when it comes to foreign investment. Tourists also spend money on services, but in that case, they are likely to spend amounts more in keeping with their practices at home. That means cab drivers, waitresses and waiters, tour guides, and others who deal directly with the public can make incomes far higher than professionals. Most people get by, using the local peso, and shop at government stores. A few have some extra money. They are likely to be involved in small businesses, some of which are operated on the side by professionals. Another way to earn extra money is to engage in services that deal with the tourist trade or to work directly on the payroll of foreign investors. But citizens must be very careful how they manage this to avoid running afoul of the authorities. It is this fringe part of the economy involving service workers that deal with tourists that is the most likely place for major drug activity."

"You're right, Jorge," said Ricardo. "We talked with a couple guys who gave us some information. They said there are customers out there, but most people are turned off because they don't want to buy bad stuff or pay full price for junk. They also said it was scary to sell stuff because the customers could come back on them or spread the word. And it was especially hard to sell anything that looked like it was local to tourists because they were also worried about getting bad merchandise. One guy said he heard there would be some high-grade prescription stuff available, but he didn't know what or where. He might have told more to a local, but he knew we were cops and not customers. He did say he thought it would be really easy for the person who had high-grade stuff to command a good price."

"This could be the hydrocodone," said Matt.

"Okay, that's our story. What did you guys find out with Dr. Rivera?" asked Pete.

"That depends," said Matt.

"On what?" Ricardo was getting more comfortable with his part in the group.

"On how sympathetic you are when it comes to a guy who seems like he is the real thing. By that, I mean he is a good friend of a man who just died, is a respected doctor, called the U.S. Consul because he thought an American doctor had been murdered, and he stuck around to make sure the scene wasn't disturbed."

"Sounds like you are making a case for someone we should be thanking," said Ricardo.

"Yes ... but, there are a couple problems," said Jorge. "First, the last two photos taken on Dr. Rodriguez's phone were erased and the phone was wiped clean of fingerprints. And second, there is some question about the do-not-disturb sign. Dr. Rivera only remembered putting the sign out after we mentioned that the maid said she saw it hanging on the door twice that afternoon. She told us that is why she didn't clean the room. And, he didn't have an explanation for taking it down before Matt and Pete arrived. We didn't press him on these issues because we didn't want to put him on the defensive, and we didn't want him to think we were questioning the truth of his statements."

"Both Jorge and I agree that someone else killed the doctor," said Matt. "The questions we have are: who erased the pictures and wiped the fingerprints—and why? And did Alejandro Rivera remain in the hotel room for the entire day, as he said he did? We are convinced the doctor's death is a homicide, and it was probably committed by a single person. That would most likely be the man who phoned the hotel twice just before the murder was committed. So we are looking for a Spanish-speaking male, most likely Cuban, who may be connected to the hospital.

"Images of a bottle of prescription-strength opioids taken in the Raul Mesa Carreras Eye Hospital storeroom were erased and the iPhone was wiped clean; which seems to tie these events together as important evidence. The Shipping and Receiving supervisor, a man named Luis Espinosa, hasn't been seen at work since Wednesday, and his girlfriend said she didn't know where he was—but that it was not unusual for him to leave for a few days without telling her. It is reasonable to suspect this man is the murderer."

Taking over, Jorge said, "The clearest path forward with this investigation is to find Luis Espinosa. He is our only connection with the drugs, unless there are other people at the hospital who know about the shipment. That is something we need to find out, Ricardo."

"Will you be watching Dr. Rivera?" asked Pete.

"Definitely," said Jorge. "I think the drug issue makes this a cart-and-horse scenario. Let's say the murderer is the horse, a local now on the lamb. He killed Dr. Rodriguez because he had the bad luck to stumble onto the merchandise. The doctor was killed because of the 'cart,' which represents the drugs. It is likely the horse and the cart are now separated. Let's say the storeroom supervisor, Luis, is the horse and he is away from his usual haunts, and likely is no longer in control of the drugs. We need to be on the alert for any activity that could be related to them, and that could lead us to the murderer. It is likely that selling this stuff will be delayed for a while. But it will be sold eventually. If not, there would have been no reason to kill Dr. Rodriguez. It is possible, but in my opinion a long shot, that Dr. Rivera is considering functioning as an opportunist and somehow derive benefit from this enterprise by keeping quiet."

"How could he do that?" asked Ricardo.

"Jorge, if I get you right," said Matt, "Dr. Rivera could be looking for what you call the 'cart'—the drugs?"

"That's right, Matt. Let's say that Alejandro Rivera saw the photos of the hydrocodone on Dr. Rodriguez's phone—he had ample time to look—recognized the location, erased the photos, wiped the phone clean, and decided on his own to track down the drugs. His friend was already dead, most likely murdered, and there was nothing Alejandro could do about that—but the drugs were there and maybe he could benefit in some way. Remember, Dr. Rivera is paid about two dollars a day. For doing the same work, his dead friend made more than fifty times that! How much of a saint do you have to be to not think about your own and your family's well-being?"

"It sounds like this could be the next piece of the puzzle," added Jorge. "The problem is, I kind of hope it is a dead end because I like the doc. On the other hand, I know we can't let our personal feelings cloud the issue. We should be able to keep track of him without much effort."

"It's been a pretty exciting forty-eight hours for us, and we have enjoyed working with you guys, but I think we have done about all we can do here; at least within the jurisdiction of the FBI in a foreign country," said Matt. "We should be heading back to Miami. The body was shipped home and you guys are on top of the investigation. I am sure you'll have this buttoned up quickly. Keep us in the loop. We would love to know how this sorts out, and we can return anytime with a few hours' notice—but I don't think we can add much right now."

Jorge spoke, clearly showing his disappointment, "We appreciate your help and we'd love to wrap this up with you on board, but we have been told you're outa here when the body goes home. Too bad, but that's the way it is. Ricardo can take you to the hotel. It's been a pleasure for both of us to work with you. If there is ever a chance for us to visit you guys, it would be great. If we do a decent job from here on, and stay cool with the U.S., we might see you guys in Miami."

"We'll be available any time and don't forget to keep us posted. Oh, one last thing," said Matt. "It's possible that Alejandro Rivera is playing amateur detective and working on his own to find the murderer. This guy was his friend and the doc could feel responsible in a way. I think we should at least give him that much slack. And, if that is the case, he really needs to be watched—for his own safety. Usually drug dealers play mean and they play for keeps."

As Matt and Pete left with Ricardo, Jorge thought of how much he had enjoyed working with the men. They were professionals. But he was glad they had made the decision to leave on their own because Jorge knew Colonel Diaz would be on his neck if they were still here tomorrow.


**Without the** urgency that was associated with their trip to Havana, the agents flew commercial back to Miami. As they settled in their seats, Matt turned to his partner. "Pete, what nice guys to work with ... But did you get it?"

"Get what?" said Pete.

"If we hadn't left on our own, their boss would have been on our tails like a cat in heat. There's no way we could have stayed to the end of the investigation or even another day. Jorge and Ricardo are good guys. They would have felt awful to kick us out. That's why I brought up leaving. I'm sure they appreciated it."

"Do you think they can finish the investigation?"

"I'm not sure, but that guy who got us involved in the first place, Grant from Washington, sounds like he has his act together and he is operating on a longer leash. I wouldn't be surprised if he figures out a way to see this thing through."

"You're probably right. But all I am thinking about now is a shower and a change of clothes."

# NINETEEN

**A**fter the officers left, Alejandro Rivera realized he faced some big decisions. More accurately, he had to face himself. He had no choice but to move ahead as events unfolded. It was impossible to erase the actions he had already taken. But there was still time to take stock of the life he now led,and what could possibly lie ahead.

At forty-seven, he practiced internal medicine with a special interest in public health at the Hermanos Amerijeiras Hospital in downtown Havana. The multi-story building was constructed in the early 1980s and towered over the city skyline. It contained nearly one million square feet of space and served the small, privileged class of the country. It had also been the centerpiece of a documentary produced by an American activist who aimed to show people in the U.S. the excellent medical care that was available to the *typical* Cuban citizen. The irony was not lost on the doctor. The only ordinary citizens associated with the hospital were those who worked as janitors and cooks. And, of course, the nominally privileged medical staff.

His renewed friendship with Mike Rodriguez had given the two men much opportunity to discuss both their shared profession and their disparate lives. One thing that haunted Alejandro was when Mike told him that of all the countries he had visited, which were many, Cuba was unique. The Cuban people were intelligent and eager, but the facilities that served the general population were as bad as any Mike had seen in his travels. Furthermore, in no place other than Soviet Russia in 1987, when Mike had participated as a very junior member on an invited U.S. visiting delegation, had he seen such an effective use of government ideology to dominate common sense and intelligence. Mike said he was just sick at heart seeing the handicap Alejandro and his colleagues had to work under. It was dispiriting to see the level of control the government had over the actions of those in the medical profession.

These revelations, from a longtime friend and someone he trusted, had stung Alejandro—but were not a surprise. By keeping his feelings buried, Alejandro had endured. But that was no longer possible. The scab had been pulled and the sore beneath revealed. Alejandro's country, the place he felt duty bound to love; the country that had lifted his family out of poverty, was now the country that had failed to deliver as promised. The first half of the Castro policy had worked to a degree. The oppressors who carried out abusive business practices, racketeering, and unbridled pleasure-seeking in a population that was ninety percent impoverished was gone. That part was good. And that is why Alejandro was a doctor. But the freedom to do the right thing, and if you could get away with it, the wrong thing and risk getting caught, had been replaced by a regime that reserved for itself the right to make *every* decision and to ensure compliance by punishing every action with which the government disagreed.

Alejandro was unsuccessful in his attempt to erase from his memory the numbers he had heard. At Alejandro's insistence, his now dead friend had grudgingly revealed his annual income. A quick mental calculation revealed that Dr. Michael Rodriguez was paid hundreds of times the amount received by his similarly trained and equally qualified counterpart in Cuba. This revelation had embarrassed the American doctor and puzzled the Cuban. How did this happen?

The image of the bottle of hydrocodone 10/325 burned in Alejandro's mind. What was he thinking when he erased the pictures from his friend's phone? Why had he wiped the phone clean? Why had he left the hotel room to go to the eye hospital and find the storeroom where the pictures were taken? Why had he asked for the name of the storeroom manager? Why had he called the manager's girlfriend and then found the shop with the crucifix?

Alejandro's younger brother made his living as an enterprising shop owner, relentlessly looking for a way to make money, and he always seemed to have plenty. Alejandro hoped that his brother's actions remained above board, but he wasn't sure. The doctor never pried, because he knew if he did, the answer would be: "In this country, is anything honest?" Two years younger, Álvaro had opened a restaurant after graduating from college. He had done quite well with this business but moved on. After selling the restaurant, Álvaro bought inexpensive properties, fixed them up, and now rented rooms to tourists. With a passport that allowed him to visit Panama, Álvaro sold men's clothing at quite a profit—maybe too much of a profit, suspected his older brother. Álvaro Rivera was a relatively wealthy man who had succeeded by his wits and his willingness to take risks. Was this the only way to get ahead in the "workers' paradise" that Castro had promised?

Alejandro needed answers, but once arrived at, they only spawned more questions. He wondered if he should take advantage of his discovery and make a profit anyway he could. No. That would betray all he had worked for. Should he threaten to expose them? No, that was extortion. Should he become a conspirator? No, becoming a criminal and working with a murderer was unthinkable. Should he turn them over to the police? No, in Cuba the police were nothing more than criminals themselves. Should he take justice into his own hands? Maybe. But how—and at what price?

# TWENTY

**A**lejandro spent the weekend in turmoil, wondering what he should do. Coming up with no better option, he made the phone call on Monday morning. He reminded Eduardo of their meeting in his shop and then asked to meet with him to discuss a business matter. The call was easy to make. Too easy. Alejandro didn't know how it would end, but he had to find out.

Eduardo Sanchez agreed to meet but said it would be better if they didn't meet at the shop. Instead they could meet in front of the tobacco shop at Trocadero and Aguila Streets at midnight. Assuming it was regarding the statue, Eduardo hinted that the art piece had a controversial history and the less said about a possible sale the better. He told Alejandro to park his car at least two blocks away from the tobacco shop and from there, they would use Eduardo's car to drive to a suitable place to talk. Eduardo apologized for the late hour, but he said he was a night owl.

Alejandro had not heard from the police since their visit on Friday. He knew he would hear from them again, eventually, but he was not worried. His main concern now was that he might be meeting with the person who had killed his friend.

**The street** in front of the closed tobacco shop was deserted except for Eduardo, who was standing just inside the threshold, looking as inconspicuous as possible; although that was a need-less precaution because nobody was around to notice. He wore a sweater against the slight chill in the air and was smoking a cig-arette that he put out, grinding it into the pavement as he saw his visitor approach.

"Hello, doctor. Let's walk to my car."

With only a nod of agreement, Alejandro fell in step beside Eduardo and the two proceeded wordlessly three blocks down Aguila Street to the only car parked on the block. In the dim light, it looked relatively new, at least by local standards. It was a Volk-swagen sedan that appeared meticulously cared for. A nice car like this was a sign of at least modest success. Eduardo opened the passenger door and Alejandro slid in the front seat. Eduardo walked around the back of the car and, as he did so, he saw Luis in a dark alleyway. Luis, now returned from Caracas, was waiting for Eduardo's signal in case they needed to do what they had discussed.

"On the phone, you said you had something important to dis-cuss," said Eduardo, who was now in the driver's seat but did not look like he intended to drive anywhere.

"Yes, I did," said Alejandro. He had decided to say no more than what was necessary.

"Is it about the statue?" Eduardo hoped it was.

Alejandro said, "It involves a bottle of pills I saw in the store-room at the eye hospital." Although it was only a picture that Alejandro saw, the look of concern on Eduardo's face confirmed the contents were what the label said they were, hydrocodone 10/325, a powerful opioid.

Eduardo drew in a breath while he assessed the situation. Luis had already killed one man over this discovery. Was this a setup? Did this man want to profit from his discovery or was he somehow connected with the dead man? Was he a man who was intent on cashing in, or did he have other motives? Eduardo feigned cordial-ity, "My friend, what, specifically, are you interested in discussing?"

"This is what I know," said Alejandro. "Dr. Michael Rodriguez saw a bottle of pills at the eye hospital, where he was serving as a volunteer. The label indicated they were a strong narcotic and not the kind of pain medicine used at the hospital. He suspected they were being sold illegally. And for that, he was murdered by people who hoped they could become rich by selling the drug illegally to people who would pay a lot for them. I think you are involved."

"Have you told anybody about this?" asked Eduardo, who made no attempt to dispute Alejandro's claim.

Alejandro was now certain this man was guilty of dealing drugs and had either committed or was the mastermind behind the death of his friend. The only way to avenge the death of his friend, and to atone for his own weakness, was to act. Alejandro, whose life work was committed to saving lives, would now take one, and do so without qualms. He reached in his right-hand coat pocket and grasped the ancient nickel-plated revolver that was the only memento from his father. It had been in the back of a drawer with a box of bullets. He had not looked at the weapon in more than twenty years. He had loaded the gun before he left for this meeting and vowed to use it if what he suspected was confirmed, and that had just happened.

Eduardo saw Alejandro hesitate and then reach into his coat pocket. Eduardo quickly leaned across the console, pinned both of Alejandro's arms against the seat, and signaled to Luis, who was standing in the shadows no more than ten feet from the car.

On the signal from Eduardo, the dark figure lunged toward the car and yanked the passenger door open. Before Alejandro could react, Luis struck him on the head with a heavy lug wrench. The first blow stunned Alejandro; two more vicious strikes pounded the life out of the doomed doctor.

Luis tossed the doctor's body in the backseat and closed the door. As soon as the big man was sitting in the passenger seat, Eduardo drove away. Luis felt he was now an essential part of the enterprise, and at the first chance, he would renegotiate the amount of payment he would be receiving.

After driving a few blocks, Eduardo stopped the car and Luis got out. He pulled the doctor's body from the backseat, emptied the victim's pockets, took off his watch and ring, and dumped the body in the gutter.

An unexpected prize, he slipped the pistol in his pocket. It would look like a robbery that went bad and turned into the murder of a man who was at the wrong place at the wrong time.

"What do we do now?" asked Luis as he returned to the car.

Calculating his next step, Eduardo said, "Before we go home, I want to check on something at the cruise ship docks."

After a short drive through deserted streets, Eduardo steered the car through an open gate at the far end of the docks. It was more than a quarter mile from the white-hulled cruise ship filled with sleeping passengers—or, as Eduardo preferred to think of them: potential customers. Entering the harbor area at the end of the dock farthest from the moored cruise ship, Eduardo stopped the car ten feet from the water and beckoned Luis to get out. Walking to the edge of the dock with a sense of urgency, Eduardo looked down at the water. His companion did likewise, although he was not sure what he was looking for. With a catlike movement, the smaller man darted to the right, placed himself behind his large companion, and shoved the unsuspecting Luis over the edge. With arms flailing and emitting a muted scream, Luis hit the murky water with a splash. The man had volunteered to Eduardo on several occasions that he could not swim. The fruitless thrashing confirmed that Luis had been telling the truth. Within two minutes, there was nothing disturbed in the water, not even a ripple.

It was almost time for Eduardo to go home, get a good night's sleep, and then get up in the morning to pursue his job as a hardworking shopkeeper with enthusiasm and diligence. But before he did that, there was one more piece of unfinished business: Isabelle. Luis's girlfriend had asked to meet with Eduardo. Eduardo guessed Luis had told her things and the bitch wanted to get in on the action. It would be best to deal with her before news of tonight's events surfaced.

His meeting with Isabelle was brief. She should have known it would be. Four o'clock in the morning was an unusual time to meet, but she was a strange woman and hours meant little to her. It would look like a hit-and-run accident, even down to the glass fragment from an auto headlight he would drive into her thigh.

But first, he delivered a blow to her head with a section of rubber hose filled with lead. Eduardo knew about this type of weapon and had fabricated it specifically for a job like this. It would be lethal, as would hitting her head violently on the pavement without causing a break in the skin. What other end could one expect for a woman of questionable character who was roaming the streets at such an improbable hour?

Eduardo felt he had done his duty as a good citizen. A man guilty of two murders had been dealt with. The other was, as far as Eduardo knew, no more than a disillusioned doctor who was eager to work himself into the drug business. Eduardo realized his actions tonight were unorthodox—or were they virtuoso? He had rid the city of a murderer, who had in his pockets the wallet, watch, and ring of a man who had been mugged and killed only hours before; and a tramp who roamed the streets at night. With this convoluted reasoning, Eduardo Sanchez was satisfied with what he had accomplished and looked forward to proceeding with a project that would make him a wealthy man.

# TWENTY-ONE

**On Tuesday** morning, Jorge entered the National Revolutionary Police Force headquarters with a heavy heart. Not only did he miss working with Matt and Pete, but he had been reassigned and could no longer look for Dr. Michael Rodriguez's killer.

On Saturday, Colonel Diaz had called Jorge into his office to say that even though the autopsy results might suggest otherwise, under the circumstances, it would be best for all concerned to list the doctor's death as being from natural causes. Colonel Diaz justified his reasoning by explaining that because the man had a serious heart condition that could have caused his death, there was nothing to be gained by stirring up a complicated series of events that would be of no benefit to anyone in Cuba. When Jorge asked what would be done about the drug angle, the Colonel pointed out there was no direct evidence that any drugs were involved. There was only a photo sent from the doctor's phone. He said, "Of course, the police will be on alert, as we always are, but we will make no special effort to look for the drugs, and if they do show up, we can talk later about how we handle the evidence." Then with a look of finality he added, "That is an American problem, not ours." And with that, Diaz signaled the end of the meeting.

Jorge left the office in a funk, uncertain about his future and his dedication to upholding the law when others looked the other way if there was something in it for them. He was sure that was the case with Colonel Diaz and the drugs.

Fortunately, this all changed when his partner accosted him at the entrance to the squad room on Tuesday morning. With an agitation that was short of exploding, Ricardo Ortiz blurted, "Jorge, all hell broke loose last night—and it might change Diaz's plan for you when he hears it! Dr. Rivera was found dead in Old Town, the victim of an apparent robbery sometime late last night! And, that is only the beginning. The man who was the supervisor of Shipping and Receiving at Raul Mesa Carreras Eye Hospital, who we never caught up with, he was found early this morning too, floating in the harbor by the cruise ship docks!" As Ricardo saw the shock on his partner's face, he continued. "And that's not all! A woman who was said to be the drowned man's girlfriend was the victim of an apparent hit-and-run!"

A stunned Jorge stopped in his tracks, experiencing an acute information overload. Immediately he asked, "Who else knows about this?"

"I don't know. For sure, the duty officer and one or two others who were in the office when the news came in only minutes ago. I don't think this has gotten upstairs yet."

"Okay. Ricardo, go back to the duty officer and tell him to keep a lid on this till I see you. I'm going up to Colonel Diaz and tell him. Hearing this news from me first might mean we can continue working the case, and maybe even get some help and more leeway. I believe these deaths are related, and I am sure the Colonel will agree. They could be part of a cover-up."

"Will do, Jorge," said Ricardo.

Jorge entered the office on the heels of the Colonel's adjutant, who had reluctantly allowed his entry. The colonel was on the phone. He signaled Jorge to take a seat. When his call was finished, the Colonel stood. He was annoyed because he suspected Jorge's impromptu visit was related to the news, he had just heard about three deaths in the city, deaths that could be homicides and possibly related to the American doctor. He anticipated the plea he would be hearing, so he greeted the visitor in a forceful tone.

"Detective Lopez, I thought we settled the issue of your future assignment when we met on Saturday. I will hear no more from you about the unfortunate death of the American doctor."

"Sir, I apologize for bursting in, but I have just received some startling news that I want to share with you first."

"I just now heard about this, Lopez, and it hasn't changed my mind." Turning his attention to his assistant, the Colonel said, "You're dismissed, Ramon. Shut the door behind you and keep it that way until I give you the okay. Now, Jorge, tell me why you are so worked up."

"Colonel, we are sure the three people who died violently last night are directly or indirectly associated with the death of the American doctor, who we are convinced was murdered."

"This has been suggested, but how do you come up with this connection, and why are you so sure?"

Seeing an opening in the argument, Jorge moved on, "The Cuban doctor is the person who found the body of the American."

"What else?"

"The man found floating in the harbor was the manager of Shipping and Receiving at Raul Mesa Carreras Eye Hospital, the hospital where the American doctor volunteered for almost two weeks. And the manager's live-in girlfriend is the woman killed by a hit-and-run driver."

"Do you think any or all of this could be coincidence?"

"No."

"The way you explain it, I don't either, Jorge. You can accept one coincidence in a situation like this, and grudgingly at that, but three is beyond any level of belief." Softening his demeanor as the shock of this disclosure settled in, Diaz stared at the ceiling for what seemed to Jorge like a very long time. Finally, he said, "Jorge, this is an extraordinary situation. It may be necessary for us to take an entirely different tack from the one I advised two days ago when we were only dealing with the American."

*Demanded not advised*, thought Jorge.

Now more conciliatory, the Colonel went on, "Since we are dealing with the violent deaths of three of our own citizens, it will be necessary to re-think the situation with the American," acqui-esced the colonel. "We need to entertain the possibility that he was murdered and that, in some way, these deaths—that now number four—might be connected."

"Sir, I would like to be re-assigned, along with Ricardo, to this investigation."

"Jorge, I think that's a reasonable request. And, it may be nec-essary to assign more people to the investigation. I will make you the lead, if you agree."

"I do, sir. And, I have one more request."

"That would be ... ?"

"Sir, I would like to have permission to consult with the two FBI agents we worked with before the American's body was shipped home."

With a look of concern, Colonel Diaz asked, "Why do you think this is important?"

"Colonel, these men were easy to work with and they were knowledgeable in techniques that they willingly and, even eagerly, shared. We worked together effectively, and I can see no obvious drawback to seeking their advice. This could be limited to a phone call or, if you agree, a return visit if we think that would be better."

"Phone calls are OK. The other, let's wait. Be careful—and keep me informed."

"Thank you," said a visibly relieved Jorge Lopez. He was eager to share this news with Ricardo, and then call Matt and Pete in Miami to tell them about the startling turn of events.

**Sergeant Ricardo** Ortiz, a new father and at the low end of the police pay scale, was not surprised when he was summoned once more by the Colonel. When he was called into the Colonel's office last week, it was a surprise. At that time, he was not sure his boss even knew he existed. Today's summons was not unexpected, and Ricardo dreaded it.

"Sergeant Ortiz," the Colonel began, "when I spoke with you

last week, you were involved in a politically sensitive investigation of a serious crime that included the possibility of drugs being involved. With the events of last night, the threat is even higher, much higher. I just want to remind you to continue to be on the lookout for any illegal drug activity and to report to me daily or even hourly, if needed, about the progress of the investigation.

"Also, in cases like this, there can be serious breaches in the chain of evidence, which can compromise an investigation. For that reason, I want you to know that I consider you my point man in the field, responsible for securing all evidence which, in this case, would be a cache of drugs someone thought was worth killing four people. You are not to share this assignment with anyone, not even your partner. Any leaks about our understanding could have serious consequences. Is that clear?"

"Yes, sir."

Ricardo Ortiz had received what, in effect, was a potentially life-changing order. He knew why the Colonel was doing this. But up to now, actions like this involved a few cartons of cigarettes or some pesos. This was different. If Ricardo remained complicit, he could be financially rewarded and, if the colonel was around, advance in his career—but at the price of abandoning his principles. It was a heavy load. He agreed, but just to end the encounter.

# TWENTY-TWO

**I**t was Tuesday afternoon. Adam Grant was in his office, but his mind was dwelling on events that had occurred last night in Havana. The news he had received from John Bridges was a shock. Yet, the fact that the Cuban police had already been in personal contact with the FBI, was encouraging. The Deputy Director said when he heard the news from Matt Hull, he felt he should immediately share it with Adam.

As Adam processed the news, he attempted to arrange events in an orderly fashion. According to Bridges, Dr. Alejandro Rivera was found dead on a deserted street in Old Havana. He had suffered lethal blows to his head that were said to have been inflicted during an apparent mugging. His body was found at 6:00 a.m. today. The preliminary examination indicated the death occurred about midnight.

Then, within an hour of the discovery of Dr. Rivera's body, a man identified as Luis Espinosa was fished out of the harbor. He was fully clothed and, in addition to his personal items, he also had Dr. Rivera's wallet, watch, and ring in his pockets. He also had a revolver, but it was not clear whose it was. It was estimated that he had been in the water no more than eight hours. And, finally, at about the time Espinosa's body was discovered, police found the body of Isabelle Menendez, his live-in girlfriend and the apparent victim of a hit-and-run.

Officer Jorge Lopez told Agent Matt Hull the local Cuban police suspected that the deaths could be related to Dr. Rodriguez's death, which was now considered a homicide. And that was why he was given permission to call the FBI. Officer Lopez strongly believed that Alejandro's death should not be written off as a coincidence; not with his ties to Dr. Rodriguez. And neither should the deaths of the storeroom manager and his girlfriend. It seemed all these suspicious deaths were somehow linked, not only to the murder of the American doctor but also the hydrocodone.

Adam felt like he had been thrust into a triangle. One side was two medical doctors, one American and one Cuban, who stumbled onto an illegal cache of hydrocodone in the storeroom of the eye hospital and were now dead. They were the good guys. The second side of the triangle was represented by two more people, also dead, who were likely involved in some way with the drugs, probably at the street level. They were the bad guys. The third side, or the base of the isosceles triangle, was the big unknown. They were the survivors and the masterminds; the suppliers who would profit from the sale of the drugs and were no doubt behind all the deaths.

If the pictures Mike Rodriguez sent in a text message to his wife were of high-quality opioids, as they appeared to be, there was a likely chance that the supplier was not peddling homemade stuff and that there might be a lot of it. Adam couldn't be sure until he saw the actual pills, but from what he could see in the photos, and was also confirmed by experts, nearly all pills like this came from the U.S. and were produced by an established manufacturer. They could have been heisted from a drugstore, but with four murders, it smelled like something bigger than a one-time event. The opening of Cuba to tourism could have been too tempting for someone to ignore. Even if Cubans couldn't afford the drugs, tourists could. Ironically, this would mean that instead of illegal drugs coming into the U.S. from Latin America, legally manufactured high-quality drugs would be going in the other direction! If this was so, how did the stuff end up in Cuba?

Adam wanted to learn more, even though it was mostly a matter for the Cubans. Should SHOP be involved until the death of the American was solved? A tiebreaker in arriving at the answer to this question was that there were overtones of an international incident with the death of an American doctor and a drug manufactured in the U.S. being shipped to Cuba illegally ... maybe it was time for Adam to run this by Bob Zinsky and Phil Stark.

# TWENTY-THREE

**"G**ood night**, Irene," said Maggie Van Berger, inadvertently using the title of a famous Kenny Rogers song that wasn't meant to extol the virtues of the person addressed. *Freudian?*

Irene Newland did not even acknowledge her assistant. She had a lot on her mind, and was leaving the office early to do some work at home before Maurice arrived for his weekly visit. Maggie would remain until five o'clock, the regular quitting time at Delgi Pharmaceutical. Irene was rigid and expected Maggie to comply.

"Have a nice evening—and don't work too hard," continued Maggie, who was not bothered by her boss's indifference. Instead, she continued this ritual on days when her boss, the Senior Vice President of Delgi Pharmaceutical, kept her weekly rendezvous. Maggie's comments were delivered in a faux lighthearted tone that masked pent-up resentment she felt for a woman she considered to be cold and self-centered. Was she being passive aggressive? *Probably*, thought Maggie, who wasn't bothered by it at all.

Maggie knew Irene had a home office and that she did some work there, but it was not likely to be much. She guessed her boss was entertaining old Maurice tonight. This was something that almost everyone at Delgi knew about but which Irene and Maurice naively considered to be their own secret. Or, Maggie thought, maybe they didn't care.

In an hour, Maggie would drive directly from the office to pick up her young daughter from daycare. Because she was required to work until five, Maggie sometimes arrived as much as twenty minutes late to pick up Mary, especially on days when traffic was extra heavy. This didn't sit well with the daycare staff but, so far, they had done nothing about it.

Brightwood Daycare was a franchise operation. Maggie preferred this to the alternative of taking her daughter to a private home. At Brightwood, what might be considered by some parents as institutional coldness, was offset by accountability and consistent practices. At almost four years old, Mary received enough warmth and love at home from her parents. What was most important to Maggie was to know that Mary was safe and well-treated, and Maggie was confident Brightwood delivered on those counts.

Monday through Friday, their lives were busy. As soon as Mary and her mother reached home, Maggie would prepare dinner, do laundry, fold any clothes still in the dryer, put everything in its proper place, and lay out an outfit for her daughter's next day at Brightwood. After dinner and a little playtime, Maggie would give Mary a bath and put her to bed. Then, after too little adult time with her husband, Ron, it was time for sleep. Fortunately, in less than two years, Mary would attend school full-time and their lives would be less stressful.

As Irene Newland's assistant, Maggie worked hard at a job she knew she was over-qualified for. With a master's degree in English, Maggie had more formal education than her boss—who made eight times as much as Maggie. Irene doled out work with a coolness and sense of expectation that created an atmosphere of pressure. Maggie was burdened with a steady diet of routine and sometimes mindless tasks that were consistent only in that they had no chance of affording the satisfaction of accomplishing something meaningful.

The reason Maggie stayed was because of the health insurance the company provided. Her husband operated his own landscape business. Family health insurance through the Affordable Care Act was not affordable in their circumstances; so, Maggie's job was not an option, it was a godsend. Ron was his own boss and Van Berger Landscape was growing. As soon as they could afford to buy health insurance through the business, Maggie would quit her job and they could seriously consider having a second child. After that, Maggie would be able to find something to do that was more in line with her skills; maybe even start her own business.

As the office door closed behind her, Irene wondered how Maggie, with all she faced at home, could worry about Irene working too hard. Then, in a nagging awareness, the woman thought of the contents of her bottom right-hand desk drawer. The drawer in Irene's desk in her office at Delgi was locked because its contents were for Irene's eyes only; it was because of those contents Irene would be doing some related work from home tonight. What she would be dealing with was something that would affect her financial well-being during her retirement—really the rest of her life.

When it came to Irene's new project, Maggie was turning out to be a perfect employee. She never asked probing questions. When Irene told her assistant that their department would be managing the paperwork involved with product orders and she would need Maggie's help, Maggie appeared pleased with the new responsibility. If she questioned the change in routine, she never let on.

The fact that her assistant asked no questions was not a reliable sign that Maggie didn't have any. In most cases, people like Maggie knew much more than their bosses suspected. For example, nearly everyone who worked at Delgi knew about Irene and Maurice. There were no secrets. The current topic of conversation was the recent visit to the President's office by official-looking people from Washington—at least one of whom was said to be from the DEA. The honchos thought they had this covered, but the people knew. Was something up?

Apart from normal office gossip and politics, things around Delgi were stable on the business side. After losing ten employees in the past six months, mostly by attrition, and a rumor that executive bonuses were being suspended, the business part of Delgi was maintained and things might even be on the up-tick. But the appearance of federal government people nosing around could be something big. In this heavily regulated business, visitors from D.C. were not a good sign. This stirred in Maggie something she had been thinking about for a while. It had started as a curiosity, but now it was a suspicion.

During her three years at Delgi, Maggie had been privy to just about everything that happened in the office. She opened Irene's mail, typed her letters, and filed all the office documents. She had access to every bit of paper, all phone calls, and the summary of private meetings. Everything that went on businesswise in the office was known to Maggie—except for the paperwork that dealt with selected orders from manufacturers, a policy that began about a year ago. Maggie knew her boss taking on more work, especially if it wasn't intended to benefit Irene personally, was not in the woman's DNA.

Another curious thing was that about this same time, Irene became concerned about locking her desk and the whereabouts of the desk keys. It would not have been a big deal, except for the first two years of working with Irene, Maggie had full access to her boss's desk, which was never locked. Initially, Maggie assumed that if Irene had something to keep private, she would keep it at her home office.

Maggie was tempted to leave early to pick up Mary, but it wasn't worth getting caught and taking all the flack. With an hour left, Maggie decided to check on some orders that she had realized earlier were missing. They weren't on her desk or in her files, maybe they'd mistakenly ended up on Irene's desk. With Irene gone and not able to chew out her assistant for interrupting, Maggie decided to look for the missing files.

The papers she went through on Irene's desk were neatly stacked; a careful search uncovered nothing unexpected nor what Maggie was looking for. Satisfied that she had missed nothing on top of the desk, Maggie tried all the drawers and realized only the bottom drawer on the right was locked.

*Did that mean anything?* Maybe now was a good time to learn what was so important that it needed to be locked up. A spare set of keys was at the back of one of the drawers in Maggie's own desk. Irene never asked about them and Maggie never thought to mention the spare set to her boss.

Before starting the search, Maggie locked the door in the outer office. This was not unusual when she worked alone. If someone came to the door this late in the day, they would not be surprised to find it locked and would simply knock.

What Maggie found in the drawer were invoices for shipments from Humboldt Pharmaceuticals. They were organized in individual manila folders labeled by the month. There was paperwork in each folder for two deliveries. One invoice was for hydrocodone 10/325 tablets delivered to Delgi at 2432 Grand Avenue in Grand Rapids, Michigan. *Looks normal.* The second invoice was also for hydrocodone 10/325 tablets, but these were delivered to Delgi #2 at 3636 West Street in Fort Wayne, Indiana. Examining the invoices, it looked like the delivery to Grand Rapids ranged between 90,000 to 125,000 pills each month. That amount seemed right to Maggie. However, the delivery of 25,000 pills—it was the same quantity every month—to the Fort Wayne address, did not. *This is weird.*

It was four forty-five. Maggie Googled the Fort Wayne address and placed a call to the business that was listed. "Hello, I am calling from Delgi Pharmaceutical to inquire about this month's shipment to Delgi #2."

This was the first time the man had received a call about the shipments he had been receiving for Delgi #2. A box always arrived during the last three days of the month. When it arrived, he would call Mrs. Proctor's cell phone. It had a 603 area code, but she didn't sound like she came from the east. After the call, she would pick up the package, always on a Saturday. Mrs. Proctor just thanked him, paid, and left without any conversation. His answer to Maggie's question was, "Unless there is a change in the schedule, the package won't be here for another ten days. Is there anything different I should do?"

"No, thank you. I'm just checking for my boss. Bye."

*Something is way out of whack,* thought Maggie. *That's a lot of narcotic floating around. I wonder what Irene is up to. It can't be anything good. Should I talk with her? Should I tell somebody else, and if I do, who?* As soon as these questions came up, Maggie decided she would tell no one, not even her husband. If the situation was as bad as it could be, it could take down the whole company and even put someone in jail. This was not likely to be a companywide operation since the records were kept in Irene's desk under lock and key. Maggie knew there was a lot of money to be made if the 25,000 pills were for street sale.

As Maggie forced herself to hold off on making any decision about what to do, uncontrolled thoughts flashed and were quickly discarded: blackmail, collusion, disclosure? None stuck. She would decide what to do only after she had given the discovery careful thought.

# TWENTY-FOUR

**f she** had been in the office and was so inclined, Irene could have answered all of Maggie's questions. But she was neither. If Irene had been willing to talk, Maggie would have learned the address was for Fort Wayne Copy and Mail. Irene visited it once a month to retrieve a box from Humboldt Pharmaceuticals.

Humboldt was paid each month with two checks, both from Delgi. The check for the larger shipment was written and mailed under the supervision of Irene Newland at the Grand Rapids office; Maggie mailed these. The second check, which looked identical to the first, except it was from Delgi #2, was drawn on a Fort Wayne bank account established by Irene. It was signed with the name of a fictitious Delgi employee and mailed from Fort Wayne Copy and Mail's address. Irene paid for the 25,000 hydrocodone with a check from Delgi #2, which she funded. She would never think of stealing from her longtime employer. She rationalized her action by calling it a "re-direction of a pharmaceutical product." She was simply making high-quality drugs—or as she thought of them, "pharmaceutical products"—available to recreational users who would otherwise get them somewhere else. Why not sell people something that was both high-quality and safe while making a profit for herself in the process?

Irene Newland did not consider herself a criminal. She

considered herself a capitalist. She was at the top of a distribution chain that supplied people with what they wanted. Working through her creation, Delgi #2, she had devised a way to sell hydrocodone to a distributor, who in turn sold it to the equivalent of a retail outlet that served the eventual customer. The process Irene had devised was patterned after Delgi Pharmaceutical's legitimate operation, which had been functioning successfully for nearly forty years. To Irene, it was only a technicality that she was distributing a controlled substance outside the law.

**A year** ago, Irene took stock of her financial situation and she was not happy. She was just fifty-nine and could withdraw from her 401(k) in six months without the ten percent penalty, but it wouldn't all be hers because of income tax. There would still be a substantial amount left after taking enough money to begin the process of purchasing her new condominium on Long Boat Key, but she would need a lot more to complete the purchase. It was being held with a $50,000 deposit. The unit she had selected would be ready in a year; and at that time, she would withdraw enough money from her retirement account, without penalty, for a down payment to obtain the largest mortgage possible. After that, the mortgage payments would be made with her "pharmaceutical" profits. She still had a tidy sum left in her 401(k) that was rolling over tax-free, and this would be supplemented with cash from her new project, which was already paying off handsomely. These funds were held in an offshore bank account known only to Irene.

Two and a half million was a lot, but her new place would be worth it. She rationalized this by recalling twenty plus years in her modest bungalow in Grand Rapids. The condo was on the eighth floor, had a private elevator lobby, and was 2,700 square feet with views of both the Bay looking east and the Gulf to the west.

The reality check for Irene was when she took a thirty percent loss in her IRA during the last recession. The withdrawal that would be required to pay for the condominium, along with the slow comeback of her recovering IRA, meant she would have less than a million in her retirement account when she quit working at sixty-five. Other hits to her savings were $100,000 she had loaned to her brother, which would never be repaid; and the $50,000 she spent each year for five years to have live-in help for her parents. Both of her parents had died in the past two years, with only debts in their estate. There was no inheritance.

Although the drain was over, the financial hit, albeit much of which was self-imposed, had already happened. She didn't regret helping her parents, or even her brother for that matter, but a dollar spent was a dollar gone. And Irene had to admit she was not a frugal person. Although her home in Grand Rapids was understated, this was a conscious decision. On the other hand, her clothing, jewelry, cars, art collection, and the vacations she took were not cheap. They were extravagant. Her one-story ranch at the end of a cul-de-sac that offered privacy was her only frugality. Irene preferred a low-key facade with an effective security system to nosey neighbors joining a neighborhood watch. Whenever she left Grand Rapids, Irene's life away from home was high maintenance.

Two important parts of her day-to-day life outside of her job were male companionship with Maurice and privacy. Her house made both possible. From the start of her time at Delgi Pharmaceutical, her twenty-year relationship with Maurice Delgi was satisfying and revenue neutral. He didn't shower her with expensive gifts, but he did reward Irene with companionship, affection, independence in her job, total trust, and absolute job security. In return, he got female companionship and good scotch. When it came to most decisions at Delgi, Irene was, in effect, on a level with the founder. A lot had happened in two decades. Irene could recite every bit of it, and that included the good and some that was not so good. There were so many things about the company that only Maurice and she knew.

Irene became Maurice's mistress shortly after she was recruited to Delgi from Big Pharma in Indianapolis. He visited her home no less than once a week, and often twice, always opening the automatic garage door that faced a wooded lot and entered unseen by the neighbors—or so the two thought. Now in his seventies, Maurice was mostly satisfied with a cup of tea or a scotch while they just talked. In the early years, he had been an ardent lover, but not so much now. Irene found this curious. Maurice had spent nearly all his working life in the pharmaceutical industry and yet could not bring himself to use Viagra or any of the other drugs for his ED.

Over the years, Maurice never shirked his duty as a good father and dutiful husband to a wife who never acknowledged but must have known about Irene and chose not to make an issue of this dalliance. The rest of the family also had to know about their relationship, but the benefits of respectability free of any hint of scandal, along with financial security, trumped any outrage that could jeopardize the status and comfort they all enjoyed. Neither of Maurice's sons gave any indication that they would enter the business. Instead they seemed to be satisfied with middle management jobs working for somebody else, something their father could never endure.

Irene made a conscious decision early in life to remain single. She had her share of beaus in college, but nothing ever clicked, and that was okay with her. After that, in her early professional life, despite many opportunities, she elected to eschew a lesbian lifestyle. The sex, heterosexual or otherwise, made slight difference; or to be honest, no difference, to her. Either was okay, but in public the social acceptability was no contest. She didn't enjoy a sexual encounter with a slobbering man more than a fervent woman. It was, for the most part, the other way around. The reason Irene was officially heterosexual was that it was easier to maneuver in a social situation with a man on your arm than with another woman. Besides, she did enjoy the physical intimacy with Maurice, which was made even better by not having to wash his socks.

Irene Newland was an attractive woman. She was blessed with excellent genes. It was the rule for her blood relatives to live well into their eighties and beyond. She played tennis once a week, in a doubles group. She was still a good singles player, but it was getting hard to find others her age that played well, and she couldn't suffer the rambunctious young upstarts who were always available. Irene enjoyed swimming and worked out regularly at Lifetime Fitness. She had a standing appointment with her hairdresser and esthetician and had used Botox sparingly but strategically on occasion. She had been a faithful daughter, good sister, loyal employee, and discreet long-term soul mate for a man she admired and enjoyed but did not love. Her life had been rich and fulfilling, and the new business she had begun was moving ahead smoothly and profitably.

**Irene's clandestine** money-making venture started on a Saturday afternoon a little over a year ago, when she picked up the phone to re-connect with Corrine Rotuno, the Senior Purser for Regal Seas Cruise Ships. Corrine served on *Princess of the Seas*, the flagship of the largest cruise line active in the Caribbean. She was about Irene's age. They had met on the first day of a week-long Caribbean cruise Irene had taken to escape the dreary March weather in Grand Rapids. Corrine had spied Irene, who the purser instantly recognized as an attractive middle-aged woman traveling alone, and from there she exceeded the prescribed role of crew when it came to fraternizing with guests. The two became fast friends, or at least as close to that as could be accomplished in a brief time. Irene even received the soft signal that Corrine was about to hit on her, but with a peremptory and fully understood, "I'd love to but I'm not there yet," Irene defused the moment. They parted with the promise to keep in touch, but as so often happens in cases like this, once back at home a person returns to their routine and these intentions are never fulfilled. But now, almost a year later, for Irene, that time had come.

With only the slightest hint of why she was calling Corrine, a meeting was arranged for the following weekend in Fort Lauderdale. Irene arrived at the motel that Corrine had selected an hour after her friend had checked in. After the customary greetings, Irene began to unfold the reasons why she had asked for this meeting by pointing out some of the things they had in common.

"Corrine, we are both single women who enjoy the good life, which we can afford as long as we continue to work and earn decent pay. Fortunately, we both have jobs that we enjoy, and we know how to mix in fun with earning a paycheck, but all this happens because we can afford to pay our own way. This is great while it lasts, but when we quit work, will there be enough? This depends on what we have salted away and how long we live, doesn't it? My guess is that when I leave Delgi, and when you split with your boats, there will be a whole lot more life ahead for each of us."

Seeing that her companion was listening intently, Irene continued. She explained that her ability to maintain the lifestyle she enjoyed now, and expected when it was time to retire, simply couldn't happen in her current financial situation. There was not enough money in her IRA or other savings. "Corrine, I wouldn't be surprised if you're in the same boat. Sorry, no pun intended," she was quick to say with a laugh.

Corrine tacitly agreed with a nod, signaling she wanted to hear more. After a few seconds of silence, Corrine said, "I know you didn't come all this way to tell me I'll be broke when I quit this job."

This was the response Irene had hoped for. It would be the first time she shared her plan with someone, and Irene believed Corrine was the perfect person. Her friend was smart and well-connected, and probably more in need than Irene. "Corrine, I'll cut to the chase. I have an idea that will allow both of us to make enough money in the next six years to build up a fund to supplement whatever we have in savings and in our IRAs. This infusion of money will allow us to live out the rest of our lives at least as comfortably as we are now, and maybe even a little better off. And, best of all, we will be able to accomplish this as an extension of the jobs each of us already has. Are you with me so far?"

"As they say at the blackjack table, Irene, hit me," said Corrine.

"The plan is that I will be able to obtain a large amount of a pharmaceutical product ..." Irene was purposely soft-pedaling by avoiding use of the word *drug* with its negative connotations. "... at a reasonable price that can be re-sold at a healthy profit for both of us."

"Are you suggesting ... ?"

"Let's not get ahead of ourselves," urged Irene, who was choosing her words carefully as she explained her plan. "The product I am talking about is entirely legal and it is manufactured by a reputable company that holds to the highest standards. When used as prescribed, in cases where it is indicated, the medication helps the recipient by easing pain and producing a sense of well-being. It comes in pill form and is used in the United States in the hundreds of millions. We would be making this medication available to a population that has a need of sorts, call it a craving, or a habit." Irene chose to avoid the real reason, addiction. "Using these pills eases whatever pain the person has and produces a feeling of relaxation that people are willing to pay a premium to obtain."

Corrine Rutuno was not naïve and had a suspicion about what would come next, but she only said, "And ...?"

Irene continued with a feeling that she had accomplished what she set out to do. "I can supply you with twenty-five thousand of these pills each month at a reasonable wholesale price. With your extensive contacts, both professionally and with the public, you should have no trouble turning these over at a price determined by you to people who would purchase them, preferably in bulk, and act as suppliers, making the product available to the individual end-user down the line."

Doing all she could to retain a neutral countenance, Corrine asked, "What are these pills?"

Eager to continue, Irene said, "The pills are hydrocodone 10/325. They have the same effect as oxycodone, oxycontin, Vicodin, and Percocet. All of these are opioids. They basically have the same effect, but some people have strong feelings about which is better. In that case, the pill can be offered as being any one of these, and they can even be priced differently if the buyer is having a special request filled. The pricing is established according to what the customer will pay."

"How much will the pills cost me?" asked Corrine.

With this Irene was sure she had made the sale. She explained to her companion that she would charge Corrine $2.50 per pill with a minimum delivery of 25,000 per month. Corrine could then sell them at whatever price she could get. Without trying to tell Corrine how to run her business, Irene suggested that the opportunity to make the pills available to passengers at a commission could be offered to other crew that worked for Regal Seas. Irene knew the line had ten other boats, with most serving the Caribbean market. Irene suggested that Corrine's best option might be to contact sellers at ports where passengers made shore-based excursions. Each boat in the Regal Seas line operating in the Caribbean made as many as a dozen trips a year and carried an average of four thousand passengers. Doing the math, this amounted to nearly a half million potential contacts each year. Added to this, selling the product to off-boat dealers would make it possible to reach tourists on shore who arrived on a different boat or in another way. "Not only are the numbers huge," Irene explained, "these tourists will be affluent, out for a good time, able to afford the pills, and confident they are receiving high-quality merchandise."

"How much money can I make doing this?" asked Corrine.

"Good question, and I only have part of the answer," said Irene. "My plan is to start with the minimum that can be expected from selling the pills I can supply, which is $50,000 a month for each of us if we can move twenty-five thousand pills. My share in the profits will be fixed. Yours will be flexible and based on whatever the market will bear—how aggressive you want to be with the pricing, and on your willingness to go retail. The easiest way to explain this is that I am assuming the role of manufacturer, you are the wholesaler, and the people you sell to are equivalent to the drugstores dealing with the actual user. Out of the more than $500,000 you could gross in a year, you will be required to incur some overhead expenses. These will lower the estimated income for you, but it could be made up by raising the eventual selling price, which you can set at whatever people will pay. There is even a possibility you could clear more than $50,000 in some months."

Corrine was a quick study. With a mind that was churning, she took up the thread. "I think I want to be more of a middle person and not sell directly to the people who will be using the drugs."

After another moment of thought, she added, "I also like the idea of working with land-based operators who will sell to passengers who have disembarked. That will get the stuff off the ship and mean a lot less exposure for me or anybody I would employ to help. I could have people on the boat direct passengers to the places where the purchases can be made on shore, but once I put the drug in the hands of the onshore sellers, none of us would be touching the stuff. From there, I will have to figure out how to collect from the sellers and to compensate the crew that direct the passengers—but that can be worked out."

"Corrine, I agree that is your best option." Irene was relieved to hear this because it would put another layer between her and the point where trouble would be most likely to occur, which was the transfer of money between the final seller and the user. "And, Corrine, I know you are good at math, but just to put a fine point on it, this partnership will mean that we can each have close to five million under the mattress, or in a bank in Grand Cayman, when it comes time for us to retire."

With that said, Corrine jumped up and gave Irene a hug. "Let's do it!"

# TWENTY-FIVE

**T**he first year of the enterprise went without a hitch. Irene handled the paperwork personally and privately in her office. She made a trip each month to Fort Wayne Copy and Mail to pick up the pills. She re-packaged them and added two dozen plastic bottles that were labeled as being from fictitious pharmacies scattered around the country. These bottles served two purposes. They could be used for purchases of more than twenty-five pills and were evidence that the hydrocodone was the same as what was sold in a drugstore. Irene then took the pills, boxed them, and shipped them to Corrine in Fort Lauderdale; alternating between using the post office, FedEx, and UPS to make sure she spread around the mailing.

Once the process started and sales began to be generated, Irene was clearing the predicted $50,000 each month and Corrine was making close to that amount. Both were satisfied with the arrangement and the operation was moving forward as if it was on autopilot. Both women were learning as they gained more experience.

Irene set up a laser printer in her home office to print labels from fictitious pharmacies that made it look like these pills might have been lifted and were for sure the real thing. Of course, most of the pills were sold in lots of less than one hundred. In that case, they were usually placed in a small envelope. For the big spender who could pay as much as $2,000 for a full bottle, what they did with the labels was their own business.

As Corrine became more comfortable with the process, she sold almost all the product in places like Georgetown in Grand Cayman; Freeport, Nassau, and Sandy Cay in the Bahamas; and more than a dozen other locations throughout the Caribbean. She was excited when a new outlet opened in Havana. These onshore contacts were managed by Greta Schmidt, the line's dining room director, who moved around all the ships while supervising the culinary operations for the entire fleet. The amount she paid Greta was well worth it for Corrine to avoid having to deal with a lot of people who could be considered undesirable. The only people Corrine dealt with directly were Irene and Greta, who had agreed that ten percent of the take would satisfy her.

The first order in Havana was delivered to the owner of a souvenir and gift shop in Old Town that was in easy walking distance from the docks. The owner told Greta at their initial meeting that he expected to purchase her entire monthly supply once his operation was fully functioning. Of course, Corrine had heard this secondhand from Greta, the only one dealing personally with these retailers. Once the contact was made and delivery started, Greta used a giant of a man, working as a deckhand, for delivery and collection. He was effective, even intimidating, when it came to collecting money from the onshore sellers. This was overhead for Greta, but she considered him well worth the cost.

Since the operation started, Irene had been able to deposit nearly $400,000 in her account in Grand Cayman. It took a few months to get the cash flow moving smoothly, but now the $50,000 monthly target was being reached regularly. Corrine was doing an amazing job when it came to finding distributors, and she had even hinted that she soon might be needing more supplies. This was good news to Irene, and she was especially pleased with Corinne's newest connection in Havana. The shop owner, Corrine said, was motivated, discreet, and highly energized, with plans to make the product available in markets that would be otherwise inaccessible to Corrine and her usual distributors. Things were looking up.

# TWENTY-SIX

"**Hello, Adam**. Great to see you. How are things going at SHOP?" was the CIA Director's greeting. It was Tuesday morning, seven days after the murder of Dr. Michael Rodriguez. The investigation was now in the hands of the Cubans and there were concerns at SHOP and the FBI that an obvious homicide involving drugs would be written off by the authorities; that the doctor's death would be called an accident and that would be it!

"Things are going as well as can be expected, sir, under the circumstances."

"Bob, please," said the director.

"Uh, sorry, Bob. Too much West Point. Some habits are hard to break," Adam apologized. "The staff is in place and the office itself, the space and furniture and equipment, are just great. Cooperation with the other agencies has been phenomenal so far—and we are already in business, so to speak ..."

"Yes, we heard about the U.S. doctor who was presumably murdered in his hotel room in Havana," said Bob Zinsky. "Scuttlebutt has it that the call to you was the first official notification to our government. Is that right?" Then, without waiting for an answer, the CIA Director said, "If it is, you must have impressed somebody, Adam."

"No, that's not correct. The way it unfolded, Bob, our office was the third to be called. The Cuban doctor who discovered Dr. Rodriguez's body first contacted the U.S. Consular Office in Havana, they called D.C., and then we were contacted. If you meant the first office that would be dealing with the issue and not just notifying others, then you may be right."

*The guy gets it*, thought the director. "I guess what I meant was that you were the first one who would do more than simply pass on the information."

"Well, yes. We did something, Bob," said Adam, who was still uncomfortable with this familiarity. The truth was, Adam felt more comfortable working in a system of hierarchy where positions were earned and authority deserved. Being on even terms with people like the director made Adam feel like he was being promoted before he deserved it, but there was nothing he could do about it. Adam added this to a list of feelings that may have been unique to him, or if they existed in others, they were too personal to be discussed. "After I heard from the Consular Office in D.C., I called the FBI's Miami field office and spoke with Deputy Director John Bridges."

Before Adam could say more, a man was ushered into the office by the director's secretary. "Chief, this is James Lawrence, from the FBI. Agent Lawrence meet Director Zinsky and Colonel Adam Grant, head of Select Home for Operational Personnel, which around here, we call SHOP."

"Nice to meet you, gentlemen. I apologize for being a few minutes late. I got turned around a bit and landed in the wrong place in the building on my first try."

"No need to apologize, Agent Lawrence. Your timing is perfect. You are right on cue. Adam just started telling me how he called the FBI in Miami as soon as he was informed about Dr. Rodriguez's death in Havana. I expect you have been briefed on this."

"Yes, sir. I have."

"Go on, Adam," said the director.

Backing up the story just a bit for the benefit of the FBI man, Adam continued. "When I received the call from the Consular Office in D.C., telling me about the death of Dr. Michael Rodriguez, which was said to have occurred under suspicious circumstances, I immediately spoke with the Consular Office in Havana to confirm details. After that, I spoke briefly with the colleague of the dead American doctor, Dr. Alejandro Rivera, who had found the body and made the call to the U.S. Consul. Rivera promised he would remain with his friend's body until he had further instructions. I had a better handle on events after I called the FBI field office in Miami and spoke with John Bridges, the deputy director."

Listening eagerly, James Lawrence asked, "When you told him about these events, how did John Bridges react?"

"Like a man of action who knew what he was doing," said Adam. "He was eager to cooperate even though I may have inadvertently put him in a bit of a box. I explained that I had already called the hotel room where the doctor died and spoken with Dr. Rivera, who had discovered the body. When I told John Bridges about the need for quick action, he couldn't have reacted any better. He told me he would arrange a charter and get two men to the hotel that afternoon, and he said he would call me back as soon as he received a report from them from the scene, and he did."

"Glad the Bureau didn't let you down," said Lawrence. "I expect this is only the beginning and there is a lot more to the story."

"Yes. A thorough study of the scene revealed that Dr. Rodriguez died in the bedroom by the desk, and then his body was dragged into the bathroom where it was positioned to indicate he had fallen and died after hitting his head on the toilet. The investigators also have photos of a bottle of prescription drugs the doctor discovered in the basement storeroom of the Raul Mesa Carreras Eye Hospital, where he was volunteering. The photos were taken on his cell phone and sent to his wife in a text message, however they had been erased from the photo gallery on his phone."

"Hmm," registered Bob Zinsky as he was thinking. "A body that was moved to make the death appear to be an accident, and pictures of a bottle of pills erased from the cell phone are not random and unconnected. Someone wanted to get rid of the doctor because he knew about the contents of the bottle, and the photos were erased from his phone to eliminate drugs as a motive. Obviously, the killer did not know Dr. Rodriguez had sent the photos to his wife in a text message."

Adam continued the story. "The agents sent from Miami connected with two local police officers who were smart and cooperative. The investigators were sure that the doctor's death was a murder. This was confirmed by the autopsy, and they were also convinced that drugs were related. In the three days the FBI had before the doctor's body was shipped home, the four men working together could only scratch the surface of the task they faced. They spoke with the hospital director, who was emphatic in saying that the pills in the bottle were not used routinely in the institution; but agreed the photographs had been taken in the hospital's storeroom. The investigators also concluded the person who erased the pictures from the doctor's cell phone must have been in the hotel room. The only persons we know, with certainty, who could have done this were the doctor himself, Dr. Alejandro Rivera, who discovered the body and alerted the authorities, and the murderer. From observation, questioning, and history, the investigators ruled out Dr. Rivera. They did encounter a slight inconsistency in his story but there was no time to work through this. The murdered doctor's laptop was in the hotel room the whole time because it was established the doctor never took it with him to the hospital. It was also password protected but when it was opened in the FBI lab it shed no new information.

"After working with the local police as long as they were allowed, and making a good deal of progress, the FBI agents returned to Miami. They were sure this whole thing would be kicked under the rug and the death called an accident or from natural causes, whichever suited the Cuban authorities best.

"Then, just this morning, I was told all hell broke loose. Dr. Rivera was found dead on a downtown street, apparently killed during a mugging and robbery. A few hours after Dr. Rivera's body was found, the storeroom director of the eye hospital was found, drowned near the cruise ship docks. And the girlfriend of the drowned man was the victim of an apparent hit-and-run vehicular accident. If something related to the pills is connecting these events, there must be a whole lot more of these pills to give rise to this carnage." When Adam finished, the three men looked at each other, allowing a few seconds of silence.

Bob Zinsky spoke. "Gentlemen, I just heard that the life expectancy in the United States has dropped one tenth of a year in each of the past two years and the most probable cause is the increasing death from drug overdose in *young* people. The opioid epidemic we are facing is becoming a serious business—a crisis."

"The reason I came here today," interjected Adam, "is to seek your advice about whether you think this business in Havana is something SHOP should stay involved in. I think I just heard the answer."

"You did," came from the staggered but agreeing comments of the two men.

"That's good to hear, and what I expected," said Adam. "I have some ideas, but they are rough and need refining. Could I share them with you when I am ready?"

Both Bob Zinsky and Jim Lawrence nodded in agreement.

Their response told Adam SHOP was facing something big!

# TWENTY-SEVEN

**A**dam preferred to start new projects on Monday and never on Friday unless there was no way to avoid what Harriet Grant called "unpropitious timing." He chuckled to himself when he remembered how much he had been affected by things his grandmother had told him. Like "The only time to get married was when the minute hand was going up—for good luck." This memory caused Adam to think of Erin and wonder when he would see her again. He missed her.

It was a week since he had met with Bob Zinsky and the FBI. Since then, Adam had developed a plan, working on his own and also in consultation with select members of his team.

"Good morning, Cissy. Are we ready for the meeting?" Adam asked his assistant as he passed by her desk on his way to his office. He already knew the answer because Cissy Friend never let him down and was usually at least one step ahead.

"You got it, boss. Everyone knows to assemble and be ready to start at the stroke of 10:00 a.m. And, guess what?"

Adam did not answer right away because Cissy could only hold the "guess what" for so long, but today she was hanging on.

"What?" Adam finally gave in.

"Your boss called and said he might be attending. I told him when the meeting would start but he warned that he might be a few minutes late. He said to start without him. He wants no fanfare."

"Did you invite him, Cissy?"

"No."

"Then how did he find out?"

"He might have heard it from his secretary."

"I don't suppose you had anything to do with her finding out?"

"As you were, Colonel," said Cissy to end the exchange.

The purpose of today's meeting was for the entire SHOP team to learn about opioids and the epidemic that was sweeping the country. This information would prepare the newly formed agency for its first major undertaking.

Adam had been doing his homework, but he believed both he and the rest of the group could learn more on this subject from Tom Hodges. Adam had asked his deputy to compile information about addictive drugs, with an emphasis on opioids. Adam knew that Tom had assembled a mound of information since receiving the assignment last Thursday; Adam was looking forward to hearing it.

**Adam believed** the first hour of each business week was best spent cleaning up your desk from the weekend and answering any phone messages, so you could start the week with a clean slate. He always did this and offered it as a suggestion to his team; which is why the meeting started at ten instead of nine.

Adam was ready to lead his team as they worked to find the reason for the death of four people, especially those of Dr. Michael Rodriguez and his colleague Dr. Alejandro Rivera. The chief problem for Adam was that the Cubans, despite finally admitting that the American doctor had been murdered, were limiting the investigation to their own police officers and only using the FBI for consultation by phone. From Adam's perspective, the best way for him to keep the investigation in motion was to pursue the drug angle. If they were able to find the source of the drugs, there was a chance this could lead to the person who was probably behind the deaths of four people.

It was time for the meeting to start. Standing in front of his team, Adam set the stage. "Two days of dedicated effort has turned this fellow next to me into our resident expert on the opioid crisis in the United States. I doubt there is a person in this room who knows more about this than Captain Hodges. Now, it's our turn to benefit as he shares with us what he has learned. Tom, it's all yours."

"Thank you, Adam."

As his deputy began, Adam hoped that the meeting would establish the concept that everyone at SHOP was part of a team that was working from the same playbook. Not everyone would be doing the same job, but all would be fully aware of the challenges and be united in working toward a successful outcome. Adam hoped that in this kind of environment, jealousies would be avoided and cooperation enhanced. He also hoped that most of those in the room would be as eager as he was to hear what Tom had to say.

"We are at the height of the deadliest drug epidemic in U.S. history," started Tom. "A large contributor to this is the abuse of prescription drugs. What I share with you today is current information, but events are moving so fast and sources are so scattered that it is not possible to guarantee precision with many of the statistics I will present. I will offer the most up-to-date information that I can. Don't hold me to specific numbers, just trends. What I am describing is a moving target and one that is moving in the wrong direction. The increase in opioid abuse is on a near exponential path. The current numbers may be soft and uncertain, but the direction is concrete and upward in a bad way. Each of you were given a fact sheet that I prepared. The numbers speak for themselves; I hope they reinforce some of what I will be saying."

With this introduction completed, the speaker noted a small commotion at the back of the room. Doing a quick double-take, Tom Hodges thought the person he saw quietly taking a seat was

Robert Zinsky, Director of the Central Intelligence Agency. A third look confirmed that it was, indeed, the Director. And he was not alone. An attractive, dark-haired woman accompanied him. Tom did not recognize her. A quick glance at Adam, to get the signal to proceed, revealed a strange look on his boss's face.

Tom Hodges started, "Can anyone tell me the difference between heroin and cocaine?" Seeing no response, Tom asked, "Anyone? It's okay; there isn't a right answer. Just tell me what you think of when these substances are mentioned."

A young woman, Valerie Gordon, offered, "When heroin is mentioned, it is usually describing an addict, not good. In the movies and on TV, cocaine and marijuana are portrayed as more or less cool."

"Right. Anyone else?"

"Meth is definitely for scumbags," said someone in the back of the room.

Marilyn Helm, who was sitting near Tom, said, "I read about the drug problem and hear about it on TV on a regular basis, like most people—but I can't figure out what is what. I am looking forward to learning something today."

With no more comments, Tom Hodges said, "Okay. Last week, I was in the same boat. Today I will share what I learned about four basic categories of misused drugs. These are the ones that are the most addictive, which too often leads to dependence, addiction, and ruination of lives. There are many others, but these comprise the core of the problem we face today."

After discussing marijuana, cocaine, and methamphetamines, Tom moved onto opioids. "Opioid refers to a class of naturally occurring drugs based on morphine. Heroin is an illegal adulteration of morphine; it is not suitable for any medical purpose. Partial and one hundred percent synthetic opioids are legally available in pill form but only by prescription. These are the drugs we will be discussing this morning.

"Morphine is a natural opioid that is the basis of this class of drug. It is derived from the poppy by extracting the sap from the bloom. Morphine, and its many synthetic derivatives, are used for pain relief, which is beneficial for a patient in the immediate post-operative period. Relief of pain in these cases not only makes the patient more comfortable but it also aids in the healing process. In some situations, patients may be able to regulate the amount of drug according to need using a self-operated morphine pump. Morphine is administered intravenously, but in emergency situations it can be injected intramuscularly. Opioids, in any form, can be addictive.

"Opioids that are available in pill form are the ones you are most likely to be familiar with—some of you may have even taken them for a short duration under the supervision of your doctor. The most common opioids prescribed today are mostly synthetic. They may be combined with other drugs, but the opioid content is the potent force. These drugs are manufactured under strict guidelines to ensure purity and accuracy of dosage. They are closely controlled during the manufacture and distribution process and are dispensed only under the supervision of a doctor.

"The foundation for opioids is the well-known morphine effect produced by the pure form of the drug that can be made even stronger in the synthetic form. Commonly used and prescribed synthetic opioid painkillers are names you are probably familiar with. They include hydrocodone; oxycodone, which is also called oxycontin; Vicodin; and Percocet. These painkillers are similar in being morphine-opioid based—differing only in subtleties, like dosage, packaging, and their additives.

"A purely synthetic opiate is fentanyl, which is said to be one hundred times stronger than morphine. Other pain management drugs are Demerol, Norco, methadone, and a few others that are opioid-based, including those used to help wean addicts. All these opioid drugs are classified as Schedule II by the DEA. This class of drugs has a legitimate medical use but only under strict supervision. Partially synthetic pills can contain as much as ten milligrams of opioid. Between one hundred and two hundred milligrams is considered a lethal dose. To put this in perspective, a prescription for these pills to be taken three times a day over seven days could be fatal if taken all at once.

"An opioid that is illegal under all circumstances is heroin. It starts with sap from the poppy but is three times more powerful. It is produced after the resin of the poppy is treated with a chemical, acetic anhydride. Heroin is listed as a Schedule 1 drug. It has no recognized medical use because it lacks acceptable safety standards for dosage. Heroin may be sold as a powder or a solution and can be combined with a tarlike substance that is called 'black ice.' It may be snorted, smoked, or injected. Heroin is frequently impure, and cut with sugar, starch, powdered milk, or quinine. The manufacture of this drug is clandestine and illegal.

"Paradoxically, the category of drugs that has become a current matter of national concern is legal when used properly. Because these medicines are manufactured in enormous amounts by legitimate pharmaceutical companies, are safe and cheap when used as prescribed, they are now being abused, in some cases because of over-prescribing, although that is not the only reason. Ultimately, its widespread availability provides an opportunity for misuse and for criminal enterprise.

"Prescription opioids that reduce severe pain can be a godsend to the sufferer. Over and above pain relief, however, they also produce a sense of well-being and relaxation that can be a pleasant and sought-after experience. This effect alone can cause a person to become addicted. People who take opioids experience a feeling of peace, ease, and pleasure, which stimulates a desire to have more. This results in an otherwise well-grounded person becoming addicted; oftentimes after taking the medication to treat a legitimate medical condition. Taking as much of the drug as the craving demands, without the exercise of will, has no recognized limits other than virtual incapacity or death.

"In the 1980s and nineties, several brands of prescription opioid drugs were introduced and touted as being safe and non-addictive. This led to widespread over prescribing, which has been difficult to get in check. Abuse of these drugs eventually takes over and ruins lives—and it doesn't matter where a person falls on the socio-economic ladder. Acute overdose will result in respiratory failure and death.

"The availability of these drugs is an example of the law of supply and demand. The drugs are effective and, when the need arises, patients expect to receive them. A person who becomes addicted to opioids will demand them long after the acute need has subsided. In some cases, doctors can be pressured to prescribe this medication because pain is a subjective matter. Furthermore, there can be bad actors, including doctors who prescribe excessive amounts for profit. As the demand increases, more drugs are manufactured, making them more available for both legitimate and illegal use. This creates a market that can lead to enormous profit for the opportunistic criminal. And that is what we are dealing with today."

As Tom finished his presentation, he saw Colonel Grant sprint to the back of the room, where he began an animated conversation with the good-looking woman who had walked in with Director Zinsky.

Could it be ... ?

# TWENTY-EIGHT

"**E**rin! What** are you doing here?" was all a flustered Adam could think to say as he approached Erin O'Leary at the back of the room.

With a small pout, mostly for the effect, Erin said, "What about, 'Hello, it's nice to see you.'?"

"Oh, okay. Hello, Erin. It's wonderful to see you—and such a surprise." Adam then turned and looked at Bob Zinsky, who was standing at Erin's shoulder.

"This is all my fault, Adam, for Erin being ..." Zinsky started to explain.

"No, Adam," blurted Erin. "This surprise is entirely my fault, not the director's. I'm sorry. I should have told you Saturday, after I got the call, but I knew you were planning a big day today, getting ready for the investigation, and I didn't want to be a distraction."

"Distraction?"

Before Adam could say more, Bob Zinsky spoke. "Adam, I assume whatever blame needs to be accepted—but I'll let Erin explain. Oh, by the way, nice presentation. I learned some things, and it looks like you have assembled a talented team that will only get better under your leadership." Turning to Erin, the director said, "I know you two have some catching up to do, so I'll leave you for now. Erin, let's meet in my office at two this afternoon." To

Adam, he said, "When you get a chance, drop by and give me an update on your plans for the next step."

Adam knew that meant the CIA Director didn't want anything coming out of SHOP halfcocked and that these first days would say a lot about the future of the team; even its survival. The director was treading a fine line between engaging in meddlesome interference and offering useful input. He was making it clear that when offering guidance was the right thing, he would be there. The director's goal was to be a useful source available for Adam as he did his job and not an advice giver imposing his own ideas. SHOP was the director's baby and Adam wanted the man who had become a mentor to succeed. Confident in himself and not threatened by Bob Zinsky's interest, Adam did not consider the director's actions as interference. His involvement was welcomed. Adam looked forward to meeting with the director before taking the next big step.

After thanking Tom Hodges on a fine presentation and introducing Erin to him, Adam and Erin headed to Adam's office. Without asking Erin what she wanted for lunch, and barely breaking stride as they passed Cissy's desk, he asked his office manager to bring two salads, one Cobb and the other taco, and two diet Pepsis to his office. Once they were inside Adam's office, Erin closed the door and the two embraced, impatient and eager to be together.

"I approve of the lunch menu. Who gets to pick first?" said Erin.

"I know you like both and that your choice will depend on how you feel at the time, so, my dear girl, the decision is yours," said Adam with a faux flourish for effect. In a serious tone, he continued, "Now, Erin, tell me what's up. Why are you back from Rome?"

"Adam, I am truly sorry for not warning you. Here is what happened. Director Zinsky called me in Rome on Saturday morning to tell me there was going to be a change in my replacement. Art Barrows has some family issues; I think they are dealing with his son who has been in and out of D.C. Children's Hospital. It might even be leukemia, but I am not sure. Anyway, the director didn't go into details, but he said he wanted to talk with me in person about my replacement. He is considering several people and thought my input would be a good tiebreaker, but only after I had a chance to meet with the candidates. I didn't tell him that he was putting a lot on me—and I think he may be giving me too much credit when it comes to this decision, but I didn't want to tell him that, especially with my new job coming up." When Erin's position as CIA Deputy Station Chief in Rome ended, she would be returning to Langley as Robert Zinsky's special assistant, a plum job and she was excited.

"Well, that's news," said Adam.

Erin wasn't finished. "When you and I talked on Saturday, I knew I would be here today, but when you told me about the big day you were planning, with the launch of SHOP's first project, well, I didn't want to have my coming be a distraction. I was dying to tell you, and I should have. Adam, I know you well enough to be certain you can handle whatever comes along, and perform better than anyone I have ever known, and by a mile at that. Trying to spare you was a mistake on my part, and it darn near killed me when I called you yesterday because I was at the airport ready to take off for D.C. Will you forgive me, my dear?"

"Erin, there's nothing to forgive. But if you insist, yes, I forgive you. And since it really is not needed, I will put it in the bank for the future."

"Adam, I saw you signal Cissy to hold your calls, so tell me what's going on here. I feel like Rome is light years away and I am completely out of it when it comes to happenings here, at home."

Before Adam could say more than a few words, Cissy knocked lightly. After Adam responded, she entered the office with a large white-plastic bag from the cafeteria, which was in another building. Adam thanked Cissy for the lunch delivery.

After his assistant retreated, he pulled out two to-go cartons and the drinks that were in a can. He set the Styrofoam boxes on his desk and passed a drink to Erin. "Erin, what's your choice?"

"I'll take the Cobb, if that's okay," she said.

"I thought you would," said Adam as he delved into the taco salad. Despite his mother's admonition not to talk with his mouth full, Adam decided to update Erin on the situation while they ate their lunches. He didn't want to waste a precious moment.

"You will now get a preview of what I will share with my team this afternoon. Tell me if you think my plan is too convoluted. I think you will recognize I am playing a long game. Sorry but I can't come up with another way." As Adam spoke, he looked with pride and satisfaction at the three-carat diamond on the left hand of the woman he loved. This ring conveyed a special meaning, the fullness of which only he could understand. First, it was a symbol of his bond with the woman he would soon marry; second, it was something he had earned at his job; and finally, it was a meaning-ful and heartfelt gift from a man whose life Adam had saved while Adam led a CIA mission to avert an attack on One World Trade Center, only months before Adam started this current job.

Between bites, Adam spoke with the enthusiasm of a man who loved his work and was excited to be with his fiancé, a beautiful and talented woman who he had met while they led a covert oper-ation with the CIA. After a brief review of the timeline of events in Cuba, Adam concluded, "The higher-ups in Havana put the kibosh on accepting the FBI's help and are ignoring the presence of the hydrocodone discovered at the eye hospital; and worse, they are ignoring or calling inconclusive the forensic evidence that con-firms the American doctor was murdered by suffocation. They are calling his death accidental."

"That's a lot of stuff to overlook," said Erin.

"Yes, it is," said Adam, who took a quick bite of a taco shell filled with ground beef, guacamole, red sauce, and sour cream as he watched Erin begin with a large bite of lettuce that was in the company of chicken, crisp bacon, tomato, avocado, and cheese. She ate like she was famished. "Then, last week, after the agents returned to Miami, all hell broke loose."

"Like?" Erin mumbled with a mouthful.

"Three people connected with the investigation turned up dead on Tuesday morning."

"Who?"

"The first was Dr. Alejandro Rivera. He's the friend who found Dr. Rodriguez, the American volunteer, in the hotel room and con-tacted the American authorities instead of the Cuban police. The second was the storeroom manager at the eye hospital, a fellow named Luis Espinosa. The FBI agents had been looking for him but never found him to question. And the third was Espinosa's live-in girlfriend, a woman named Isabelle Menendez."

"How did they die?"

"Dr. Rivera's body was found on a curb in Old Town, that was said to be an unlikely place for him to be, especially late at night. He died from a beating during an apparent robbery. His wallet and other possessions were missing. Luis Espinosa was found fully clothed, floating in the harbor near where the cruise ships dock. His wallet and other personal items were still on him, plus he had Dr. Rivera's wallet and a watch and ring that were later identified as belonging to the doctor. Isabelle Menendez, Luis' girlfriend, was found in a street near her home, the victim of a hit-and-run."

"This is no coincidence," was the near automatic response from Erin.

"I couldn't agree more," said Adam.

"Is there something that ties these deaths together?" she asked.

"Yes. I think it's the bottle of hydrocodone Dr. Rodriguez saw in the eye hospital's storeroom. Dr. Rivera told the FBI that his friend wanted to discuss something with him but did not want to talk about it over the phone. This knowledge links Dr. Rivera, the storeroom manager, and his girlfriend—plus we know how lucrative it can be to sell opioids illegally. That's what I think is behind all of these deaths."

"Did you see the pictures of the hydrocodone?"

"Yes. They had been erased from the doctor's iPhone, but he sent them to his wife in a text message. Of course, they were still on his phone messages but apparently nobody, including the killer checked. The FBI lab in Miami sent the pictures to us last Thursday. It is unlikely that anyone other than Dr. Rodriguez could have taken them or sent them to his wife. He may have done it for safekeeping, so that the photos were saved on two devices. His laptop was password protected, but the lab found no pictures on it. Our conclusions about the timing of the photos being taken and sent clearly link the sighting of the bottle of pills with his murder. Of course, we are assuming the label truly indicates what the bottle contained. And remember, the box the bottle was sitting on is missing. Based on everything that has happened, we are operating under the assumption that the bottle was labeled accurately. People just don't get killed for taking a picture of a miss-labeled bottle of aspirin."

"Who erased the picture?" asked Erin.

"We don't know."

"Who could have done it? Who had access to the phone between the time the last picture was taken and the FBI confiscating it?"

"Good question, Erin. The best answer would be Dr. Rivera, the killer, and the dead doctor himself. Since Dr. Rodriguez thought the photo of the bottle was important enough to send it to his wife, he could have erased it from his phone—but then, why no fingerprints? Oh, I forgot to tell you, the phone was wiped clean."

Erin was warming to the task. "The pictures were eliminated by someone who did not want anyone to see them. That person had to be unaware that Dr. Rodriguez had already sent them to his wife. My guess is the person who did this has plans to sell the pills, and possibly a lot more than was in the bottle. And it should be pretty obvious the person didn't know that much about an iPhone."

"That means Dr. Rivera; Luis ,the storeroom manager; or someone else deleted the pictures and wiped the phone of fingerprints."

Erin asked, "Who do you suspect?"

"Between these two men, the most likely culprit is an obvious choice: Luis. Dr. Rivera was an upstanding citizen and a longtime friend of Dr. Rodriguez. Comparing him to Luis, a marginal character who worked in the hospital's storeroom and who may have called Dr Rodriguez's room twice only minutes before the murder, makes the choice a no-brainer. My hunch is that getting rid of the photos confirms the contents were hydrocodone and suggests that there are more bottles like this. The pills were important enough to someone that he or she has killed four people who knew about them. That's serious stuff."

Erin said, "You haven't told me much about the drugs."

"Our best guess is that the bottle could hold one hundred pills, but the label was in the way, so our best guess is that it was at least half full. The street value of this much hydrocodone would be a minimum of six hundred U.S. dollars, possibly a lot more. In a country where medical doctors make the equivalent of a dollar or two a day, and a successful businessman might make sixty dollars a month, having these to sell would be a big deal. The influx of tourists since the travel embargo was lifted means there are more people with money to pay for this stuff. We may be looking at a perfect storm of opportunity for an expanded illicit drug trade in Cuba. I can't help but think there are hundreds of bottles like this, and that would mean a big payday for someone."

"Do you have any theories yet, about how all of this is linked?" asked Erin.

"Yes, but we are a long way from closing the loop. You could say we have some promising loose ends, but they are still dangling."

"Okay, Colonel Grant, tell me how you are going to put this all together from your position here, in the States, and with no jurisdiction in Cuba."

"First, we are reasonably sure that the native-speaking Cuban male who called the Hotel Sevilla twice asking for Dr. Rodriguez's room was Luis Espinosa. It is also likely he was in the storeroom when Rodriguez took the photos. Whatever transpired, we suspect the killer went to Rodriguez's hotel room shortly afterward and killed the doctor because of what he saw, or what the killer suspected Dr. Rodriguez knew. The association of the victim, the probable perpetrator, and the bottle of pills makes it likely that this whole thing is about drugs. Luis or somebody else involved might have thought Dr. Rivera, being a friend of Dr. Rodriguez, might have known too much and killed him as a precaution.

"When it comes to Luis's and Isabelle's deaths, I can only guess someone acted in desperation to get rid of anyone who had any knowledge of the opioids. I believe we are dealing with a local Cuban whose plan for setting up a profitable business selling opioids has been compromised and that his plans are now on hold. If he is smart, this person should be lying low, which will make it harder for us to find him. Or her."

"Adam, with no U.S. presence in Cuba, it looks like you are not going to make any progress by going after the murderer."

"I agree. And according to my compass, that means we start from the other end and find out how the hydrocodone, which we are sure is the real thing and from an American source, got into Cuba. Why don't you put your mind back to the way you were thinking in Pyongyang last year and tell me what you would do?" said Adam, remembering the dangerous adventure the two had succeeded in, an event known to only a few in the CIA and even fewer in the federal government.

Happy for the task, Erin began. "Well, for starters, I would try to find out where the pills came from. If they are the genuine article, they should be traceable to a legitimate source in the U.S. where all or nearly all of these are made. I would begin by looking at established manufacturers and follow the trail from there. There are a limited number of producers. If, however, the pills are homemade, then it will be necessary to pursue a different course. But based on what you have told me about the bottle in the photos, I think they are likely to be the real deal. We know an illegal market for the real stuff exists in the U.S., and this could have spread to Cuba and beyond. If you can find the manufacturer, you can work with them to find a path that fits the scenario you are facing." Erin paused and looked at Adam. "After the origin of the hydrocodone is determined, you should go to Cuba and act like a cop, whether the powers that be like it or not. That, my dear, is about as far as I can go—and frankly, I am jealous. I wish we were working on this together. From what I read in the papers and hear on the news, there must be millions of these pills around. I don't know what method, if any, the companies have for tracking their product once it leaves their facilities. The large pharma companies must deal with dozens of wholesale distributors, and that will take a lot of work to sort through, but it is doable. Anyway, that is where I would start. And, even though he comes across as a good guy, I think you should find out everything you can about Dr. Rivera."

"Erin, you aren't making it easy for me to decide whether you are the most beautiful woman I know or the smartest person I have ever met. Actually, I think you are both."

"I'll take that as a fine compliment; especially coming from the smartest and handsomest man I know. I really wish I could work with you on this. What you are doing makes my job in Rome seem like tiddlywinks. Do you suppose Bob Zinsky would let us work together when I get back?"

Letting that delicious but unlikely option hang in the air, Adam said, "Erin, I will be sharing a plan with the team later today; pretty much along the lines of what you just said. Then, tomorrow, doing essentially what you suggested, I will assign teams to check out sources for the pills, starting with hydrocodone manufacturers. Most are in the east and should be accessible. I will start this afternoon to lay out our plan and make individual assignments. I think it will be good to move ahead now, while everybody is gung ho. "

"Adam, it's almost two o'clock. I'd better get moving."

"Wait a minute, Erin. What about tonight?"

"I haven't even been to my apartment yet," said Erin. "And I packed light, so I'll need clothes. Let's have dinner there. If it's okay with you, we can order a pizza."

"And then?"

"Bring what you need because I'm not letting you out of my sight. We decided to keep our own apartments but that doesn't mean we have to use them every night."

After Erin left for her meeting with Director Zinsky, Adam returned to the conference room and reassembled his team to go over what they had heard in the morning session.

**While the** two were eating a mediocre cheese and pepperoni pizza, seated across a small Ikea table in Erin's apartment, Adam listened to the news about her meeting with Director Zinsky. "The director said his choice for my replacement was Sam Thrall. I couldn't think of a reason for not choosing him, so Sam will be replacing me in Rome. He has been with the agency for twenty years, mostly in Central and South America, and his record is clean, even if unremarkable. Rome should be a fresh experience for him, and I think he will do just fine. There isn't all that much going on. The director asked me to spend two days briefing Sam and then return to Rome. Sam will arrive in eight weeks, which is when I can come home. It can't be too soon for me! Adam, how did your team react when you spoke with them this afternoon?"

"We mostly discussed the crimes and the evidence collected so far. Nobody was as smart as you though. We decided to begin with the major manufacturers of hydrocodone and oxycodone, and from there, if we are lucky, work our way down to the distributors they supply, and then maybe find the source of the Cuban activity."

"Anything else?"

"There was general agreement that we should have someone return to Cuba but not right now. Marilyn Helm, the young woman who helped with the boat monitoring last fall, pointed out something that was obvious but so far had been overlooked. She said that there are only two ways to get a commodity into Cuba in quantity: either by air or by sea. She suggested that we could ask Cuba to help in beefing up security at its airports; but that when it came to boats and ships, the Coast Guard has been active and successful. Although, she did say that most of their interdictions dealt with cocaine coming in from South America. And, she pointed out that there is an increased presence of cruise ships from the States since the travel ban was lifted, which raises the possibility that this could be the way the drugs are getting in. With the crush of passengers coming and going, it would be impossible to accomplish comprehensive screening."

"That girl came up with a winner," said Erin.

"I agree," said Adam. "My dear, now let's make up for some lost time and just enjoy ourselves. No more work tonight."

Erin did not argue.

# TWENTY-NINE

**C**issy Friend knew her way around the bureaucracy in Washington, D.C. and could get things done. This morning, she would connect her boss with the head of the Drug Enforcement Administration. After Adam's productive day yesterday, this afternoon he would be meeting with the team to set their plans in action. But before he did this, Adam wanted to speak with the head of the DEA to seek his guidance and cooperation. Having successfully made the connection, Cissy buzzed Adam and said he could pick up his phone. The Acting Director's secretary, following protocol, would get her boss on the line as soon as she was connected to Adam.

"This is Colonel Grant."

"Thank you, Colonel. I will connect you to Mr. Williams."

Having done his due diligence, or more accurately benefiting from Cissy's efficiency, Adam knew that Bill Williams had been the Acting Director of the DEA for only four months, but his history with the organization went back almost to the beginning. He joined the agency in 1980, in its seventh year. Since he had been with the Agency for thirty-eight years, this interim appointment was not unlike a military retirement promotion and was probably well deserved. The DEA was considered an important addition to the bureaucracy when it was established during the Nixon Administration, and was getting only more so with the way society was behaving. There were nearly 11,000 employees. The mission of the organization was to investigate and enforce regulations dealing with controlled substances and illicit drug trafficking at all levels. They worked with federal, state, and local authorities in the U.S. and cooperated with their international counterparts for investigations that were beyond local or limited federal jurisdictions and resources.

"Bill Williams here. Colonel Grant, how can I help you?" was the friendly greeting.

"Thank you, Director Williams," Adam responded. "I am director of the new Select Home for Operational Personnel based at CIA headquarters in Langley. SHOP is not specifically associated with the agency, instead our purpose is to coordinate the activities of governmental organizations, us with them or them with us, whenever working together will make it easier for each to achieve a successful outcome; mostly in the areas of security and law enforcement."

The director spoke up. "Glad to hear from you, Colonel Grant. How can the DEA be of help?"

Adam answered by giving a quick rundown of the situation.

"Sounds like a mess," said Williams. "What is the time frame?"

"The American doctor was killed two weeks ago. The other three murders occurred six days later, and all appear to be related to hydrocodone. After only three days in Havana, the FBI agents were sent back to Miami. The Cubans, at least those higher up, have not been as cooperative as the two who worked with our men originally.

"Ouch," said Bill Williams. "Do you have a plan?"

"Yes," said Adam. "There is something I want to run by you."

"Okay. I'm eager to hear it."

Encouraged by what seemed to be an openness to cooperate, Adam sketched out to Williams what SHOP was planning. Adam felt like someone who was riding a bike while building it, or like a Hercule Poirot wannabee. "Based on the belief that the drugs in question are prescription opioids that were manufactured by a legitimate source in the U.S., and the number of people who have been killed, makes us think that this could be a large illegal operation."

"What you say makes sense," Williams said. "With the hundreds of millions of opioids being produced and put on the market each year, it would be silly to go to the expense of making counterfeits. Diverting just one percent of the legitimate production of opioids means millions of dollars in profit could be realized from selling them on the street. I think you are correct in assuming these are quality drugs in the hands of bad guys. Tell me what you need. If I can do anything for you, I will."

"There are two ways for illicit drugs to enter Cuba in a high volume, and both involve tourists. They can come in by air or by boat. Several airlines have regular flights to the island, and there are now hundreds of cruise ships in the Caribbean and many that dock in Havana and several other ports around the island on a regular basis. Our idea is to do two things: work with the Cubans to screen at the Havana Airport, where all travelers from the U.S. arrive, and plant agents on some of the larger cruise ships to see if they can uncover any drug action on the boats. If the hydrocodone is coming into Cuba by way of cruise ships, it is possible that there could be some selling on board also."

"If it would help, several of our people could work the ships, along with your team," said the DEA Director.

"Thanks, sounds like a plan." Adam continued, "Our other idea is to learn how manufacturers distribute these drugs. Is that something you could also help with?"

Bill Williams responded after a few seconds. "That could be touchy, and would require some voluntary efforts on their part. These guys make a lot of money selling opioids and they have a legitimate claim that they help a lot of people with severe pain. At least, that is always their response when we ask them to justify sending more than a hundred million opioid pills to a town with three thousand people. They tell us that where the pills are sent is up to the distributors and the public—not them. The manufacturers point out that they have broken no laws. And, in case we forget this, we are reminded by a virtual army of lobbyists working on their behalf. Without saying it, they can hide behind the hypocrisy of there being more than seventeen million people in the U.S. seriously abusing a product that is advertised during the Super Bowl and a thousand other outlets."

"Every coin has two sides. Can we approach the manufacturers in a way that is not confrontational?" asked Adam.

"Yes, we can. My suggestion is that we contact the largest companies first, with a request that they look at their own records to determine if there have been any unexplained changes in the pattern or the volume of the drugs they supply to their wholesale distributors. It is a bit of a longshot, but if the drugs are being diverted, they will first have to go through somebody who sends out products to retailers in manageable lots. In the case of an unscrupulous wholesaler, one of these outlets could be putting the drugs on the street and sharing in the extra profit."

"How can we best get this cooperative effort started?"

"I will ask one of my top field guys, Arnold Phelps, to contact you. He will have full authority to move ahead along the lines we have discussed. And Colonel, I owe you an apology. While we were talking, I remembered that Arnold told me he went to a meeting at Langley a few weeks back and he was very impressed with the guy who was heading the new operation there. He said he wasn't sure we needed the help but was convinced the head guy was for real—and that must be you. He said he was eager to see what would come of the new group. I guess he will find out. Thanks for the call. I am looking forward to hearing more from Phelps, and from you."

Adam was pleased with the results of this conversation. Today would be the first day of real work for the team once he handed out assignments—but first he was heading over to the Starbucks in the old building for a quick lunch with Erin. He was looking forward to hearing what she might have learned about her new duties once she returned to Langley.

# THIRTY

**E**rin said she had spent most of the morning with Sam Thrall. Being the type of person, she was, Erin said she was embarrassed to be in the position to pass judgment on a man who was so clearly her senior in the agency, and a good guy at that. "I guess I flunked the Title IX part of life because I never felt like I was discriminated against for being a woman. In many ways, being female has turned out to be an advantage for me, or at least a draw when it came to competition with men. Of course, I never tried out for the Bears or any other activity that required more strength than my anatomy or physiology could provide. And, although I was never selected, I always knew it would have been easier for me than my date to be prom queen ... bad joke," said Erin, who was trying to say that both privileges and opportunities came with being female. "And, I should make it clear, I did go with a boy."

Adam smiled at her humor, but he was disappointed there wasn't more news about what Bob Zinsky had in mind for Erin when she returned to Washington, D.C. Maybe that news would come tomorrow.

"What did you learn from the DEA, Adam?"

"I spoke with Bill Williams, the acting director. He seems like a good guy. He made it clear that we are on the same team and the DEA will be glad to help. I just have to tell him what we need."

"What do you need?" asked Erin.

"That's a good question, and I am going to wait until after my meeting this afternoon with the team before trying to come up with an answer. In just the few weeks we have been together at SHOP, I have been tremendously impressed with the quality of the people we have recruited. For the most part, they are young, but there are a few older, steady hands. Cissy Friend is the most important."

"Should I be jealous?"

"Erin! She's the big sister I never had."

"Sorry."

Adam continued with what he had started. "Overall, the people we have on board seem to be smart and eager. To be honest, I am looking for them to provide important input. They aren't dummies. I will start with a general outline of what I have in mind and let them go as far as they can when it comes to filling in the blanks."

"That sounds like a good start. How much will you explain before you turn the team loose?"

"Enough but not more than I have to. Our approach will be two-pronged. First, we learn who manufactures hydrocodone and then we look for a pattern to help us figure out how the drugs are getting into the hands of the street sellers. We will do both with a very light touch to cause as little fuss as possible. And, with a separate strategy, we will find a way to uncover potential sellers in the greater Caribbean which, of course, includes Cuba. How does that sound?"

"Sounds like a plan that will give your team an opportunity to fill in the blanks about the drug part and also help you in solving the murders," was Erin's enthusiastic approval.

Looking at his watch, Adam was between being sorry his short lunch date with Erin had to end and his excitement at finally getting underway with the challenges ahead for SHOP. In his mind, he had already established a sharp demarcation between the two parts of the task that lay ahead. First was the manufacture and distribution of hydrocodone and second was connecting the deaths of four people who were likely killed because they were connected to the drugs. The question remained how cooperative would the Cubans be in the continuing investigation of the deaths, or would there be any at all? Would they reveal their findings to the FBI? Adam hoped that if his team made progress following the trail of the hydrocodone, events would naturally segue into finding the murderers.

**Adam looked** at the group assembled in the conference room. It included Cissy, Tom Hodges, and Maha Kamal, their receptionist who had asked Adam if he objected to her wearing a hijab. Although he said no, it was her choice to not wear it at the office. Adam was sticking to his philosophy that inclusion produced cohesion which led to cooperation, teamwork, and progress.

Adam began the session. "We have a big task ahead of us. It will take effort from all of us to work with the DEA, the FBI, and possibly the Cuban police. You can look at SHOP as creating symbiosis. Those of us in this room must do everything in our power to work as professionals while we team up with several resources to root out an illegal drug operation and solve four murders. With that, I open this session. Are there any ideas about where we go from here?"

Adam saw a collection of blank faces. Maybe he hadn't started this correctly. Then, a tentative hand came up in the middle of the group. It was Marilyn Helm. "Colonel Grant, I think we need a little more to go on before making any worthwhile suggestions about what to do next."

"You're right, Marilyn. Here is what I have been thinking. We will tackle the drug supply and distribution simultaneously. That means six of you will team up with a person from the DEA. Each team will work two ten-day shifts. On the first shift, three teams will each visit three of the largest manufacturers of opioids and three teams will be assigned to a ten-day Caribbean cruise. For the next ten-day session, the teams will trade places. This phase of our operation will require three weeks. With a chuckle Adam said, "Anyone who doesn't want to be assigned to a cruise ship, please raise your hand." None were raised. Expecting this Adam said, "To be clear, each of the groups will have a chance for a Caribbean-cruise experience. The program will begin this coming Monday. Are there any questions?"

"Who will be selected for the teams?" asked Donna Fisher.

"Cissy will post the assignments by the end of the day. If, for any reason, you are selected for a team and find it impossible or inconvenient to be away from home for three weeks, let Cissy know and we will do our best to accommodate. For those not assigned on a team, realize that SHOP's mission is to run a marathon not a sprint. Over the long haul, there will be other opportunities, and everybody will have a chance to do their part. For those not assigned for this mission, there will plenty of work to be done here, and know that your time will come."

The remainder of the meeting was productive, with nearly everyone contributing in a positive way. By four p.m., after two intense hours of discussions, plans were set for the conduct of the interviews with the manufacturers and for how the people on the cruise ships would interact with fellow passengers and the crews. With plans in place, the next step was to spend the rest of the week working out the details.

# THIRTY-ONE

**D**onna Fisher, representing SHOP, and Phil Deegan from the DEA sat in the waiting room outside the office of Humboldt Pharmaceuticals' Distribution Manager. The company was located in Providence, Rhode Island. It was 10:15 and they had been waiting for nearly forty-five minutes. It was Monday morning of the second week, and this was the second of the three manufacturers they would be visiting.

The two were told to not discuss their experience with the other two teams visiting pharmaceutical companies. Adam stressed it was essential to carry out all inquires without any preconceived notions. If one of the teams thought it had uncovered the source, that might signal there was no need for further search. Adam made it clear to everyone that there could be more than one supplier, or someone could make a mistake. He told the teams that every possible source deserved a fresh and thorough review.

Their first stop, at Argon Pharmaceuticals in Wooster, went well for Donna and Phil. The people who greeted them were pleasant and couldn't have been more helpful. They felt all the staff they worked with recognized the seriousness of the problem and believed they had a responsibility to be accountable and transparent. This morning, at their second stop, Humboldt Pharmaceuticals, the wait seemed overly long. Donna wondered if the distribution manager was acting warily, as one might do when told the IRS was dropping in, even if everything was in order.

Finally, the door behind the secretary's desk opened. A pleasant appearing woman, who looked to be about fifty, walked briskly into the waiting area where Donna and Phil were now standing. "I hope Sandi offered you coffee."

"Yes, she did. Thank you," said Donna Fisher. As a feminist, she was pleased to see that Jaye was a woman in charge of this important part of the business.

"I am so sorry that I kept you waiting so long. My name is Jaye Wood. I'm the distribution manager at Humboldt. The reason for the delay is that this request was dropped on me only two hours ago. I have been scrambling to have something ready for you as quickly as possible, and I finally decided that I couldn't finish in a reasonable time, so I am inviting you to come in now. It's going to require some work in the trenches, if you have the time. If it's okay with you, we can review this material together."

Phil Deegan made it clear that he thought this was a good idea and was happy to see from her look that Donna agreed. It occurred to Phil that it might be more productive to see raw data and sort through it rather than be given a polished report that said everything was in order. This might even have been planned by the company—not giving a person time and opportunity to tidy the books.

As Ms. Wood had warned, the table in the conference room had stacks of order forms, invoices, bills, and records of payment. It looked orderly, but there was a lot of paper. What Jaye Wood didn't say was it had taken her nearly two hours to sort through the pile of records to locate the actual drug shipments she was looking for. She had been able to deal with the electronic information easily, but the hand recording done in the shipping office, appearing in triplicate, was not so easy to dispose of. She tore into the jumble of records, some of which had been misfiled in the shipping department and found the orders she was seeking. Then she put the files on the bottom of a stack that she would say she had already checked. The work done by the investigators would simply give the two from the government assurance that Humboldt had cooperated and was totally forthcoming.

With the three sitting at a table stacked with papers in a small conference room off the manager's office, Jaye Wood said, "Before delving in, it would be good for me to know specifically what you are looking for."

Donna took the lead, adhering to the practice she and Phil had agreed on when they prepared for this assignment. They would alternate roles when beginning the interview. In other words, there was no lead person, they were a team. Deferring to Phil's experience, Donna told him to interrupt any time he felt the need.

Satisfied with this arrangement Donna began, "We are looking for a possible supply chain of prescription opioid medication occurring outside the usual distribution patterns. Several teams like ours are meeting with your company and five others, all major producers. We have no reason to suspect Humboldt or any of the others of wrongdoing. We are here only to find out if you have noticed any unexplained increase in the number of pills, specifically hydrocodone, being sent to an individual distributor or a region. We realize that you don't record retail distribution, and it is possible that is where the problem lies, but we are starting with manufacturers because there are fewer of you and the tallies are more likely to be obtainable and accurate. I should also explain that we are investigating a sudden and alarming increase in the illegal sale of prescription opioids in a geographic area of significant political consequence. As I say this, please excuse what may sound like mumbo-jumbo, but we are from the federal government and are operating under considerable constraints in what could be a serious criminal investigation."

With a studied look at her two visitors, Jaye Wood picked up several folders from a large pile of forms and showed each of them what to look for in the final delivery column on the back page of each stapled packet. Individual pages represented one month of deliveries and each packet covered a twelve-month period ending six months ago. She explained that this kind of data was unique to Schedule II drugs and the records they would be reviewing were limited to hydrocodone. This information was stored on the computer, but she thought "pick forms" used in the warehouse might be the best way to determine out-the-door numbers. "This material is not the whole story and it doesn't include the most current data, but my guess is this will not be a problem because if you are just now investigating, it is likely that what you are trying to uncover has a history of a year or more. What we will be doing now is the fastest way to uncover the first clue. Each stack represents one year of deliveries to a specific distributor and at the bottom of the pages you will see the total number of hydrocodone pills sent in the current month. Are you two willing to help?"

"Absolutely," said Donna, speaking for both.

"It is great to actually have something to do," added Phil.

The three got to work. Based on her experience and familiarity with the forms, Jaye worked at more than twice their speed, but having them help with the task was a boon. And she was glad that the two government employees would find nothing amiss with the hydrocodone shipments she had relegated to the bottom of the finished stack. By lunchtime, they had found nothing, as Jaye knew would be the case. At the suggestion of their host, the three ordered in for lunch so they could continue with their task after the shortest possible break. When lunch arrived, the Humboldt executive excused herself, explaining that she had a short conference call and would be gone no more than a half hour.

When Jaye Wood closed the door behind her, Phil offered to his partner, "She's been extremely helpful, even more than the last guys. And they were good." Phil said this with a satisfied look that lasted only until he saw Donna Fisher reach for the stack of files that had been checked by Jaye Wood before they were invited into the room to help. Phil continued to work away at his original pile and didn't comment on what his partner was doing.

After fifteen minutes, Donna said, "Phil, I may have found something."

Looking up from the stack of files he was checking, Phil said, "Let me see."

Donna slid a stack of twelve months of deliveries of hydrocodone 10/325 to Delgi Pharmaceutical in Grand Rapids, Michigan. In March, the shipment increased from 100,000 to around 125,000, but the entire order was not shipped to Grand Rapids. Instead, starting in March, 25,000 pills were shipped to an address in Fort Wayne, Indiana, to Delgi #2, identified as a new distribution hub for the company. The shipment to Indiana was always the same: 25,000. The remainder of the order was shipped to Grand Rapids and the number of pills in this order varied somewhat. This pattern continued for the remainder of the year. As Phil looked at the report, Donna Googled Delgi Pharmaceutical.

"Phil, I see a nice website for Delgi Pharmaceutical in Grand Rapids, Michigan, but there is no mention of a branch in Fort Wayne, Indiana. What do you think we should do with this?" asked Donna.

"Nothing now," said Phil, after looking around the room to see if there was a copy machine. There wasn't. "I'm going to take some photos with my phone. We won't mention this to Jaye. We were told to bring any information that could be useful back to SHOP in D.C. Once there, it will be looked at carefully by the investigative team and followed up if something is uncovered."

When she returned from her call, almost apologetically, Jaye Wood asked, "Will Humboldt be identified in any way as having provided this information?"

"Absolutely not," said Phil, who wanted to field the answer because he was not sure Donna was ready. "We are fully authorized to gather this information, but we are also duty bound to honor the confidentiality that your business dealings promise to your customers. As I am sure you know, we can get this information in several ways, so ultimately everything you give us today, we could get with a search warrant. In the case we are investigating, other factors make it necessary that the process be expedited, but at the same time confidential. Being able to review these records, and to do so with your help, has made our job quicker and easier. In addition, the way this information will be used, the only people who would have any reason to object would be the bad actors, of which we know you and your company are not included."

With their work at Humboldt finished, Phil and Donna offered profuse thanks to Jaye Wood and prepared for their last visit to a manufacturer in Sommerville, New Jersey. After that, they were looking forward to a Caribbean cruise that would begin the following week.

As they were leaving the office, Donna Fisher saw an expectant look on Jaye's face. Before Jaye could say anything, Donna explained to the woman, who she had instantly bonded with, "Under no circumstances will anything that transpired here today be divulged, as Phil assured you. If it turns out that information obtained here leads us anywhere with our investigation, you will be informed first and none of this will surface without your input."

"Thank you, Donna and Phil. Good luck."

Phil was glad Donna had provided additional reassurance because he had also noted the concern on Jaye's face.

As soon as Donna and Phil left, Jaye Wood phoned Irene Newland back, as promised when they spoke a short time ago. The first call was made when Jaye excused herself when they paused for lunch. "Should we be worried, Irene?"

Irene responded confidently, "As long as you kept the pick lists out of their hands, we should be okay. The digital tallies are just fine because you changed them on your master computer. The hard copy files can now be destroyed or buried in a stack of old files in the shipping room. It seems like Humboldt got a clean bill and that means we did too. Good job keeping your cool. Let me know immediately if there are any new developments."

Not as confident as she sounded on the phone, Irene wondered if this was the first crack in the system. Then, admonishing herself, she thought, *Irene, get a grip. We're fine.*

# THIRTY-TWO

**A**fter ten cold, fruitless days in New Jersey and eastern Pennsylvania, visiting three pharmaceutical manufacturers, Marilyn Helm, on team two, was looking ahead to the promised time in the tropics. Even though disappointed at coming up blank in the first half, she was having difficulty corralling her excitement at the prospect of a delightful Caribbean cruise.

The brochure said the cruise ship she would be on could accommodate up to five thousand passengers, on seven decks, plus a below-decks area that included a small infirmary and quarters for some of the crew. According to a friend, there was also a morgue down there, but it was not advertised. This made the cruise liner equivalent to a small city. A Google search revealed to Marilyn, who was into statistics, that there were more than 16,000 cities in the U.S. with populations under 10,000; her guess was that more than half of those were under 5,000.

From the information she had studied, everything about the upcoming week on the boat, including the planned excursions on shore, was aimed at ensuring the passengers had the most enjoyable experience possible. For Marilyn, who was a down-to-earth person, the best part might be that she would unpack and repack only once while having a new experience brought to her every day; as if it were traveling to her and not her to it. Additionally, she would have a whole week without the hassle of going someplace in her ten-year-old, hand-me-down Volvo, and having to find a parking place.

Marilyn would board *Princess of the Seas*, the pride of the Regal Seas Cruise Ship Line, at three on Saturday afternoon in Baltimore Harbor. The ship would depart at five p.m. Her travel from D.C. on Amtrak was only fourteen dollars. By avoiding the airfare to Fort Lauderdale, Adam decided it would be okay to apply the savings from two cheap train tickets to book an outside stateroom with a balcony for Marilyn.

When Derek Fuller was assigned an inside stateroom that cost three hundred dollars less, Adam saw the disappointed look on the man's face. "Derek, while you and Marilyn are on the job for the next week, I think we can cast a wider net if the two of you assume profiles that make you entirely different sorts of travelers. A single woman bent on having fun, with the finances to have a more expensive room, and a single guy on the prowl, pretty much covers the bases when it comes to providing bait as likely prospects for buying drugs. Besides, you both will be making hay on the prowl and not in your rooms."

Only half convinced, but eager to do his part, Derek, who also wanted to be a good representative of the DEA, lit up with a good-natured smile and said, "That sounds like a good strategy, and I'm willing to do whatever is necessary for the team."

**Inside SHOP** headquarters, Adam met with the six teams, twelve people in all, equally divided between SHOP and the DEA. This briefing marked the halfway point of the investigation. The teams would be switching roles from probing manufacturers to hunting distributors in the Caribbean and vice versa. Adam knew that one of the teams checking with the manufacturers had come up with a hot prospect. According to protocol, this was not revealed by Adam or the team that had made the discovery. Having this information was comforting to Adam. If it panned out, they were halfway home. There had been no hits on the cruise ships.

Adam felt it was like being in the lead at halftime during the Super Bowl. He didn't know how this predicted the odds of winning, but he was sure it was better than being behind. For the team, this was not the time to let up. In effect, he had the scoreboard covered. Only Adam and two other people knew they only needed to make a score on the retail side of the drug operation to win the game. Addressing the group, Adam incorporated some of the experiences that had been shared with him during individual conferences, and that included a refined strategy for the teams that would be on the cruise ships. He did his best to get across that they should not behave as they would in their own persona. Instead, they should try to behave like someone who would be receptive to an offer to buy drugs, whatever that was—he didn't really know and could only guess. He was pleased to hear that several of the team members had devised their own strategies, and he was most impressed by Marilyn's plan.

"You may think this is silly, but I remember from the sorority house at school that you could tell a lot about a girl from the way she kept her room," shared Marilyn. "I don't think it would be much different while on a cruise."

"Now, that's an interesting concept, Marilyn. How will this play out?" asked Adam, who was eager to hear more.

"The way I see it, some people are more prone to addiction than others and three big addictions are smoking, drinking alcohol, and taking drugs. If I left things on display around the stateroom suggesting I was into some or all of these, it could generate some interest on the part of a seller. I am told that maids and sometimes even stewards come into staterooms daily—I am sure they would notice things like that."

"What exactly would you do?"

"For starters, I could keep a half bottle of scotch and maybe a dirty glass in plain sight, and an opened pack of cigarettes, and maybe a butt or two in an ashtray on the balcony, where I think it is okay to smoke. I could also leave a couple pill bottles in plain sight in the bathroom. It might be too obvious to have them clearly labeled, but the pills could be real, and anyone interested in finding out could look at the code on the pill and a dealer would know what they were."

"Marilyn, I can tell you have given this a lot of thought. I am impressed. Good job," said Adam.

"Actually, I didn't spend much time on this at all. It just seemed obvious."

**At noon** on Saturday, Marilyn Helm and Derek Fuller boarded Amtrak at the station in Washington, D.C. They each had a medium-sized bag and a substantial carry-on. Traveling together to the harbor would be the last time they acknowledged they knew each other in public for the next week. They would each be trolling for the same thing, but in different waters on the cruise. They shared cell phone numbers and agreed to talk once a day but never when in sight of other passengers. Derek told Marilyn that in case of an emergency, she should call anytime.

**Marilyn's room** was a pleasant surprise. She had seen the diagram in the brochure, but it didn't hit her until she was in it how nice the room was. It was twelve by sixteen feet, 196 square feet, and had a balcony that was five by ten feet. There was a queen bed with a night stand and lamp on each side, a loveseat, a small desk with a chair, and a TV and computer hook-up. The closet was more than adequate for the clothes she had brought. A bathroom with a stall shower and a toilet, along with detailed instructions for its use, completed her living space for the duration of the cruise. Her accommodations were everything she would need. The sliding door to the balcony was at least eight feet wide and let in ample light when the heavy drapes were opened.

The room was better than she expected. Not a bad way to spend the next week; too bad she couldn't show it off to Derek. After unpacking, she sat on the loveseat to look again at the itinerary, the arrangements for food, and the entertainment that was available. The first two days they would be at sea. The main activity for most of the passengers during that time would be eating, drinking, and partaking in what looked like a sparse option for entertainment. One of the venues promised a karaoke event on steroids and the other a potentially X-rated comedian well-versed with use of the F-word. Marilyn remembered several of her friends telling her about the lavish entertainment on the *Queen Mary 2* during a five-day Atlantic crossing. There were extravagant stage performances, with dozens of dancers performing in Broadway-quality musicals; and top-flight performers, from comedians to concert pianists; along with an orchestra with more than thirty musicians. Caribbean cruises, she realized, catered to a different clientele; the cost was much less than anything Cunard offered.

Putting the brochure down after reading it for possibly the tenth time, Marilyn had a little talk with herself. *What in the world got in your head to make you think you could suddenly begin acting like a temptress and entice drug sellers to feel comfortable coming on to you? You were a big talker when you spoke with Adam.*

Returning to the present, and doing so with resolve, Marilyn walked into the bathroom and took a good look at herself in the mirror. She was twenty-five, five feet six inches tall, and had a good figure, on the athletic side. Her looks wouldn't make her a slam dunk for any beauty contest, but she was confident when it came to her appearance. She would like to get married someday, but she just hadn't met the right guy. She was still three years below the average age for women marrying in the United States, so there was no need to panic.

Looking in the mirror, she saw an uncomplicated face with a light dusting of freckles, rich-brown hair in a short bob, and eyes that were green bordering on blue, depending on the lighting. Her eyes were Marilyn's unique feature; people commented on them regularly in a complimentary way. She dated but nothing serious had developed, and now, busy with her job and not much else, she was in a dry spell.

She had been told that guys might be afraid of her because she seemed so capable. If that was true, it was okay with Marilyn, who privately believed that a lot of guys acted like wimps, especially the ones people referred to as metrosexuals. *I know what I am going to do. I will just be myself. I am alone, so it is all right for me to make friends and I think on a cruise like this there must be lots of single people. Cruise-ship personnel must know this and do everything they can to get single people together. One thing I will do, in addition to booze, cigarettes, and drugs, that is not in my nature, is I will be friendlier with the cabin steward than I ordinarily would be. I have heard these fellows can be wheelers and dealers, ready to fix people up with what they need in order to have a good time.*

With that settled, Marilyn opened the bottle of J&B Scotch and poured a third of the contents in the sink to make it look like she had had her own welcome-aboard drink. She then put an opened pack of Marlboro Lights next to the bottle on the dresser. In the bathroom, she opened her makeup kit and took out two bottles. One with hydrocodone 5/325 contained only five pills. The other bottle was full and contained Ambien, a popular sleep-aid. She hoped the hydrocodone bottle with only five pills would convey the message that more were needed.

While she was setting up her room, Marilyn had felt a slight jar but paid no attention. Now done with her staging chores, she decided to go out on the balcony to take her first look at the harbor from her elevated perch on the fifth deck. To her amazement, the Baltimore skyline was on the distant horizon. The boat had moved at least two miles outside of the harbor. She was at sea! That slight jar must have been all that registered when the boat departed. The itinerary said that after two days at sea, they would anchor at Sandy Cay, where they would spend the day with the option of going ashore, carried by small launches, that doubled as lifeboats, that she knew would be described during the safety drill their first morning at sea.

She was tired in the aftermath of the day's activity, and hungry. There were several options for dining, some included an extra cost. Marilyn decided to eat in the dining room that was included in the price of her ticket and requested the first seating because she wanted to be in bed early. She also selected the option that she was willing to dine at what was described as a "get to know others" table. The brochure said these tables usually accommodated six. Beginning to feel like a real undercover agent, Marilyn wondered if she'd see Derek. Who would hook up with the drug peddler first? Would either of them make a connection?

She had an hour before going to dinner. While Marilyn tried to decide what to do next, read, try the TV, or take a nap, there was a knock on her door. She answered and saw a nice-looking man slightly taller than she. He was attired in a spotless white uniform with a jacket that had brass buttons—very official. She guessed from his appearance he was from the Philippines, as were many of the crew. With perfect English that had a twang that confirmed where he was from, he introduced himself as Ralph, the cabin steward. He told Marilyn he would be available at any time in the evening if she needed anything, and in the morning a maid would make up the room. It would have been too obvious to invite him in, but Marilyn did thank him, although not before saying this was her first time on a boat like this and that she was looking forward to finding things to do, and she would be taking something to help her sleep tonight. As she closed the door, Marilyn wondered if everyone received this kind of attention or was it reserved for an unaccompanied woman?

**The next** two days were uneventful, and, as it turned out, Marilyn's main activity was reading *The Cellist of Sarajevo*, a book that had been highly touted but didn't live up to the hype. There was only one deck where a person could sit in the sun and it was contaminated by a waterpark-type contraption that was way too complicated and not big enough to do what it was intended to accomplish—a rip-roaring good time. It was used mostly by adults who were working hard to convince themselves they were having fun.

In the late afternoon, the day before they were scheduled to anchor at Sandy Cay, there was a knock on her door. When Marilyn answered, she saw Ralph standing in the narrow corridor. This was the first time she had seen the steward since their initial encounter.

When she asked him if he would come in, after a split second of indecision, he did, but the door didn't close completely behind him. A rule on this line and all cruise ships for that matter, explained to Marilyn in a briefing at SHOP, was that the staff were trained to attend guests but never fraternize. Not comfortable making small talk, especially in this situation, Marilyn told the steward she was looking forward to Sandy Cay. Ralph said, "Miss Helm, we don't have a pharmacy, per say, on the boat, but we do have some medicines available for special purposes on a limited basis. If you were to need anything, such as a sleeping pill that really works, or pain medication stronger than aspirin or Tylenol, I can direct you to a source when we visit Sandy Cay. I remember you saying the first night that you needed a sleeping pill to get a good night's sleep. For all the crew, the number one job for us is to do everything we can to make your trip the most enjoyable experience that it can be, and that is why I am here."

"That's very kind, Ralph. I may take you up on that offer," said Marilyn who was trying not to act too eager. She looked at the floor for a second and then raised her head, looking past Ralph toward the door behind him as though she were giving serious thought to what she would say next. "Ralph, I have to believe there will be a lot going on when we leave the boat for the day and go ashore tomorrow, and I am sure you will be busy. Maybe if you could tell me where the pharmacy on Sandy Cay is now, I wouldn't have to bother you tomorrow."

Ralph never ceased to be amazed at the gullibility of the people, mostly women, like the one he was dealing with now. They were so predictable, or maybe it was that he was getting better at picking out likely customers. Either way, working at this extra job, which was solely for himself, was proving easy and profitable. *She is doing my job for me by asking for the drugs*, he thought. "That's a good idea, Miss Helm."

"You can call me Marilyn."

"Okay. Then it's Marilyn. Here is a card showing the location of Tony's gift shop. Sandy Cay is a small place and this shop is just off the beach. It is a short walk from where you will be dropped off by the launch. As you can guess, the owner makes his living selling gifts and souvenirs. His small pharmacy is simply offered as a service to cruise ship passengers who visit the Cay." After a brief pause, Ralph added. "Marilyn, you probably know that in some businesses like this, a lot of licenses and things like that are needed, and I am not sure where Tony stands with that, so it would be best if you didn't mention this to anybody. I am doing this for you, as a favor. And, before you can do any business with Tony, you will need to show him this card." The steward handed her a business card describing the shop. On the back was a space where Marilyn could write in her request.

With a knowing glance, Marilyn said, "No need to even say that, Ralph. Mum's the word, I promise. And thank you for taking the time to tell me all of this. I really appreciate what you are doing to make this cruise more enjoyable for me."

As he left the room, Ralph tallied up the number of cards he had given out. This was the tenth, and there was a good chance he could give out three or four more before the evening was over. He still had the comedy club crowd to work, which was a much raunchier group; not at all like Marilyn, who came across as an innocent. In a fleeting brush with conscience, Ralph hoped she didn't mess up her life, but enough of that stuff. This was turning out to be a good sideline business for him. He didn't know all the details, but the closest he could come to figuring out what was going on was that someone on the ship, probably high up, someone besides his boss who answered to Greta, was supplying prescription opioids to sellers at the ports. These sellers would have the stuff available for passengers who would be referred by people like Ralph who had direct access to the guests. He suspected he wasn't the only one on the boat digging up customers, but no one else had talked about doing this and he certainly wasn't going to mention it to anyone. His kickback was anywhere from ten to fifty dollars per referral. His profit had been an average of one thousand dollars for the past three trips. Not bad considering the small amount of effort required on his part.

# THIRTY-THREE

**t was** six o'clock Tuesday morning. Marilyn had a wonderfully restful sleep and was prepared to do her best today. The sliding door to the balcony was open, admitting the faint rush of the water and a mild breeze that wafted intermittently. The freezing weather in Baltimore had given way to semi-tropical breezes as the ship neared the end of the first 1,000-mile leg to the Bahamas. In the next hour, the boat would be dropping anchor off Sandy Cay.

Marilyn fingered the business card Ralph had given her. It advertised a shop that was called Tony's Tropical Isles Gifts. At the bottom it named the owner as Giuseppe Scala. Marilyn would look for him specifically, guessing that if her visit to the gift shop involved a drug sale it would be with the owner and not a clerk. A picture of the shop's exterior was included on the back, along with the words "Take home a piece of paradise, and never forget."

Looking at the card and checking the address against the map of Sandy Cay included in the cruise information, Marilyn could see that the shop was only a short walk from the drop-off point. The Cay was said to be fifty acres, which was probably a bit of an exaggeration. Nothing was far away. The first launch would deposit passengers shortly after 8:00 a.m. and the last launch returning to the ship would be at 5:00 p.m. sharp. That meant a maximum of nine hours on shore. Marilyn had a job to do and she was a con-scientious person who would never shirk duty, but she would also have lots of time to enjoy the experience, and that is what she planned to do. Then, indulging in what she had to admit was pure rationalization, she reminded herself that she was supposed to give the appearance of a traveler on vacation who was looking for a good time, not a government sleuth outing a drug dealer.

Putting the card in a special wallet that was to be used when a drug buy was imminent, Marilyn took another look to re-familiarize herself with the contents. The driver's license, credit card, and health insurance cards that had been prepared at SHOP said she was Carol Stifel. She lived in Washington, D.C. and was employed, according to an ID card in the wallet, at a publishing company. SHOP used her regular name and credentials for booking the cruise, but this subterfuge was deemed necessary for her own protection when it came to make any drug purchase. In addition to the usual trappings, her special wallet contained three new $100 bills plus another hundred dollars in smaller denominations. Marilyn, or Carol as she would be for the possible buy, was satisfied with this part.

She considered the activities that were available: snorkeling, fishing, renting a paddle boat, a dune buggy ride, a tour around the island on a banana boat, renting a small air-conditioned villa that looked like a metal industrial building, sit under an umbrella on the beach and swim when you wanted, and take a glass-bottom boat ride around the coast for an hour. In addition, there were two restaurants, one barbecue and the other fish; two bars; and two gift shops. It seemed like the cruise line wanted to offer alternatives when it came to the big three that were eating, drinking, and buying souvenirs.

Marilyn surveyed her ample canvas bag packed with what she would need for the activities she planned during the day on shore. Besides the most important task, she would take a long walk, spend an hour on the glass-bottom boat, visit the other gift shop, have lunch, and spend the rest of the time on the beach before heading back to the ship by 4:00 p.m., but not necessarily in that order. Added to these touristic covers, would be the important and obligatory job she was here to complete: visit Tony's Tropical Isle

Gift Shop and, if possible, make an illegal purchase of a controlled substance. She would start the process by visiting Tony's in the morning and attempting to find out if Tony was around. If he was not, she would try to determine the person that was in charge. She would not give anyone the card on her first visit, instead she would do that when she returned to the shop after lunch, and after she had thoroughly checked things out.

With the day's activities determined, Marilyn re-checked her packed bag. It contained her bathing suit; sunblock; an extra T-shirt and pair of shorts; the book she didn't like very much but was the only one she had brought; sunglasses; a large, floppy, canvas sunhat; New Balance walking shoes; and a pair of flip-flops for the beach. With the preliminaries taken care of, Marilyn went down to breakfast at 7:00 a.m. and then got in line for the first launch. She suspected she could have avoided the "cattle call" if she had waited until nine o'clock, but that wasn't in her nature. When something needed to be done, she wanted to get at it, which today meant she would be in line with the masses. These lifeboats would be transporting what, in effect, were the inhabitants of a small city, and most everybody would want to be on the first launch.

Once on land, Marilyn took a brisk ninety-minute walk, during which she saw most of the buildings noted on the map, including the second gift shop, which she visited. After this, Marilyn went to have her first look at Tony's store. The building was sizable and made of the same ribbed-metal siding as the small huts that were available for rent; its exterior walls were painted yellow, pink, and baby blue. There was nothing obvious to differentiate it from the other gift shop. Inside was the standard array of conch shells, flip-flops, sunglasses, T-shirts, and a thousand other inexpensive items. The store was so packed with merchandise, it was impossible to see the interior walls.

**After eating** lunch at the barbecue restaurant, Marilyn wished she had opted for the fish instead. *Can't change the past*, she reprimanded herself. It was now time for Marilyn Helm, aka Carol Stifel, to get to work!

Once back inside Tony's Gift Shop, Marilyn browsed the merchandise while assessing the people who were working in the store. She spied a man who was clearly set apart from the others. She hadn't seen him on her first visit. He looked to be about forty, with dark hair, a ready smile, and he was wearing a gaudy island shirt. He seemed to meander the store, observing the customers. There were three other clerks in the store and one cashier; all were younger and looked local. This fellow, who she suspected was Tony, was now helping a man who didn't seem to be buying anything off the shelves. As she continued to observe the encounter, Marilyn saw the person she had decided was Tony retreat to a back room. A few minutes later, he returned with a small envelope that the man quickly put in a pocket before leaving the store. There may have been more to the transaction than Marilyn observed, but she had seen enough to convince herself that this could be what she was looking for. Marilyn forced herself to remain neutral and not jump to any conclusions. She would continue with the plan she had laid out for herself and approach the man she considered was Tony, present the card Ralph had given her, and see what happened.

As Marilyn walked closer to Tony, their gaze met. He greeted her with a pleasant, "May I help you?"

Marilyn replied, "I hope so," and handed him the card Ralph had given her. As she gave the card to him, she noticed R-11116 written on the back in very fine print in pencil. She had not noticed it before and hoped the notation would show up in the pictures she had taken last night with her cell phone camera. She guessed she would have to give up the card if she made a purchase.

As Tony accepted the card, he said, "Did you and Ralph discuss what you might be purchasing?"

"He said you had access to some pain medicine that could help me."

"Did he say what?"

"No, but I think he knew I had a bottle that was just about empty. He said that a prescription for these pills couldn't be filled in the ship's dispensary but that you operated a convenience pharmacy exclusively for passengers, and that you could help me. He also said that because of licensing issues, I should keep this to myself."

"What was it you were expecting?"

"I have been using hydrocodone 5/325 but I ran out." Marilyn was glad she hadn't written anything on the back of the card that she might have had to explain. Tony was making things easy.

"I have something better. Tens."

"How much?" As she said this, Marilyn did her best to contain her excitement.

"Ten dollars each for up to ten pills; nine dollars each for fifty; and eight dollars each for one hundred."

Marilyn said, "I'll just need ten."

The owner said, "Good. That will be cash, and no sales tax. I'll be right back."

In less than five minutes, the man returned and handed Marilyn a small white envelope, and she handed him a crisp hundred-dollar bill.

Behind a display of garish T-shirts, a man, obviously a passenger from the ship, was wearing a silly hat that he had taken from a rack and seemed to be trying out. He was wearing large sunglasses and holding out his phone at arm's length taking a selfie, but the view on the screen was not of himself. It was a burst of shots recording the transaction taking place ten feet away.

To say the rest of the day was an anticlimax for Marilyn would be an understatement. As planned, she spent the rest of the afternoon on the beach, enjoying the sun and reveling in the fact she had been successful in her quest. Under a beach umbrella and away from prying eyes, she opened the envelope and saw the small, tan pills with "X" engraved on one side and 06 09 on either side of the scoring. She knew this was the kind of marking that identified both the drug and the manufacturer. It was Humboldt and hydrocodone 10/325.

**At six** p.m., Derek Fuller and Marilyn Helm sat in her stateroom. They were no longer concerned about being seen together. They had accomplished what they needed to and could now act as friends who happened to take the same cruise by chance. That would justify their being together if they were seen or questioned, although they agreed after this to revert to the no-contact mode for the rest of the cruise. Marilyn showed Derek the pills. They looked like the real thing when she compared the type of marking and the apparent quality with the legitimate pills she was using as a decoy.

"You did great, Marilyn," enthused Derek. "And now, I have a surprise for you."

"Wow, a surprise! This must be my lucky day," said Marilyn. "I can hardly wait."

Derek took an iPhone out of his pocket and held it. "Marilyn, when we talked last and you told me you would be going to the gift shop with a card the steward had given you, I decided to be on hand, just in case. I was there in the morning and nothing happened, so I decided to hang around in case you came back. When you did, after lunch, I followed you in, and when I saw the transaction taking place, I took some pictures."

"But I didn't see you."

"That's the idea, Marilyn. We're undercover! I was that goofy guy with the funny hat and sunglasses who was taking a selfie while you were paying for the drugs."

"Let me see."

Derek handed over his iPhone with a clear picture of Marilyn and Tony in the gift shop. It showed the small envelope clearly and there was just a hint of the hundred-dollar bill she was handing over. The burst captured four pictures, and all were good. "And now, the nerd who took them," said Derek as he showed her the selfie he had taken after he recorded the transaction. "Do you remember seeing this guy?"

"Sorry, no," said Marilyn. "I guess you are a good spy, Derek."

**The two** enjoyed the rest of the cruise doing their own thing. Marilyn did not see the steward again except from a distance in the corridor. She suspected from the notation on the card that he would have been contacted by Tony for his kickback, and Ralph's connection with Marilyn was over.

The two agents didn't see each other until they reached their pre-arranged rendezvous after leaving the boat at the dock in Baltimore Harbor. From there, they took the train back to D.C. Both were excited and could hardly contain themselves as they looked forward to the de-brief that would take place with the rest of the team on Monday, their first day back in the office.

The last thing Derek said to Marilyn as they parted was, "I hope someone was luckier than we were when it came to the manufacturers."

"Me too," said Marilyn.

# THIRTY-FOUR

**E**rin returned to Washington, D.C. from Rome on Saturday. The transition with Sam Thrall had worked out well, so Director Zinsky called Erin back several weeks earlier than originally planned. Adam met Erin at Dulles and the two went to her apartment for a long-anticipated reunion. They had faithfully continued their weekly dinner dates via Skype and almost daily phone calls, but the physical separation was getting old. They missed being together.

Adam was comfortable at Erin's apartment and saw no need for two dwellings, but Erin insisted they stick to their agreement. "I'm an old-fashioned girl who can act modern, but I am who I am when it gets down to it. We are going to have a long life together, and I want to start that life as something really special in our own home."

*How can you argue with a person like that?* Adam thought.

**On Monday** morning, Adam would assemble his team in the conference room. But, adhering to the routine he had established, the first hour of the work week was spent cleaning up desks and putting things in order. Of course, Adam knew that two of the teams had succeeded, one on the drug manufacturer side and another at the retail sale. He knew both teams were bursting to share their news with the rest of the staff—and that everyone was anxious to learn if anyone had been successful.

On this special morning, Adam found it hard to adhere to his own rule by waiting an hour to start the meeting. Finally, it was 10:00 a.m. and everyone was gathered in the conference room. Adam suggested that Marilyn start.

"Prompted by an overly friendly cabin steward, I was able to purchase prescription hydrocodone 10/325 at a gift shop at the first shore excursion in the Bahamas. The steward described the gift shop as a 'convenience pharmacy.' It was said to be for the benefit of passengers only."

Donna Fisher and Phil Deegan then described their success at Humboldt Pharmaceuticals, where they obtained information pointing to a small Midwestern distributor as the likely source for the pills reaching the illicit market.

After listening to the two reports, Adam assumed a satisfied smile. "Thank you, Marilyn and Derek. And thank you, Donna and Phil, for partnering at a job that I know was a team effort. To the rest of you, I offer my equal thanks and praise for a job well done. I want you all to know this was a team effort and all of you should consider yourselves winners. I would like Marilyn, Derek, Donna, and Phil to come forward. We will hear more from them firsthand and then have the chance to ask questions. After that, we will discuss our next steps and strategies based on their information."

When the four finished, several staff members asked questions and some shared their observations. Adam felt he should put some issues into perspective. "What I have heard about the responsible behavior of the manufacturers is encouraging. The issues regarding what happens to the product after it leaves their jurisdiction is where we must limit our interest and activities. What Donna and Phil uncovered is the probable pathway from Humboldt Pharmaceuticals, likely involving a single person or small group in the company, supplying a local wholesale distributor who is re-directing a significant number of pills each month for sale illegally.

Marilyn and Derek uncovered the retail part at a cruise ship destination. Now, it is our job to find out how these pills get from the distributor to the point of sale."

Looking at Marilyn and Derek, Adam said, "You two have discovered at least one way a person can be led to the point of sale. Our job now is to identify the chain of events that ties all of this together. When we do, I am sure this will lead us to Havana, where the wheels came off the buggy and eventually to solving four murders. I have some ideas, but I also want to hear from the rest of the team. So, does anyone want to start?"

A man raised his hand. He was not a member of SHOP. Adam was pleased at this because it meant that even though he was with the DEA, he must have felt like he was a part of the team. Cissy had prepared a roster of the people from DEA along with their pictures. Adam had studied it and was able to connect a name and a face in most cases, but to be sure, he glanced quickly at the paper on the table. Double-checking the names confirmed he was right. "Dave, what do you think?"

Pleased to have the chance to speak, Dave Provisor said, "I see a situation like I sometimes encounter when I'm doing woodwork, which is a hobby of mine. You have a couple well-worked parts, but neither is useful alone. They only work when they are joined and can be kept that way under stress. Think about four legs and a large table top." He looked around the room, expecting to see people nodding their heads in agreement and understanding, but he saw none.

Adam thought he knew what Dave was getting at and looked forward to hearing more to see if he was correct.

"What I am trying to say," continued Dave, "is there needs to be some glue when dealing with a situation like this." Finally, seeing a few grins, he went on more confidently. "The way I see it, the two solid parts are the manufacturer and the seller. The glue in this operation should be the distributor or an extension of an activity that could connect with both parts. In this case, that could be Delgi Pharmaceutical." Looking at the pair who visited Humboldt, Dave said, "Donna, you said the distributor was in Grand Rapids,

Michigan, and they had recently opened a branch in Indiana. I think we should start there."

Donna said, "Yes, we did find the likely manufacturer. Records we were shown confirmed that Humboldt Corporation, for more than a decade, sent an average of one hundred thousand hydrocodone 10/325 to Delgi Pharmaceutical on a monthly basis, but the number increased slightly in the last year, to averaging one hundred and twenty-five thousand. Then Phil asked if we could see some sample shipping records. Tell them what we found, Phil."

"It was just like Donna said, but when the woman we were working with left the room for thirty minutes to take a call, Donna got the bright idea to have a look at the stack of charts that we were told had already been checked and were said to be okay. In a few minutes, she found a double set of shipping orders for a company called Delgi Pharmaceutical in Michigan that got around 100,000 each month but the number always varied. In the second folder for Delgi, twenty-five thousand were shipped to Delgi #2 in Indiana. The order was always the same. This didn't pass the smell test and that is where we are now."

After almost an hour of animated discussion and hearing nothing that made more sense than Dave Provisor's comment, Adam spoke, "This has been a constructive discussion which essentially boils down to what Dave suggested in the first place. We need to identify the glue. And that is right in line with our plans to find out more about Delgi Pharmaceutical's operation in Grand Rapids. But first, we will visit their new operation in Fort Wayne and work back up the line from there. Now, I want to express my sincere thanks to all of you; especially the group from DEA, that has worked so effectively in the first part of this investigation. I would like each team to provide a brief written report to me by the end of the day. Please, don't go to great lengths with this. Effective now, we have concluded this phase of the operation and will, in the words of Dave, go after the glue. I invite all the DEA folks to stick around and use your time and our offices as we continue to partner with you on this project. Now, let's get to work. There is a lot more to do before we can wrap this up."

**Adam asked** Cissy to place a call to Bill Williams at the DEA. He would deliver the good news that the initial task force had uncovered both the likely manufacturer and at least one of the retail outlets for the hydrocodone. The DEA Director said he was pleased to hear that his team had performed well. What he also believed but was not ready to say at this early stage, was that having his operation facilitated by SHOP made his job a lot easier. Working together, the DEA and SHOP had accomplished in three weeks something that could have taken three months if the DEA had worked alone. Bill Williams was impressed that Adam Grant had kept his word and was willing to keep his team in the background. The Director of SHOP was living up to his promise. Not all that common in the environment they worked in.

"Where to from here?" asked Williams.

"Bill, we need to find out more about Delgi's operations in Fort Wayne and then look into Delgi's principal operation in Grand Rapids. I think four people should do this; two from the DEA and two from SHOP. Of course, we will need the DEA's support for research and background. If it suits you, the team could be based in your offices."

Bill Williams was impressed that Adam was able to check his ego at the door and just wanted to get things done properly. "Adam, this sounds like a good idea. If you can have your team put together a summary of where we are now, this will be the starting point for any action that we plan when it comes to investigating the two operations."

"Will do, Bill." After a slight pause, Adam said, "I haven't made an issue of it, but this whole thing started with the death of a doctor from the U.S. It happened in Havana about six weeks ago. He was murdered, and it might have been done to cover up an illegal drug operation. We have been shut out of this investigation. The FBI wants to bring the murderers to justice, but this is not likely to happen until we solve the drug part and nail this action to the deaths. We believe what happened in Havana is only the tip of an iceberg that could lead us to where we need to be with the murders. Our hunch is that we may be looking at a big operation in the

Caribbean with drugs behind it. I also believe we will need the FBI with us on the U.S. side as we move forward."

"We are with you all the way. Send your guys over with a road map and we will be back with you in a week," said Bill Williams.

# THIRTY-FIVE

**T**he plan the DEA and SHOP devised was straightforward: two agents, one from each organization, would visit Delgi #2 in Fort Wayne, at the address Marilyn and Derek found on the shipment orders. Shortly after that, another team would visit Delgi's offices in Grand Rapids to continue the investigation.

And so, two weeks after the Monday-morning debriefing at SHOP, a team arrived at 3636 West Street in Fort Wayne, the address for Delgi #2. They were surprised to discover it was a small business called Fort Wayne Copy and Mail. When the men entered the establishment, they identified themselves as representing the DEA and explained they were interested in a regular mailing received at this address each month. The men assured the proprietor they were interested in the sender, not him.

Facing them from behind a low counter, the man gave no hint of any reaction to what he had just heard. He was of medium height, wore horn-rimmed glasses, had a full head of dark hair, and a facial expression that was blank. It revealed nothing. After a few seconds, he told the men a large part of his business was as a transfer agent for FedEx and UPS, which also included preparing materials in a suitable form for shipping. As the man said this, he motioned to his left, indicating a large array of corrugated material ready to be shaped into boxes in a variety of sizes, bubble wrap,

Styrofoam balls, brown paper, and tape dispensers. The store also had an array of copy machines, including one large enough for blueprints. Shelves in the center of the store held an array of copy paper, pens and pencils, staples, rubber bands, and almost everything else a person would need to function in a small office. As expected, the items were priced higher than Staples or any other big-box store. This was no doubt offset in part by the convenience this small store offered.

That convenience, along with the confidentiality that came with a proprietor, for the most part working alone, were the reasons Irene Newland had chosen this place after finding it with a Google search. It would be an ideal conduit for her to receive shipments sent to Delgi's new branch. There would be no reason for Humboldt to question this, but to be sure, the distribution manager, Jaye Wood would cover the shipments from Humboldt and be on hand to field any questions. The added expense of paying her a few thousand a year was well worth it for Irene.

As the two men looked at the proprietor, who said his name was Chester Greene, "with an e," Walter Fish, from the DEA knew they were at a crossroad. If Chester Greene dug in his heels and refused to cooperate, it could take weeks to get the information they needed. If the man chose to do so, he would only be exercising his rights. Agent Fish knew he needed to say just the right thing to put Greene at ease, but the man's behavior wasn't giving much in the way of a clue about how to proceed. These thoughts turned out to be moot as Chester Greene said, "I know that I can stonewall this, and I also know that I will have to answer your questions eventually; so, let's get on with it. But first, I'd like to ask you a question."

"That is your right," said Michael Kim from SHOP, a first-generation son of Vietnamese immigrants.

Chester Greene said, "It is this. If I receive mail for someone and it is unlawful or has a criminal purpose, am I liable if I don't have foreknowledge?"

"I can't give you a legal opinion, but it is my understanding that as long as you are dealing in good faith, the answer is no."

"Now," said Walter Fish, "we are specifically seeking information about a quantity of goods shipped here on a monthly basis addressed to Delgi #2 Pharmaceutical. They were sent from Humboldt Corporation in Providence, Rhode Island."

"I think I can help you, gentlemen. I was approached about a year ago by a woman. I am not sure where she came from, but the phone number she gave me has a 603 area code, somewhere in the northeast, Maine or New Hampshire. Her name was Proctor and she always paid in cash. Her request was simple. She would receive a shipment once a month from Humboldt Corporation. I was to accept the package, hold it, and contact her when it arrived."

"How big are the packages?"

"Not big," said Greene. "It is always a corrugated box that measures twenty-four by twelve by eight inches, and it always weighs the same, eight pounds." Mr. Greene was accustomed to making precise calculations like this for mailings. Michael Kim did some quick mental math and concluded that this size box could hold as many as twenty-five thousand pills.

"What does your customer do with the box?"

"She usually gets here within a day or so. She just takes it from me and leaves."

"Do you have any idea what is in the boxes?"

"No. Is there any reason why I should?" asked Greene, for the first time sounding on the defensive. "That's the responsibility of the sender. It was mailed. I received it. And passed it on. I was only doing what is done probably a million times a day with packages like this."

"How much do you charge for this service?" asked Walter Fish.

He was paid in cash. There was no record. Chester knew that the amount he charged was a lot and the men might suspect something was fishy. If he lied, he might get caught and they would think he was guilty of something. Weighing his options, he decided to tell the truth.

"The woman pays me two hundred fifty dollars."

"Do you do anything extra?"

"No, just what I told you."

"Isn't that a lot?"

"Yes. There isn't a set price for this kind of service, but I usually charge about a hundred bucks. She made the offer and I accepted it. This kind of thing is not unusual, but she was more particular than most. She told me to keep the package dry, at room temperature, and in a safe place. She was specific in her demands. This made me think I might just be earning the two fifty."

"Do you have any idea what she does with the packages?"

"Other than walk out of the door with them, no."

With a good feeling about what had just transpired, Walter Fish said, "Thank you, Mr. Greene. We appreciate your help. Here is my card. If you think of anything else or have any questions for us, do not hesitate to call." Then the two men left the store.

"What do you think Mike?" said Walter as the two were getting into their rental car, ready to head back to the airport for a one-stop, five-hour flight back to Reagan National Airport.

"This guy had to suspect a shenanigan, when a customer offers to pay that much for about two minutes of work. It looked like there was plenty of space in his store, so keeping a small package for a day or two would be no problem for Greene. The guy must be just scratching out a living. The main thing he has to offer is convenience, and in this case, individual attention. That is how he justifies the payment. I'd probably do the same thing. For my part, I'd give this guy a pass. And, he didn't break any laws that I know of."

"I agree," said Walter. "What about the woman?"

"Remember that guy who talked about finding the glue?"

"Yeah."

"Well, I think today we unscrewed the top of the glue bottle. The next thing that needs to be done is to find that woman and give that bottle a squeeze."

# THIRTY-SIX

**M**aurice Delgi sat behind a splendid mahogany desk in his unadorned office at the headquarters of Delgi Pharmaceutical in Grand Rapids. This was the same office he had when he started his own company nearly forty years ago. During the first five years after college, Maurice entered a diversified-industry training program in a large pharmaceutical firm, which he left after determining big pharma was a bad match for him. After that, he worked as a salesman for a company that sold environmental control systems, which he learned was a fancy name for thermostats. This didn't work either, so he returned to the family business, joining his father in Grand Rapids, where he worked for a year supplying independent drugstores. Then, when he saw an opportunity to produce a quantum leap in business, Maurice suggested that his father expand the operation to supply large chain operations and increase their scope from local to regional. Faced with the decision to change or stay the same, Maurice's father bid his son good luck and said he would continue his small local business. In a gesture of parental support, the senior Delgi invited his son to launch his venture using space that was available in the family operation. Maurice accepted.

Over the past four decades, Maurice had guided the now consolidated Delgi Pharmaceutical to $400 million in annual sales, while doing business as a regional supplier. Despite the growth, Delgi remained a family-owned business. Several larger operations, with annual sales in the billions, had approached him over the years, but Maurice, as his father had done forty years earlier, eschewed the overtures and continued the business he had built. In all these years, Maurice had never run afoul of the law or attracted the attention of any of the enforcement agencies that were ever more watchful, some would say intrusive. Would this morning's visit, the second dealing with this issue, be the end of that exemplary run of ethical business practice?

The message that his secretary had relayed to him was that the man who he had briefly met with last week, wanted to arrange a second visit, at his earliest convenience, and would be accompanied by some colleagues. Maurice interpreted this to mean sooner rather than later. The worst part of this morning's experience was that Maurice suspected they must have found something. In the past few years, with all the hubbub about drug prices, the enactment of Medicare Part D, and now what the media was heralding as an opioid crisis, the pharmaceutical industry was in the public cross-hairs. Increasingly in the past few years, leading up to his seventieth birthday, or entry into the eighth decade as he thought of it, he had put his trust in a lot of people. Most were honest and loyal long-term associates. But some were new, and there were several who he did not know well. His job, this morning, would not be to take on the posture of innocence or denial, or even ignorance. He would listen carefully and divulge only what was necessary. He would give his visitors every confidence that he and his company would cooperate.

Maurice knew it would be his responsibility to develop a strategy for damage control, regardless of the outcome, in order to protect the good name of the company; and if there was a bad apple, to do everything possible to avoid having this person take down his enterprise. Maurice took a deep breath and told himself to slow down. He was getting way ahead of the situation. It could be nothing and yet he was already acting like the sky was falling.

Maurice was taken aback by the number of people who arrived

for the 10:00 a.m. meeting. He recognized Derek Fuller and the man from the DEA, whose name he had heard but couldn't remember; and there were also two other men and a woman with them. Maurice signaled for his secretary to bring in an extra chair.

"Good morning, Mr. Delgi," said Derek. "I would like to introduce my two associates representing the U.S. Drug Enforcement Administration, Phil Deegan and Donna Fisher; and Orville Bradley, who is with the FBI." After a few pleasantries about the weather, what an enterprising city Grand Rapids was, and how friendly everybody they met had been, Derek began the meeting in earnest. "We are here to ask for your help in understanding an irregularity that is attributed to your company regarding the illegal purchase and handling of a controlled substance."

Derek Fuller began a concise rundown of what the agency had learned. "Hydrocodone 10/325 was purchased by an undercover DEA investigator on a shore excursion during a Caribbean cruise. This drug, produced by the same manufacturer, is also associated with multiple murders in Cuba. We learned that distribution of this drug has been linked to your firm by a person or persons using the fictitious business Delgi #2. The most obvious explanation is that someone hacked into a system using your name and is selling the drug in the Caribbean and in Cuba. There is no solid evidence tying all of this together right now, just suspicions. But there are too many coincidences. I am sure you can appreciate that it is our job to find answers that will lead to locating the perpetrator and clearing the good name of Delgi Pharmaceutical."

Maurice Delgi immediately recognized this as a potentially serious problem for him and his company. After a few seconds, he spoke. "Well, this is the first I have heard of something like this happening. I am shocked. This is serious. I will have my people investigate what you have just described. My first thought is, and I could be completely wrong, is that someone has hacked into our computers and is ordering drugs in our name and diverting them for their own use. I can assure you that if that is the case, we will uncover the irregularities immediately. I am just as eager as you are to find out what is happening. Can you give me a week to do a thorough review of our records?"

"That's good for us, Mr. Delgi. We agree that someone could be ordering the hydrocodone using the name of your company and making you a victim of what could be a large-scale criminal enterprise. Our presence here, today, is in no way an indication that we believe you or your organization is responsible. But we do need your help to uncover the truth. When are you available for us to return next week?"

A somewhat relieved head of Delgi Pharmaceutical said, "How about next Thursday, at ten?"

"Great! We will see you a week from today."

Derek and his companions left, confident that in a week they would have some solid answers.

Maurice was shaken by the news. It sounded like the DEA had done a thorough investigation and his only hope was that Delgi's records did not corroborate the possible intrusions they had described. He reflected on the conversation he had had with Irene a week ago about the financial situation of the company. Business at Delgi had not been good for the past four years. Sales were down by more than twenty percent; mostly due to the large chain drugstores acquiring and merging with smaller stores. These companies had gotten so big and their merchandise so varied that they found ways to manage their supplies in-house without the need of a traditional wholesaler like Delgi. There was an opportunity to expand the variety of goods that Delgi supplied, but Maurice could not bring himself to seriously consider adding such trivial fare to his offerings. The chain drugstores were becoming more like expensive Dollar Generals, and he didn't like that.

His stubbornness may have cost the company, but it was too late to do anything about it now. This business downturn had made it necessary to reduce and finally eliminate management bonuses, and to reduce the workforce by fifteen percent across the board. Added to this was the unwelcome news he had just received. Something new was in the wind. Could it be linked to the overall downturn in business?

Maurice had not revealed the first meeting to anyone, not even Irene. Now, after the second meeting with the DEA, in a situation exacerbated by the presence of the FBI, Irene was the only person Maurice trusted to root out the truth. With the information she could provide, Maurice hoped he could get through next week's meeting and put this whole thing behind him. What he had heard this morning shook his confidence. He needed reassurance that only Irene Newland could provide.

When Maurice asked Irene to organize a team to analyze the previous year's records of shipments from Humboldt Pharmaceuticals, their only supplier of hydrocodone, Irene told him she could do it better herself. "Of course," she said, "that will include my assistant, Maggie Van Berger. We are the only ones who will know what to look for." This satisfied Maurice, who hated to put the extra work on her shoulders but was glad when she decided to do this on her own. He knew Irene would be thorough as well as discreet.

Irene was certain the shipment documents at Humboldt to Delgi #2 had been dealt with by Jaye Wood and the records at Delgi were safe in her office, so there was nothing to worry about. Any records of payments recorded at Humboldt would connect to a phony bank account which would lead to a business that knew nothing about her or the transaction.

Irene asked Maggie to review all the records of Humboldt's shipments to Delgi, especially the Schedule II controlled substance hydrocodone 10/325. Irene knew nothing would come to light about a monthly shipment of twenty-five thousand pills sent to Fort Wayne, Indiana. Jaye Wood had taken care of that. Irene also knew that the invoices for the twenty-five thousand pills sent separately to the mail drop in Fort Wayne were locked in her desk and had only been seen by her. The Fort Wayne bank account for Delgi #2, which was used to pay Humboldt, was opened under a fictitious name, Emily Proctor, that could not be traced to Irene. However, just to tie things up, Irene decided to give Jaye a heads up.

Maggie placed the call, connecting Irene with the manager of the Humboldt Shipping Department. Confident that the contents of this call would answer questions Maggie had about the information she had uncovered in her boss's desk drawer, Maggie kept her line open when she buzzed Irene. Hearing both sides of the conversation would help Maggie decide what she would do with the information.

Anticipating Jaye Wood had done her job destroying the shipping documents, Irene expected Humboldt would have no record of Delgi #2. Information about inventory and payment would be on the main computer of the company, so there would be no discrepancy with product and payment, but information about shipment would not exist. Irene was pleased to hear the shipping manager say, "Ms. Newland, our records don't show any shipments to Delgi #2 in Fort Wayne, Indiana. Is that a problem? We don't keep specific records of orders or payment. Accounting would be responsible for that. As far as I was told, the product was paid for, and that would be strange if we didn't send it."

This raised another problem, but it was for Humboldt not Irene. Jaye had taken care of the important part. Records of payments for something they had no evidence of being shipped would come back to bite someone, but not Jaye or Irene. Irene thanked the manager, hung up, and sat back in her chair, going over the plan, trying to find any holes in it, and then figuring out how to close them.

Irene had provided a forwarding address in New Mexico to Chester Greene, just in case things got hot, and now they had. The address was a homeless shelter, and any inquiries would result in a dead end. Irene told Greene that anyone who asked about the shipments should be told the arrangements had been made by a man, not a woman. He would pick it up within a day or two and that's all. The proprietor could say this was an unusual arrangement, but that is what the customer wanted. Chester Greene was not to say that he earned an extra fee for not questioning the transaction, and he would offer only a sketchy description of the *man*—a point Irene insisted on. What Irene did not know was that she hadn't paid the man nearly enough for him to lie, so he had already told the investigators exactly what he knew, not what he was told to say.

This was not turning out exactly as she planned, but Irene was confident her exit plan would work. The extra money coming in would stop, but she had worked out an excellent business model and it was entirely possible that she could re-start with a new supplier and maybe Jaye could help with that. Her explanation to Maurice would be that an unknown person or persons had posed as Delgi #2 and had hoodwinked Humboldt into making the shipments. It was unlikely the person who carried out the scam would ever be found, but the good news was the scheme had been outed, and it was unlikely Delgi would ever be bothered again. To reassure Maurice, Irene would tell Maurice she would set in place procedures to guard against scams like this to ensure that Delgi was never harmed again.

Hoping the scheme could be restarted, Irene would have to get back with Jaye Wood and discuss the possibility of finding a new location for whatever they called the replacement for Delgi #2.

# THIRTY-SEVEN

**W**hen the phone rang, the caller ID indicated it was Jaye Wood. Irene knew Maurice was expected momentarily and she could only guess that this call would bring more bad news. Instead she heard Jaye say, "Irene we're in the clear. The last possibility of Delgi in Grand Rapids being implicated as part of Delgi #2 has been taken care of."

"How?" was all Irene could say.

Jaye continued, "I realized that even with the shipping records eliminated, the main computer records in accounting would show the shipments to Delgi #2 and the payments that were received. With the books balanced in accounting, there is no reason for anyone there to check on actual shipments and vice versa. But that doesn't mean it couldn't happen."

"So, what did you do?" asked Irene.

Jaye continued, almost breathless. "I got a guy in IT to delete both the shipment record and the payment information from the main computer. He's a bloody genius and he needed the money."

"How much?"

"Ten thousand."

"Under the circumstances, that's a bargain. I'll get the cash to you ... damn good work on your part, Jaye. Now, it's time for us to lay low, but the good part is, we still have our distribution network in place and we can find another source in time. Let's take a break for a couple months to re-group. And, thanks for all you have done."

The call ended and Irene told herself, *That's it. The last evidence of any connection between Delgi and Delgi#2 is gone. Maurice will be able to tell the investigators with confidence there is no connection. Humboldt will be left to face a conundrum. Their company is implicated in selling a controlled substance but there is no evidence, except for the ten pills bought in the Bahamas. It was a close call, but she was $500,000 richer.*

**Maurice pressed** the door opener and parked his Mercedes in Irene Newland's garage. Irene had always been there for him and he was sure she would have some answers tonight. Their weekly trysts took a variety of forms. On this evening, it would be all business. He needed to be properly armed for his meeting with the people from Washington. He was sure Irene would have the answers.

After accepting his usual Black Label Scotch with a splash of water, Maurice Delgi settled in his accustomed green-leather chair and put his feet up on the matching ottoman. Looking troubled, the man said, "Do you know of any reason why we should be worried about the attention we are receiving from these government people? Have you found anything new?"

This man had been a combination mentor, father, companion, and lover for twenty years. Irene was relieved, even overjoyed, that she was now able to provide Maurice with assurance that whatever was happening with the drugs had nothing to do with him or anyone at Delgi. The news she had received in a phone call only minutes before, let Irene know that the last loose end had been taken care of. Anything that could possibly connect Delgi to the clandestine operation was gone.

Irene analyzed the ways she could be connected to the drugs sent to Fort Wayne Copy and Mail, and she found none. Greene knew a package came each month from Humboldt, but the company had no record of sending the shipment. He had no way to identify the person who picked up the package or make contact because the burner phone with the East Coast area code had been destroyed. She had worn sunglasses and a wig during their brief encounters, and the Fort Wayne bank account had been closed.

Irene looked at Maurice, knowing she had spared this man who meant so much to her the unspeakable anguish of losing both her and the good name of his company. "Maurice," she said, "I have done a thorough study and I can say, unequivocally, that except for some scumbag using our name, Delgi has no connection whatso-ever to any clandestine drug operation. By that I mean *none*—and that should be the end of it."

"Irene, I knew I could count on you. I can't tell you how much this has weighed on my mind. I feel ten—no twenty—years younger." Then he thought, *No not really. I still can't get it up.*

# THIRTY-EIGHT

**M**aggie Van Berger sat at her desk, unable to work and barely able to sit still in anticipation of what she was facing. Sometime between ten and ten thirty this morning, the FBI was going to interview her privately in a conference room. The notice informed her that she could expect the interview to take no more than fifteen minutes, which was confirmed by several of her coworkers who had already been interviewed.

When it was time, two agents greeted Maggie as she entered the conference room. She had been in this room several times but never under circumstances like this. It had a polished wooden table, a dozen chairs, a credenza, and a projection screen that was rolled up above a white board. The two agents stood behind the chairs where they had been seated at the end nearest the door.

"Thank you, Ms. Van Berger. My name is Orville Bradley, and this is my partner, Bill Bellows. We are from the FBI. We are here to gather information about a controlled substance that may have gotten into the wrong hands. This has nothing to do with you personally or with Delgi. We will be speaking with you as someone who is familiar with the company and its ordering procedures. We suspect somebody used Delgi's name to procure a Schedule II controlled drug, which they may be selling illegally. Again, we want

you to know we are just gathering information. I want to emphasize that this interview is not about you."

Bradley had been involved in the investigation for several
weeks. Agent Bellows was just now joining him. So far, they had
uncovered nothing that advanced the investigation. Only three
more people remained to be interviewed. They started this process hoping, but not expecting, to obtain useful information. So
far, everyone was cooperating, but none had anything of substance
to share.

Without waiting for a question, Maggie spoke, mostly to see if
her voice worked. "I heard something about this. You know how
things get around in an office." After this test, Maggie, was eager to
get on with the interview. She had made up her mind about what
she would say but decided to choose her words carefully. Maggie
had given a lot of thought to what she knew for sure, and how she
would tell it. At first, this seemed like it would be easy. She would
say she was sure of her facts and then pronounce judgment. Her
boss did it. But that wasn't Maggie's nature. It was more like her to
give people the benefit of the doubt. Was she relishing the chance
to get back at her boss? Was it something petty, like Irene making
her work until five even when Maggie was caught up in her work
and Irene knew she would be late picking up Mary? Or was it
Irene's enduring coolness and preoccupation? That was only part.
Instead, all Maggie could think of now were the times Irene had
complimented her on a job well done or encouraged Maggie to
pursue a real career in business, telling her assistant she had the
stuff to be a leader. Would this meeting be the relief valve for the
pressure cooker that had been Maggie's life since she had discovered the papers in Irene's desk drawer? As these thoughts churned
in her mind, Maggie was jolted back to the present when Agent
Bradley spoke.

"Ms. Van Berger, you are the assistant to Senior Vice President
Irene Newland."

"Yes. And, please, call me Maggie."

"Maggie, what is the principal activity in your job?"

"Our office is responsible for placing orders, monitoring,

following up, and maintaining supplier relations. I am involved in a little bit of everything ..." Before she could finish the thought, Maggie spit out, "There is no reason for me to make you pull out of me what you will get anyway." With that said, Maggie explained the ordering process at Delgi and told the men that most of the drugs were ordered and accounted for in their office and that included all of the controlled substances.

Agent Bellows asked, "Has there been any changes recently in the way controlled substances have been handled?"

Fidgeting in her chair and trying to control her breathing, Maggie said, "Yes."

Agent Bellows continued, "Can you tell me what changed?"

Maggie felt the floodgates were about to open, but she fought the feeling and tried to retain her composure. "About a year ago my boss ..."

Interrupting, Agent Bellows said, "By that, you mean Irene Newland?"

"That's right. Irene Newland was given responsibility for all aspects of handling the controlled drugs in our office. It worked out all right and there were no problems."

This time Agent Bradly asked, "Did anything change recently?"

"Yes."

"What was that?"

Maggie was starting to dread her predicament and wished she could disappear. "I found several months of orders for hydrocodone 10/325 in a drawer of my boss's desk. She started locking it about a year ago."

"Did locking the drawer begin about the time of the policy change for controlled substances?" said Agent Bradley.

"Yes. I suppose so. But a week ago, I opened it with some keys I saved for an emergency. I did it without her permission. That was wrong, I know. I was looking for some papers that were missing from my office. When they weren't on Irene's desk either, I looked in all the drawers in her desk, including the one I unlocked. Maybe I just did this to get back at Irene for making me stay late. I was being nosy."

With an expectant look, Bill Bellows asked, "Did you find anything unusual?"

More in control Maggie continued, "There were nearly a dozen folders, one for each month from the past year. There were notes about hydrocodone 10/325 deliveries and payments. I saw the name Delgi #2. These files didn't look right. I knew something was wrong. I could have asked Irene, but I didn't know what she would do. I have to keep my job. I have a young daughter and my husband is starting a business." With this Maggie slumped. Not a crier, she was only just able to maintain control.

After giving her some time to regain her composure, Orville Bradley said, "Thank you, Maggie. What you have told us is vital to the investigation. It confirms what we already suspected about Delgi #2. You are brave to tell us. None of this will be shared now, but in time, this information must be disclosed. I am sure you understand. We will do everything to support you and your family in this ordeal. In the long run, you could be the one responsible for saving the company."

Maggie quickly regained her composure and returned to her office with a great sense of relief and some questions for herself. *Would I have done this if Irene had talked to me first and offered me money?* Maggie knew this question was unanswerable.

After conducting several more interviews, Agents Bradley and Bellows were finished at Delgi. Based on the information Maggie had provided, they were directed by their boss, in consultation with Bill Williams and the guy from SHOP, to drive three hours to Fort Wayne, where they would spend the night in a motel and visit with Mr. Greene first thing in the morning.

**The proprietor** of Fort Wayne Copy and Mail was not surprised to see more government men in his store, but he approached them warily. He had told the first two all he knew. He had hoped that was enough and he would be left alone. Visits like this were not good for business, even the legitimate business he maintained.

Sensing this, Agent Bradley attempted to assuage the man's fears. "Mr. Greene, we read the notes from your previous interview and we will not go over this material. Actually, we have just one question to ask you." With this, Bill Bellows pulled a brochure out of his pocket, one that he had picked up at Delgi. It had headshots of the management team and several group pictures of workers in the various departments.

As Agent Bellows handed the brochure to Chester Greene, he asked, "Do you see the person who engaged your services initially and then picked up the package each month?"

"Is this some kind of game? I said it was a woman when I talked with the other fellows, and there is only one woman here."

"I'll restate my question. Do you see the person who claimed the boxes, and was it the same person every time?"

"The answer is yes, it is the woman here," he said as he pointed at the picture of Irene Newland. "Except she said her name was Proctor, Emily Proctor. And she had dark brown hair, not like the woman in this picture, but it could have been a wig. She always wore sunglasses, but once she took them off and put on glasses to read a label. I got a good look then, and that person is on this brochure. Irene Newland."

"Thank you, Mr. Greene," said Orville Bradley. "We may need your help again, if this case goes to trial."

"I hope it doesn't," was Chester's comment to himself as the agents left the store.

# THIRTY-NINE

**More than** a week had passed, and Maggie had heard nothing new. There was lots of buzz around the office, but nobody knew anything—or if they did, they weren't sharing. Typically, Maggie had no interest in office gossip, but this was an exception. She made sure she was in the best place to listen at strategic times. She did this with care and avoided speaking. In this case, the person who knew the most said the least, and Maggie was determined to keep it that way.

The hard part for Maggie was not telling her husband. She longed for Ron's counsel. She could tell him, but if she did, it would be selfish. He would have nothing to add and would only take on extra worry, when he had enough of his own. His business was growing, but she knew he endured the anxiety of a person who was his own boss and provider, and not just for himself, but also for his wife and child. If Maggie blurted the news, it would mean that two people would worry, and neither could do anything more than what Maggie was already doing: wait.

Maggie continued to do her job and saw no perceptible change in Irene's behavior. *How long could this charade last?* Maggie wondered.

The answer came at precisely ten thirty, when Maggie looked up to see Agent Bradley and Agent Bellows walk into the office. "Is Ms. Newland in?" asked Agent Bradley.

The door to Irene's office was closed, she had been in there alone all morning. No calls had come in and Irene had made none, which was unusual. Before Maggie could inform her boss of the visitors, the agents approached Irene's door and knocked firmly. After a muffled "Come in," the men disappeared into the office, leaving the door more than slightly ajar.

Maggie could distinctly hear Agent Bradley. "Ms. Newland, I am Agent Bradley, and this is Agent Bellows. We represent the FBI. We are here to issue a warrant for your arrest, citing you for suspicion of distribution of a controlled substance in violation of the federal law. You have the right to remain silent. Anything you say now may be used against you in a court of law. You have the right to speak to an attorney and to have an attorney present during questioning."

Maggie was familiar with these words but realized she had only heard them on TV. It was chilling to hear in a real-life situation. The agent continued. "We will be taking you to a federal facility for questioning. You will be scheduled for arraignment, and after that, appropriate action will be taken. You need to come with us now."

Maggie did not hear a single word from Irene, who apparently was invoking her right to remain silent. Under normal circumstances, having your boss arrested in the next room and hearing every word would be a big deal. But, with all that had gone on in the past few weeks, starting when Maggie discovered the contents of Irene's locked desk drawer, today's events were both an anticlimax and a huge relief for Maggie. *What next?* she wondered.

**Two days** later, Maggie was called into Maurice Delgi's office. Maggie thought he looked like death. His face was drawn and his voice was hoarse. He sat behind a large desk with not one thing on it. He leaned forward, resting his upper body on his elbows. "I should know the answer, Ms. Van Berger, but I don't always keep up on these things. How long have you been with the company?"

"Three years, sir."

"That's what I thought. Do you like your job?"

"I do. But to be honest, I have two jobs. I'm also a wife and mother of a three-year-old. I like both, but it takes some juggling to serve two masters."

"Goodness. May I call you Maggie?"

"Yes, of course."

"Most people would have said they loved their job, liked the mission, and a bunch of other stuff that amounts to a snow job. I have to say, I like your honesty. If you had a choice, what would you change about your job?"

"Since you ask, I will tell you there are two things that would make my job better: more responsibility and flexible hours."

"I see you have a graduate degree, and that it's in English."

"Yes, sir. Most of what I know in business, I learned right here, at Delgi. As I said, I can do more. And if I had flexible hours and even a chance to occasionally work from home, this job would be just about perfect."

"Maggie, I wear cuff links, occasionally sneak a cigar in the office, and like to wear a tie. This makes me old-fashioned and the idea of flexible hours and working at home seems inconceivable to me ..."

*Ouch*, Maggie thought. *Did I overstep?*

"... but maybe I should start thinking more about how things are now. My dad wore detached collars in the office and thought my regular dress shirts with attached collars were too informal. I'll tell you why I called you into my office. I was going to offer you the job of Purchasing and Distribution Director on an interim basis, working regular hours, like the company has always expected. Now, I am not going to do that. Instead, I will offer you the job with the option of flexible hours, including working from home when you think it is necessary—but no more than twenty percent of your time. The position will be *acting*, of course. After that, we will discuss your future with the company. How does that sound?"

"Just about perfect, Mr. Delgi. If you are really offering me the position, I accept with enthusiasm. I promise, you will not regret this."

"Then it's a deal, Maggie. You can move into Irene's old office and start the interview process to find an assistant. I must tell you this has been a great shock for me. Irene Newland was a special person, and I and the rest of Delgi will miss her greatly. This is not the end of her life, but it is a significant and tragic detour. I will do everything in my power to help in any way that I can, but things will never be the same.

"I hope you will continue all the good work Irene has done and forgive her for the rest, like I have. By the way, a big reason why I am offering you this opportunity is because Irene's evaluations of your work put you on top of anyone she ever had work for her. Pretty high praise I should say, and something that made my decision an easier one."

Hearing this, Maggie doubled down on her hope that the authorities would be easy on Irene. As for the results of her dealing with the contents of the drawer, Maggie felt that telling the FBI had helped both her and Irene in the long run.

# FORTY

**A**dam put the phone down after a thirty-minute conversation, or really a listening session, with Bill Williams. The DEA Director thanked Adam for all the work SHOP had done to help thwart an operation that threatened widespread illegal distribution of opioids in the Caribbean. Then he recapped the end of the interdiction, at least as far as the DEA was concerned. Williams told Adam the operation ended with Irene's full confession, including the fact that Havana was one of their ports of call. Both the DEA and FBI were convinced that neither Maurice nor anyone else at Delgi had been aware of the scheme.

Williams said, "When the Senior Vice President was confronted with the information we received from her assistant, she readily admitted to what she had done. She stated emphatically that Maurice Delgi and the entire workforce at the company had been kept entirely in the dark. The only connection Delgi had with the criminal enterprise was through Irene. She also revealed that she had been Maurice Delgi's paramour for most of the twenty years she was with the company. When she was confronted with the bogus orders for the hydrocodone that had been diverted to Fort Wayne, Irene realized there was no escaping the truth and admitted her involvement in the scheme. At the time of her arrest, she said she was ready to admit what she had done and throw herself on the mercy of the court."

The director explained that Irene Newland was an otherwise good citizen who wanted to build up her retirement savings to supplement a 401(k) she had raided both for family needs and her own pleasure. Her goal was to accomplish this before her planned retirement in seven years. He laughed and said, "She was like the widow who was supplementing her social security check by growing marijuana in her backyard, only on steroids."

Because Irene Newland had been cooperative, it was likely she would be required to pay a fine equal to the money she had made selling drugs, along with serving time in a federal penitentiary. That jail time would probably be short, but that was up to the courts. Director Williams admitted that when it came to the people who were involved in the promotion, distribution, and actual selling of the hydrocodone, things weren't so clear-cut. Although they had arrested the purser and the head of the dining department for the cruise line, the trail diluted and got colder as it left the ships—although they had been able to arrest a few of the retailers. The role of Humboldt was unclear, but they were certain senior leadership had no role in this scheme. The company would be working with the DEA as they carried out an internal audit.

The director said he was sure others on the cruise ships had played minor roles, but they were hard to identify and would likely get away with their involvement, at least for now. "When it comes to the lower end of the operation, we will have to take what we can get and hope these people will be gun shy when it comes to doing something like this again," was William's conclusion. Then, almost as an afterthought, he asked, "Did anything come of the doctor's murder, the one who was killed in Havana?"

"Nothing conclusive," said Adam, "but it's good to confirm there was a connection with the Delgi#2 operation."

With his question about Dr. Rodriguez's unsolved death, Williams had pulled the scab off an excruciating spot for Adam. Sitting behind his desk, with his chair swung fully left, Adam stared out the window, seeing evidence of the early spring the calendar promised. Winter had finally given up in Washington, D.C. The season of hope and change was at hand. Adam should be happy. His team at SHOP had been instrumental in the successful completion of its first major undertaking. Most of the credit had gone to the DEA, with a pat on the back for the FBI. That was the way the play was drawn up. The role of SHOP was more like the oil that made the engine run smoothly. SHOP was the drive train that transferred power from the engine to make the wheels spin. It was the transmission applying just the right torque to get things moving. In other words, SHOP was the unseen essential that made things happen.

When he took this job, Adam knew he would be leading a team that worked hard while remaining unheralded and often behind the scenes. Success would depend on the unsung efforts of people who would be on the ground, developing and then assisting with operations, supporting an entity that was known. Adam was satisfied with this role and was eager to continue helping others accomplish their goals and letting them get the credit. But he admitted this didn't always come naturally and this was especially so for the team, but they would learn, or they would leave.

Enough of these thoughts. Adam's work was not finished. It was time to get on with what he knew he had to do.

# FORTY-ONE

**A**dam pivoted to face his desk and asked Cissy Friend to come into his office. As she walked through the usually open doorway that connected their offices, Adam motioned for her to sit down. "Cissy, I want to thank you for all you have done to make our first operation a success. Having you with me has meant a lot."

"Thank you, Colonel Grant." Cissy had a keen sense about when formality was needed. This was her own call and Adam never interfered.

"Cissy, is there anything that has been left undone that needs our attention? You know, something only SHOP can do?"

"Well, that would be a yes and a no. Is there anything we are *obligated* to do? The answer is no. Is there something I think you are pretty fired up to do? That would be a yes. To be honest, I think you are about to tell me what you think needs to be done—and you expect me to agree with you before you even tell me what you're up to."

"In that case, Cissy, are you going to leave me hanging? You go first."

"Colonel Grant, I don't think you are going to be satisfied until you find out who killed Doctor Rodriguez. And, for the record, I would like to catch the bastard too. Pardon my French."

"In that case, Cissy, I'll take your suggestion. Please, get Jane Rodriguez on the phone. I want to meet with her. When she agrees to a time for me to visit, I will need you to make reservations for me to fly to Ann Arbor."

Pleased to hear this, Cissy said, "I'll make the call. As far as getting there, you will have to fly into Detroit Metropolitan Airport, and from there it is about a forty-five-minute drive."

Cissy made his reservation for a 5:10 p.m. flight from Reagan to Detroit Metropolitan the following day; with a return flight the next day at 9:00 p.m. Then she prepared to take Adam off the grid until his return. Cissy knew he would be operating solo and it was her job to make him and what he was intending to do invisible. What transpired would be a nonevent as far as anyone else was concerned. If anyone asked, Cissy would say Adam was at home with his ringer off, or if it was during the day, she would say he was playing golf. There would be no announcement or explanation about this trip to the staff. It wasn't officially a secret, but as Adam said, "This visit is nobody's business, at least for now."

Adam's plan to re-open the murder investigation was his own doing. His boss and a few others said they regretted not support-ing Adam when he suggested resumption of the investigation in Cuba, but they made it clear that SHOP had achieved its objective and the matter was finished. Adam didn't push it, but he registered what he had heard only as an implied no and did not want to risk an implicit verdict. He was certain his efforts would take him back to Cuba.

His quest would start by visiting Jane Rodriguez. When Adam spoke with her on the phone, she said she would be happy to meet with Adam, and was glad to know somebody was taking an inter-est in her husband's death. She suggested they have lunch in her home and she asked if it would be all right if her friend Dottie Plaice was there. Adam agreed, saying it would be a good idea to have the support of her friend.

**Adam checked** into the Bell Tower Hotel on the University of Michigan campus a little after 9:00 p.m. He had told Cissy he wanted to get a feel for the place, and the hotel Cissy selected could not have been better. It was in the heart of the old campus; it made him feel like he was back in school. Adam was justifiably proud of his years at West Point, but while growing up, he had been a fan of the University of Michigan's football team. He loved the Wolverine's maize-and-blue uniforms, especially their helmets with the winged front and three yellow stripes. He gloried in the winning seasons and suffered when the team lost—his devotion to the maize-and-blue never waned.

In addition to experiencing the academic campus, he planned to visit the Big House after meeting with Mrs. Rodriguez. The University of Michigan had the largest college football stadium in the country, with a capacity of over 107,000. He had only seen it on TV. Tomorrow he would enjoy the stadium in person, even though it would be empty.

**Adam arrived** at 1432 Heather Way at the appointed time. A thin woman, whose facial expression brightened to a gracious and welcoming smile as she opened the door, greeted him. Adam sensed that her smile was painted on a canvas of despair. "Hello, Mrs. Rodriguez. Thank you for agreeing to see me. And, please, accept my condolences for the loss of your husband. Everyone I have spoken with has told me he was a truly outstanding doctor and a wonderful man. I am sure you miss him very much."

"Thank you for coming, Colonel Grant. I am so happy to see you. These past two months have been hell for my family. You are the first person who has contacted me with anything other than hand-wringing and frustration because the Cubans are blocking all attempts to move ahead. It is so upsetting that they are calling Michael's death an accident."

"Mrs. Rodriguez, as I told you on the phone, my goal is to get to the bottom of the events surrounding your husband's death—and find the person or persons responsible—and bring them to justice. I want to help bring closure to the uncertainty that you and your family must be feeling."

This brief and spontaneous interchange established an equi-librium as the two stood inside the still open front door. Both knew this was only a Band-aid on a fracture, but they appreciated the respite. With a quick change of expression, that became more reso-lute than peaceful, Jane Rodriguez said, "I am sorry, Colonel Grant. Sometimes the pressure can build up only so far before the steam has to be let out, and that's what I just did. Please, forgive me. Come in. I want you to meet my good friend, Dottie Plaice. Let's eat lunch before we talk more about what brought you here."

After a light lunch that consisted of a cup of tomato bisque, a chicken salad with mixed fruit, and iced tea, the three left the small dining area off the kitchen and settled in a cozy study. The women sat on a small sofa and Adam sat opposite in a leather Queen Anne arm chair. The position of the three suggested that Adam was there to deliver a message while the two women would listen and respond. Sensing this, Adam began.

"Mrs. Rodriguez and Mrs. Plaice, I am the director of a new federal government organization called the Select Home for Operational Personnel—or SHOP for short. The responsibility of the department is to act as both a facilitator and ombudsman for government operations and those they serve; mostly dealing with matters of law enforcement, investigation, and protection of our country's citizens and guests. We operate, for the most part, in that gray area that sometimes exists between similar depart-ments and in cases where there is no explicit responsibility but definite need.

"In the case of your husband, Dr. Rodriguez, I am assuming a unique role, one that can be considered vital but off the books. For this reason, I am asking both of you to keep this conversation strictly between us. Cuba has insisted that the FBI not be involved, and our government has no jurisdiction when it comes to solving your husband's murder. I will be calling on others for help when the need arises, but for now, I will be working alone. As you know, after your husband's body was returned home, the Cuban authorities asked the FBI to leave Havana—and have since cut all ties. It seems the Cubans have closed the case, calling it accidental."

"Is that the end of it?" asked Jane Rodriguez. "Can the President do anything? What did you mean when you said you'd be working alone?"

"The best way I can answer is to say yes, the President could do something—but as things stand, it is likely the Cubans would only harden their position about not wanting our involvement, making things even more difficult, which is why I am here."

"Does this mean you are in a position to do something the President can't do?" asked Dottie.

Taken aback by her frankness, Adam shifted in his seat and said, "You ask a very good question. The answer is no, I can't even remotely compare my effect with that of the President's. However, from a practical standpoint, I can do more by being less. I can move about freely in Havana and obtain the needed information much faster without a target on my back. My work in Havana will start with the certain knowledge that your husband stumbled onto an illegal drug operation while he was in the storeroom at Raul Mesa Carreras Eye Hospital. Our suspicion is that he was killed as part of a cover-up."

Jane Rodriguez spoke. "Was it the bottle of pills in the photograph that got him in trouble?"

"We think so," said Adam. "For the past two months, we have been investigating the drug angle. During that time, we have uncovered an elaborate scheme to sell opioids illegally in the Caribbean. Some of the people involved in this operation have already been apprehended and are now in the hands of our legal system. These people started a process that eventually led sellers, including someone in Cuba, to murder four people, of which your husband is one."

With a startled look, Jane said, "I knew about what happened to Alejandro—but are you saying that there have been more deaths?"

"Yes. Two people who we suspect were involved in selling the drugs were also murdered. When it comes to Dr. Rivera, we believe he was a victim, like your husband, and was killed because he also knew too much."

"What are you going to do?" asked Dottie.

"I will visit Havana on my own and conduct interviews, starting with the two policemen who initially worked with the FBI. From there, I will go where the information leads me."

Satisfied that finally someone from the government was going to investigate what happened to her husband, Jane Rodriguez made a request. "Colonel Grant, please tell Rosa Rivera I send her my love. She is grieving like me. We have talked, but that's not enough. I know she will welcome your visit.

After asking the women once more to keep everything they had discussed confidential, he promised to keep them informed of any developments, then he said goodbye.

Before starting his drive back to Detroit Metro, Adam visited the football stadium. Thanks to a friendly woman who didn't say what her job was, he was escorted down to the field where he could stand on the artificial turf and look up at the massive array of seats and the elegant, commodious press box. The woman said, "You can go to Google, where you will be told that women were not allowed on this surface before 1968. Sounds chauvinistic, and it's wrong. I know it's true because my mother graduated from medical school at the University and her class was seated on folding chairs in the middle of the field for her graduation ceremony in 1960. Only then, it was real grass not artificial turf."

With that bit of information in tow, Adam headed to the airport, and looked ahead to his visit to Havana.

*I'm back in the saddle*, Adam thought.

# FORTY-TWO

**T**he following morning, Adam called the FBI field office in Miami and asked for John Bridges. "John, have you heard anything more from the Cubans?"

"Not a word, Adam," replied the Deputy Director. "I think that's the way it's going to stay unless we make some noise. I'll bet they've put this whole thing to bed. The only real loss for them is Dr. Rivera. The American is of no concern to them, and as for the other two, well, they got rid of a couple of lowlifes. Too cynical?"

"Not at all, John. Would you agree that our hands are tied?"

"Absolutely. The Cubans are happy because of the increased tourist trade and they'd do anything to keep that business going. They have zero motivation to solve the murder of an American."

"John, I just paid a visit to Jane Rodriguez in Ann Arbor. She's still taking the loss of her husband very hard, and I get the impression she is frustrated by the fact that nobody in the government seems to be doing anything about finding his killer. She understands that your guys did splendid work when they had the chance, but she only wishes there was a way to get to the bottom of this."

Bridges said, "We'd be down there in a heartbeat if it were possible. My guys assure me that the two men they worked with would be happy to see them and finish what they had begun as a team, but that's not even remotely possible. Their bosses have said no, not now, not ever."

"Which brings me to the reason I called," said Adam.

"Shoot."

"The operation I run, SHOP, is one hundred percent legal and accountable, but it was also designed to be low-profile. When we work with the FBI, you guys get the credit you deserve and when we work with the DEA or anyone else, it's the same. Our job is to be useful and not just helpful. I'll explain what I mean by that later but let me just say that being useful is what I want to be now."

"How?"

"I'm going to Havana on my own, as a private citizen, a tourist. I'll be talking with Dr. Rivera's widow. It's a hunch, but I think she may have something. Maybe he had been acting funny or he told her something she didn't understand but now it makes sense. I don't think the doctor had anything to do with the death of his friend, but the iPhone found in Dr. Rodriguez's room, with no fingerprints and deleted photos of the pill bottle, has to be explained."

"That sounds like a reasonable plan," said Bridges. "When do you go?"

"With your blessing and my promise to share anything I come up with, I will leave in the morning. I hope to have something to share in a day or two."

"Go for it."

"Thanks."

**Adam arrived** in Havana just after 1:00 p.m. the next day. He flew from Reagan to Fort Lauderdale and then to Jose Marti Airport on a United Airline's Express CRJ. From the airport, he went directly to the Hotel Sevilla in Old Town. His plan was to begin his efforts where the doctor had been murdered. He didn't think he would find anything there, but the hotel's association with the event would add to his experience. Jane Rodriguez had provided Adam with Mrs. Rivera's address and telephone number.

When he called Rosa Rivera, it was clear she had been alerted. When she heard his name, she expressed satisfaction and relief, and invited Adam to come to her home. They would have coffee mid-afternoon.

After a twenty-minute cab ride from the hotel, Adam was deposited in front of a modest duplex. From the address, he selected the right-hand door. Before he could even knock, it was opened by a woman who had obviously been watching for his arrival. "Hello, Mrs. Rivera. I am Adam Grant, who you spoke with on the phone."

Responding in excellent English, she said, "Please, call me Rosa. Welcome to our home, Mr. Grant. Please, have a seat. Can I get you some coffee?"

"Thank you, Rosa. That would be nice—black would be fine."

Rosa returned almost immediately with a cup and saucer in each hand. *The coffee must have been ready*, Adam thought. After handing Adam his coffee, she sat and looked expectantly at her guest. It was clear she would welcome any news he had.

Adam briefly reviewed the events that had occurred around the hydrocodone and its distribution by a rogue executive and telling her their theory that the deaths of both hers and Jane's husbands were related to the illegal sale of the drug in Havana. "Dr. Rodriguez's association with the drugs was his apparent discovery of a bottle of opioids in the basement of Raul Mesa Carreras Eye Hospital. We believe his discovery was observed by the man in charge of the storeroom and that this man followed Dr. Rodriguez to the Hotel Sevilla, where he killed him. After that, we have no solid information that can lead us to who is responsible for the death of your husband or two other suspicious deaths that occurred on the Monday after Dr. Rodriguez was killed. We do believe that whoever is responsible still remains at large, most likely here in Havana."

"Are the local police helping?" asked Mrs. Rivera.

"The two local officers who worked with our FBI agents for the first three days were very helpful, but after Dr. Rodriguez's body was returned home, it is our understanding they were taken off the case. As far as we know, the Cuban police, at the direction of the officers' superiors, are doing nothing."

With a look of concern Rosa Rivera offered, "I remember one officer came to the house with a man from the FBI to see my husband on Friday, three days before my husband was killed. Both seemed very nice."

"Mrs. Rivera, can you think of anything that your husband said or did that could shed any light on this?"

"No, Mr. Grant, not really. Alejandro was very upset on Wednesday, when he spent so many hours at the hotel, watching over the body and meeting with the Americans. He stayed around the house on Thursday and didn't go to the hospital. Friday was the day he met with the Cuban officer and the man from the FBI. Not much happened over the weekend. We stayed home. My husband stayed at home and didn't go to work on Monday, but after dinner, he went out. He said he had an errand, and nothing more."

"Did he say what he would be doing?"

"No."

"Was it usual for him to do something like that?"

"No, he never went out after dinner. But he had been so upset and our lives were in such turmoil, I thought it would be best if I didn't press him. My husband was a very sensible, honest, and straightforward man. I never knew him to engage in a reckless act. He was brave, but at the same time, timid. I think in the American jargon, you would say he was laid-back. I trusted him, and when he left, I didn't ask where he was going. I just told him to be careful."

"Is there anything else you can think of?"

"There was something—but I don't think it can be important."

"Please, tell me anyway."

Mrs. Rivera continued, selecting her words carefully. "We are Catholic, but religion is not something that can be practiced easily in Cuba, so I guess you could say we have fallen away, at least in our practice if not in our hearts. Just before he died, Alejandro and I were talking about a recent visit by the Pope and how much we were encouraged by his words. In this discussion, Alejandro said he had seen the most remarkable statue. He described it as two shackled wrists with the hands holding aloft a crucifix. He said it was beautifully carved from a single block of wood, done by a local artist. It was the trunk of a tree and the proprietor said he had counted more than sixty rings. The man said it was pre-Castro. Alejandro told me I should see it some time, but he didn't say where it was. My husband was the kind of person who would share something like this immediately. He wasn't a person who kept things like this to himself. He would have told me about something like this right away, I am sure of it—but when did he have time to see it?"

Adam got the feeling that the widow was searching for some higher meaning which, under these bizarre circumstances, he could understand. "Thank you, Mrs. Rivera. I want to assure you that we will be doing everything in our power to find out who is responsible for the death of your husband and Michael Rodriguez. These investigations are never easy. And with this being out of our jurisdiction, it becomes even harder. My presence in Havana is as a private citizen. I will be operating independently while gaining as much information as I can before I can contact the local authorities. My work will start by meeting with the police officer who visited with your husband here, in your home."

"Thank you, Mr. Grant. And God bless you in this work."

Adam left the Rivera home and re-entered the cab that had brought him there an hour earlier. Adam had arranged for the driver to stay, paying him for his waiting time. As he scanned the nearly deserted street, Adam was glad he had thought to do this.

# FORTY-THREE

**O**n the drive back to the hotel, riding in the front seat of the cab, a bright-yellow KIA that looked almost new, Adam thought about what he had learned from Rosa Rivera. He had to admit most of his observations and the result of their conversation had merely confirmed what he already knew or thought he knew. On the positive side, when it came to collecting clues for his investigation, Mrs. Rivera had shared two things about her husband's behavior: his telling her about a unique wood carving he had seen and his uncharacteristic departure from their home without telling her where he was going on the evening he was murdered.

Based on what she knew about her husband, Mrs. Rivera was sure he had seen the wood carving recently. Her husband's leaving the house at night was most disturbing to the grieving woman. She now felt that she had let her husband deliver himself to his murderer. In no way did she believe he was the victim of a robbery. She said with absolute certainty that her husband would not go to Old Town at night without a specific reason.

During the ride back to the hotel, Adam came up with a plan. He told the cab driver he wanted to continue using his services for the rest of the afternoon and would pay him appropriately. The driver, Jose, who spoke acceptable English, agreed. After a price was settled, Adam said, "Jose, let's park this thing and you come into the hotel with me. We can get a cup of coffee and make some plans. Do you have a city map?"

"Si ... yes."

"Good. Bring it with you. We are going to take a tour of Old Town Havana."

Entering the hotel and walking through a lobby that had colonnades on each side decorated with colorful Moorish tiles at their base, the two men walked the length of the lobby that gave way to a spacious open-air courtyard with a dozen tables, none of which were occupied. The two men sat at one that offered partial shade and Jose spread the city map and folded it so that they were looking mostly at Old Town and the harbor. The area they studied was the tip of a small, broad-based peninsula that was adjacent to where the cruise ships docked and discharged thousands of tourists on an almost daily basis. The area was west of Paseo Martí, bounded in the north by the Malecón, and in the south by the rail yards. The cruise ship docks were to the east. This area included the Hotel Sevilla, where they were seated.

Adam did a quick mental calculation and determined that this approximately 200-block area, which comprised most of Old Town, would be within easy walking distance of the cruise ship docks. It was also the most likely place for a souvenir shop, the kind of place they knew was being used to sell drugs to cruise ship passengers. These drugs were supplied to a retailer monthly by a crew member who had set up the sale. This was confirmed by SHOP team member Marilyn Helm. Carrying his hunch further, Adam decided the wooden carving was his only lead to the store, and that was what he would be looking for today.

Adam realized that Old Town wasn't small if you were planning to search it on foot while looking for the proverbial needle in a haystack, but it was manageable. The area he delineated was approximately twenty by nine blocks. The plan he laid out to Jose was that they canvas the entire area. They would start traveling on successive streets north to south and then would switch moving east to west. They would be singling out gift shops, art galleries, and any other establishment with a window display.

"We can't do it all from the car," volunteered Jose. "Many of the streets with the busiest shops are closed to traffic and can only be reached on foot."

"That's okay," said Adam. "You can drop me off at the beginning of these streets and then you can go to the next parallel street, drive down it, and then pick me up at the end of the street I just checked. I'll give you my cell phone number in case we miss a connection. How long do you think this will take?"

"We could finish in about four hours," guessed Jose.

"Okay! Let's do it."

The two started traveling from the north end of a street named Cuba Tacón. Halfway down, Adam was surprised to cross a street named O'Reilly, but that was the exception. Other names were consistently Compostela, Picota, Lamparilla, etc. In a little under two hours, they completed the north-south grid. With aching necks from constant craning and bleary eyes from their yet unsuccessful quest, the two stopped for a Coke before beginning their east-west search. Attacking the grid in this direction, Adam was forced to exit the car more than half a dozen times to search on foot while Jose navigated to collect him at the other end where cars could travel. This part took a little over two hours and delivered no results.

A weary Adam looked at an equally weary but richer Jose and said, "Okay, now plan B."

"Which is?"

"First, drop me off at the hotel. I will wait for you there. Then, I want you to go back to the dozen or so places that look the most alive and prosperous. You can use your best judgment about which places to visit but keep track of them in case you come up blank. That way, we will not have to check those shops twice. For this part, I want you, operating alone, to ask the proprietor or someone who looks responsible, if they have ever seen a wooden carving of two hands with shackled wrists holding up a crucifix. Tell them you had an American fare who described this object to you and he was eager to purchase it. Say that the man you are representing never saw the statue himself, but it was described to him by a person who came across it. The man who saw it, left Cuba yesterday and the potential buyer couldn't remember where the store was exactly, only that it was somewhere in Old Town. If you find a person who can provide the location of such a piece, tell him the customer will pay for the information. You don't know how much, but it could be as much as twenty dollars. Tell him the American you are working for is leaving tomorrow and really wants this art piece."

"I can't be sure how long the stores will be open," said Jose. "It's now after seven. When do you want me back?"

"First of all, I want you to come back the minute you find a lead. Don't go to the shop itself. Come back here first and we will go there together. If you find nothing by nine o'clock, come back and we will decide what to do next."

"This has been a long day and ..."

"Jose, you have earned at least a hundred bucks so far, and you deserve more, I know. Don't worry, I'll be fair."

"Sorry, I was sure you would be." With that, Jose left Adam at the hotel and set out on his quest.

Suspecting it would be an hour or two before he heard anything, Adam went to his room. He was tired enough to need a nap but was too focused on the immediate goals to think about anything beyond Jose learning something. All he could think about was locating the statue and its owner. Adam was now convinced this would put him one step closer to identifying the killer. Barely thirty minutes later, his phone rang. Adam heard an excited Jose, who was calling from the lobby. "Boss, I think we got it!"

"I'll be right down."

Exiting the elevator in the lobby, Adam was met by a man who looked like he had just won the lottery.

"The third shop I visited was on Compostela Street. The owner said he had seen that statue many times in the window of a store only three blocks away, but he said it had not been in the window recently. I told him that if my customer found it, he would be taken care of. The man said he hoped we found it. I could tell he was excited about the money!

"Then, I did what you told me not to, but I did it carefully. I drove by the store where the man said he had seen the statue.

It wasn't in the window, so I stopped the car for one minute and peeked in from the sidewalk. There it was, just as you described it. The carving is prominently displayed on a shelf, and in very clear sight of any customer inside the store."

"One last run, Jose," said Adam. "It's only eight. We should have plenty of time to at least see it tonight."

"For sure," the driver said. "The guys who own these shops don't open early in the morning, but they keep their shops open as long as there are people on the street, and there are a lot of tourists out tonight."

Adam decided that Jose should park the car and stay with it while Adam walked to the middle of the block where the store was located. Jose said it had a sign over the window that said Regalos. Adam's limited Spanish told him this word meant gifted or handsome. Not a bad name for a gift shop, but under the circumstances, he didn't believe he would have much good to say about the owner. When he looked inside the shop window, Adam saw the carving displayed where Jose had described. Not wanting to call attention to himself, Adam continued walking to the end of the block, checking all the windows. At the end, he crossed the street and walked leisurely back to the cab and Jose.

"You nailed it, Jose. That statue is exactly what we have been looking for. This has been a great day—and your efforts have been above and beyond." Adam pulled out two crisp hundred-dollar bills and handed them to the smiling driver. Then he handed Jose a twenty and told him to give it to the shop owner who had tipped him off to the location of the statue. Adam wondered if Jose would do it; then immediately felt bad that he had even harbored this thought.

At the Hotel Sevilla, Adam thanked Jose, who was never told the significance of the day's work and said goodbye. It was just part of what needed to be done but an essential one. Adam was convinced the wooden carving was key to the investigation. He looked forward to a good night's sleep in anticipation of a big day tomorrow.

# FORTY-FOUR

"**J**ohn Bridges here."

"John, this is Adam Grant. Sorry for calling so late. Have you heard how things are proceeding on the Justice side?"

"I heard from our guys in D.C. They say that Justice is moving at a pretty good clip, both the Department and justice, small "j". The head of the drug operation is making their job easier by cooperating on all fronts. She is singing like a canary. All the bad actors, at least the big ones, are in tow, and the people who manufacture and distribute the hydrocodone have been notified about what happened. They said that this experience made them realize they need to keep better tabs on the distributors they supply. The ones we spoke with promised they would do their best to keep something like this from ever happening again. I am confident there will be a tightening up across the industry, but time will tell." Then, after a pause, he said, "That's about it."

"Thanks, John. Full disclosure, I am in Cuba now. I arrived earlier this afternoon. I am flying under the radar, so please don't share this with anyone now. I could get pulled off this if my boss knew. When I'm done, I will fess up and get my butt chewed, a small price if we can get the murderers."

After weighing the potential consequences for himself, Bridges replied, "I'll be keeping everything you tell me today under my hat, and I will help you in any way I can. Can you give me the down and dirty?"

"Well, I met with Dr. Rivera's widow. She's pretty broken up, but she was cordial and freely told me a lot of things I already knew—but she also provided some information, which could lead us to someone her husband was dealing with right before he was killed. This might not lead us directly to the killer, but I believe we are getting closer to a person who, for sure, knows who the killer is. That's the good news. And another good thing is that I can operate pretty much independently down here and not mess up the reputation of any government organization because SHOP is small, and nobody knows us anyway. But the problem is, I need to meet with the Cuban police, preferably the men your guys worked with, and then meet with the owner of a gift shop. He is a person of interest, but we must find him first. I can't move the ball forward on my own though. It will take help from the locals to get the job done. John, can you make a call and get me lined up with these guys?"

"I can do better than that, Adam. I will ask Matt Hull to make the call, and when he has, I will have him phone you directly and let you know the best way to contact the Cubans they worked with. You hang tight, Adam."

"Thanks, John."

Less than an hour later, Adam's phone rang. "Colonel Grant, this is Inspector Jorge Lopez. Matt Hull just called me and told me the good news, that you are here in Havana. My partner, Ricardo Ortiz, and I will help in any way we can to bring Dr. Rodriguez's killer to justice; and hopefully solve the three other murders—which we think are connected."

"Wonderful," said Adam. "Can we meet at the Sevilla? I am in room 412."

Jorge agreed quickly and with relief that at least one American hadn't caved in to political expedience. "Our shift will be through in an hour. We can meet right after that. And Colonel, it will be best if you don't mention to anyone now or later that we are working with you. Ricardo and I will be 'off the clock.' We are cops, Colonel, and we want to get the killer as much as you do."

"I'm in the same boat," said Adam. "Let's just say none of us exist, at least for now."

**A little** over an hour later, Jorge Lopez and Ricardo Ortiz were in Adam's room listening as he explained how they exposed the drug-distribution scheme and the arrest of the leaders, who he described as formerly upright citizens who had succumbed to greed regardless of the cost to others. Adam emphasized that now it was their job to find the person who was selling the hydrocodone in Havana, and who was also most likely behind the deaths of four people.

"Do you think you have found the seller, Colonel Grant?" asked Jorge.

"I have a pretty good idea. We identified a gift shop on Compostela Street that we believe Dr. Rivera visited some time before he was murdered. I think this explains why Dr. Rivera was killed in a part of town that he was not likely to visit. His death and the shop could be connected."

"Have you seen the shop?" asked Jorge.

"Yes, but I didn't go inside."

"Are we going to do what I think you have in mind?" asked Ricardo.

"If that is to confront this guy together; then yes, you are right."

The three agreed to meet at the hotel at nine o'clock the next morning.

# FORTY-FIVE

**dam met** Jorge and Ricardo at precisely 9:00 a.m. in front
of the hotel. From there, the three walked to Compostela
Street and stopped on the sidewalk opposite Regalos. After
a few minutes, they saw a man flip the sign hanging on the door
so that it now said Open, and retreat to the back of the store. They
crossed the street and entered Regalos. When the men entered,
Eduardo was in the backroom, which was separated from the front
of the store by a flimsy curtain. It was nine thirty.

Eduardo heard the door open and sensed the presence of his
first customers of the day. He knew traffic on the street was slowly
building. It was nothing like it would be when the crowds of tourists from the cruise ships began their quest for souvenirs and, he
hoped, other things. Early people like this were more likely to be
spending a few days in the city and staying in a hotel. In his experience, these people generally purchased more expensive items
than people who only came ashore from the ships. They were also
more likely to bargain, which was not a problem because if they
bargained to half price in dollars, Eduardo would still realize a
hundred percent profit.

These thoughts fled Eduardo's mind when he realized three
official-looking men had entered his shop. They were focused on
him and not the gaudy merchandise. Eduardo Sanchez's heart
sank. A second look at the men told him it couldn't be more

obvious who they were if they had POLICIA emblazoned on their chests. Eduardo was a good talker and most of the time, he could get himself out of a jam—but today it struck him that his luck may have run out.

"Gentlemen, how can I help you?" Eduardo offered brightly as he emerged from the back room where his real treasure was. Before the visitors could respond, he moved past the trio and positioned himself between them and the door. To make this move look innocent, he repositioned a vase on a nearby shelf and took a second look to confirm it was now where he wanted it. His mind raced as he thought of escape. Selling drugs was one thing—four people dead was going to be hard to beat. The decision for Eduardo wasn't just the lesser of two evils. It was all or nothing. There was no back door to the shop, which was why he positioned himself on the other side of the men. His only hope was the front door.

Just as one of the men started to talk, Eduardo bolted through the door, swung the slotted arm of the hasp through the metal loop, and thrust his pen in the opening. This took only seconds. The men were already at the door as Eduardo was securing the closure. The door was now locked from the outside. Eduardo knew it would not take long for the men to break through. He wheeled and ran south to the next cross street, brushing by when he could and pushing people when they slowed him, until he reached the end of the block. All his life, Eduardo had been a multitasker. As he ran, he planned his next moves. His brother could liquidate the store. That would gain him a few thousand dollars. The pills would probably be confiscated, but he had one thousand at home that would be worth five thousand dollars clear because he would not be paying for them. With his brother's help, he could get to Central America and would have nearly ten thousand dollars to start over. He wouldn't be deserting Cuba, only taking a "vacation" while things cooled like he knew they would.

Inside the store, the startled men rammed the door. On the third try, the hasp broke free from the partially rotted wooden door frame. They had seen the man run to the right, so they started in that direction, running through the groups of tourists. As they reached the corner, a crowd was gathering at the next cross street. There was alarmed chatter. When they joined the gawkers, they saw the man they were chasing sprawled in the street with his legs and torso on the sidewalk. His head rested near a solid metal post. At its base was what looked like fresh blood and hair.

Jorge identified himself as a police officer. He crouched next to the man and felt for a carotid pulse. There was none. Jorge signaled this to his companions.

Adam said, "Ricardo, you stay here with Jorge. This is a local matter. His death will be considered an accident. At least for now. Let's get rolling and make the most of the time we have now. I am going to check the shop and you two can pick me up at the hotel. Call me on my phone before you come."

Ricardo didn't have time to respond before Adam bolted in the direction of Regalos. As soon as Ricardo realized Adam was going back to the shop to look for the drugs—alone—Ricardo relived the last meeting with his boss, Colonel Diaz. Diaz had announced, "Ricardo, deliver any evidence you collect to me here, in this office, and discuss this with no one. If these murders are related to drugs, it is essential that this matter be handled properly. I am giving you this job because I trust you and know you will follow orders."

Of course, this meant Ricardo was supposed to give any drugs he found to Colonel Diaz—and say nothing. Ricardo was sure the evidence would then become the personal property of his boss, who would probably sell it. If Ricardo didn't do as he was ordered, he knew there would be hell to pay, including the strong possibility of losing his job or even worse. These thoughts represented a dagger at his heart, with the threat that if things got as bad as they could be, he would leave his children without a father and his wife a young widow.

Adam heard the ambulance siren wail as he prepared to re-enter Regalos. He knew Jorge and Ricardo would handle things at the scene. He had briskly walked back to the gift shop but not running or in an apparent hurry. When he reached the building, Adam pushed aside the mangled lock, entered, and turned the sign to display to Closed.

He had already decided what he was looking for would not be in the front of the store. He looked again at the wood carving of shackled hands holding a crucifix that had led him here; then he parted the curtains and entered a cluttered backroom. It was filled with assorted merchandise in an array of boxes. His aim was to look for the hydrocodone. If the drugs were in the store, they would most likely be in one of the boxes—but which one? He did not have much time before someone would recognize Eduardo and come to the shop. Adam had to finish his search before this happened.

Following his instincts, Adam's attention was drawn to a stack of boxes that looked slightly askew. He opened the two boxes on top, but they only contained trinkets and other small merchandise that would be sold to tourists. In the third box, he found colorful scarves. What seemed odd was that instead of being neatly folded, they were in a state of disarray. He soon discovered why. Plunging his hands deeper, Adam felt and then extracted two one-gallon plastic storage bags crammed with scored white pills and a third bag with a dozen empty pill bottles that looked like they might hold a hundred pills each. The labels on the bottles said they were from Ametz Pharmacy in Albuquerque and the contents were hydrocodone 10/325.

Adam put the three plastic bags in a large shopping bag he found among the clutter. Leaving the closed sign in place, he walked back to the hotel. It took just fifteen minutes. Entering the lobby, Adam was surprised to see Ricardo waiting for him. He must have left Jorge at the scene to sort things out. Adam said quietly, "Ricardo, let's go up to the room. I have something that you will want to see."

In the room, Adam placed the shopping bag on the bed and removed three plastic bags. Two were crammed with white pills about the size of a typical aspirin and the third contained a dozen empty medicine bottles. Ricardo's face took on a concerned look; the opposite of what Adam expected to see for this job well done.

"Adam, I have a problem," said Ricardo. "Colonel Diaz told me I would be personally responsible for any physical evidence. I am supposed to give everything to him and discuss this with no one. If Jorge complains, I am to say these are the Colonel's orders." The look on Ricardo's face was one of concern, pleading, and embarrassment. Ricardo continued, "He knows Jorge is an honest cop, and he knows I am junior. Honest or not, I can be gotten rid of either by being fired or having something happen to me."

Adam understood. "Ricardo, I'll take a handful of them just to close the book on the drug angle from our end. Then, do what you need to do with the rest. I think the decision should be made by both you and Jorge. Whatever you two decide will be the way I remember it."

Before Ricardo could respond, there was a knock on the door. As soon as Adam opened it, Jorge burst into the room. "What did you find?" he asked.

Adam showed Jorge the handful of pills he had just gotten from Ricardo and said, "This is what it was all about."

Jorge asked, "Was there more?"

Adam ignored the question.

When Jorge looked at Ricardo, he saw a look of terror in his partner's eyes, and an unspoken message: "Don't push it."

Jorge decided to not pursue an answer, instead he told them how things had wrapped up at the scene. "Nobody seemed to be aware that we were chasing the guy. The witnesses I spoke with said the man was hurrying to cross the street and ran into the path of a car. The car was not going fast, but the driver had no chance to stop. My guess is that it would have been no more than a bump and a sore leg if it hadn't been for the post that his head hit. The identification in his wallet identified the man as Eduardo Sanchez." Pausing to look directly at Adam, Jorge said, "Adam, tell me again what you found at the store."

"The pills were there, in a box in the backroom," answered Adam. "I brought them here and took a handful as evidence to take back to my guys. You can see there could be as many as a few thousand left."

"What should we do with them?" asked Jorge.

"This is your bust. I am assuming that Eduardo was a one-man operation and when his plan was threatened, he committed or was directly responsible for four deaths. His suppliers, at least the ones at the top, are already being prosecuted in the U.S. The small operators are just that, minor crooks. Some will continue this kind of thing if they have a chance and others will get scared and hang it up. My guess is that the three of us are the only ones who know about these pills." Adam said this in a way to test the two Cuban police officers. He wanted to believe they would do the right thing but ...

Ignoring Adam's last comment, Jorge asked, "Do you think Eduardo killed the doctor?"

"Which one?"

"The American."

Adam said, "No. I think that is when the trolley got off the track and the whole thing started to come apart. My guess is that his henchman, Luis Espinosa, killed Dr. Rodriguez and Eduardo wasn't at all happy about it."

Ricardo remained quiet.

Ignoring further talk about the pills, Jorge pushed on. "What about the Cuban doctor?"

"That, my friends, is your crime to deal with. From our standpoint, I am satisfied to say that Luis Espinosa killed Dr. Rodriguez and Eduardo killed or supervised the killing of the other three. Or maybe Eduardo killed everybody. Either way, we got the killer or killers. There is nobody left."

"But why Dr. Rivera?"

Adam paused. He wanted to say this to Jorge and Ricardo in exactly the right way. "I'm going out on a limb, but this is what I think. Only two people had the opportunity to erase the fingerprints and the photos from the phone: Dr. Rivera and the killer. If Luis had been interested in Michael Rodriguez's phone, he would have taken it, got what he could and tossed it, not wipe it clean and leave it on the desk. I don't think the killer ever saw the photos. Instead, I think Dr. Rivera checked his friend's phone to see if he could find anything on it that would offer a clue about what happened. Remember, Dr. Rivera was in the hotel room a long time by himself. When he saw the photos of the bottle of pills, he realized they were taken in the storeroom at Raul Mesa Carreras Eye Hospital. The doctor didn't look at the text messages on his friend's phone, so he didn't know that Dr. Rodriguez had sent the photos to his wife. She wouldn't know their significance, so he essentially sent them to himself. Dr. Rivera erased the photos from the phone, wiped off his fingerprints, and then decided what to do with the information.

"Between finding his friend dead and meeting with the FBI, Dr. Rivera had time to visit the eye hospital; learn that Luis, the storeroom manager was gone; and found the name of his girlfriend, who may have tipped him off to Eduardo. The only way Dr. Rivera would have seen the crucifix would be for him to have seen it in Eduardo's shop. And remember, he did not leave his house between Wednesday night and after dinner on Monday. His wife was positive her husband had not seen this statue before the time of the American doctor's death. She was adamant in saying her husband would have shared something like that with her as soon as he saw it. He might have confronted Eduardo on Monday night and been killed for it. Luis and his girlfriend were killed the same night as Dr. Rivera, clearing the deck for Eduardo. Unfortunately, with Eduardo dead, it might be impossible to confirm this."

Taking a few seconds to let this sink in, Jorge asked, "Then what was Dr. Rivera's involvement? Why did he meet Eduardo at a strange time and in an unlikely place? And when he got there, why was he killed?"

"Gentlemen, I leave that up to you. As I said, this is your investigation. I am here only as a tourist who has offered some help, and it was accepted. I am not here in any official capacity. I have met only you two and there is no reason for me to go further than what I have just explained."

Jorge looked searchingly at Ricardo, who simply nodded. Looking directly at Adam, with a straightforward and non-conspiratorial countenance, Jorge said, "Ricardo and I believe that Dr. Rodriguez was brutally murdered by Luis Espinosa because the doctor stumbled on evidence of an illegal drug-selling operation.

Dr. Alejandro Rivera believed the pictures he saw on the doctor's phone had some special meaning, so he erased them and wiped the phone clean of any fingerprints because he wouldn't want it known that he knew about the pictures and the drugs in the basement of the hospital. He went to the storeroom and learned that Luis Espinosa was gone. He then got the name of Luis' girlfriend, who told him about Eduardo. We know the only time Dr. Rivera could have been in Eduardo's shop was Wednesday because the doctor described the details of the carving to his wife and he had not been out of the house all day Thursday and Friday, or over the weekend. He had to have seen the carving on Wednesday or before.

"His conversation with Eduardo on that day must have set the stage for a second meeting, which took place on Monday night. Was Dr. Rivera equivocal about turning Eduardo in on Wednesday, or maybe even complicit, only to change his mind on Monday and be murdered for it?"

Adam nodded his head in agreement. He thought all Jorge said was a plausible explanation of what happened.

"How do we write up your involvement in our report?" asked Ricardo.

"You don't—unless the superiors you spoke with want more information, which I doubt they will. This is your thing."

"We will say that Dr. Rivera was a brave man who foolishly confronted a dangerous criminal and was killed for it. His bravery helped us foil the plans of a drug dealer and society will benefit from the doctor's actions." Jorge paused, then asked, "But don't you have to file a report about this, Adam? Wouldn't it be useful for you to have our thanks and appreciation in writing?"

"All I need is what you just said. I didn't explain to you the whole deal with SHOP and, to be honest, I don't even have enough answers to explain it to myself. All I know for sure is what I was told when this operation started: that the Select Home for Operational Personnel is an agency designed to help others in the government get things done but not be worried about taking credit. You have my word that the work we have done will be reported and seen by those who need to see it, and only by them. This will earn me a pretty good chewing out, but the whole thing will stay in-house. Handling information this way is the only way I can stay in business" Looking at the two men who were digesting this information, Adam said, "So long, fellas. It's been a pleasure. Let's stay in touch. I'll walk with you down to the lobby, so I can check out and get back home."

"But wait," said Jorge, "There is one more thing." He looked at the two bags of pills on the bed. "We did a good job at answering my second question, but what about the first? What about the pills?"

Adam replied with a pleading look, "I know what I am going to do with the dozen or so I have. When it comes to the rest, that is up to you guys."

Jorge looked at Ricardo and said, "Ricardo, it will take both of us to agree on what to do with them. The options I see are turn them in at the station following protocol, make a hundred thousand dollars selling them, or dump them in the toilet. As senior officer here, I relinquish my vote to you."

With this, Ricardo walked over to the bed, picked up the bags, and went into the bathroom. Not wanting to plug the toilet, he emptied the bags in six batches and flushed the toilet six times. As this was happening, Jorge was glad he had not revealed that the bastard Diaz had approached him first. Jorge was proud of his partner for doing what was right.

# FORTY-SIX

**A**dam was in his office, writing a confidential accounting of the events in Havana, for Bob Zinsky's eyes alone, when his cell phone rang. He sensed who was calling, and his hunch was confirmed when he saw the name on the display. "Hi, Erin. What's up?"

"Adam, can I see you now?"

"Where?"

"How about Starbucks?"

"When?" asked Adam.

"Now."

"I'll be there in ten." Adam wondered what was up. Why were two people with nice offices meeting in a public place? He knew Erin would have a reason, she always did.

As Adam walked over to the old building, he contemplated the rumblings he had been hearing about cybersecurity, and especially a conversation he had had with Eddie Freeman. A lot was being said in the government about election security, but there was an equally persistent undercurrent in Washington, D.C. about the grid, air traffic control, and a variety of industrial and health care entities that were vulnerable. A lot of bad things could happen, and the country had already been introduced to this in a violent way on 9/11. The digital imprint had fully engulfed society and American lives could be held hostage in many more ways than could have even been imagined a generation ago. But there was more. Home-grown terrorists shooting up public places, school shootings, and the conflict with Immigration and Customs Enforcement (ICE) were in the news almost daily. His walk to the old building ended before Adam could list more challenges—but he was sure he hadn't covered them all.

He was glad he was meeting Erin because these thoughts were the kind that he liked to share with a woman who, among her myriad attributes, was always levelheaded and insightful when it came to sorting out the feelings that Adam was prone to harbor.

Entering Starbucks, Adam saw Erin perched on a stool at a round high-top table for two, with a tall cup in front of her and another like it in front of the empty seat opposite. Erin had beat him to the spot and was set with what looked like her usual latte.

"I ordered you a latte and held a table, okay?"

"Absolutely, Erin. Now, tell me what couldn't wait until tonight."

"When Bob Zinsky and I were talking this morning, he asked me what the best thing about working in D.C. was for me."

"What did you say?"

"I asked him if he meant ever or now and he said ever. When I asked if he wanted me to be totally honest, he said absolutely, so I told him."

"What did you say?"

"I told him it was when you and I worked together preparing for and then going to North Korea on assignment. I said I liked the excitement and I liked working with you."

"Thanks, Erin. I liked working with you more than I can say, but where does this get us in this scenario?"

"He asked if I wanted to try it again."

"He said what?"

"I know your hearing is excellent, Colonel Grant, so I won't repeat what I just said."

"Is he serious, Erin?"

"You know the boss doesn't kid around. He means it, and he said that it was our decision. He said he thinks enough of us to at least give it a try. And, in case you didn't know, he was not at all happy about your recent freelancing in Cuba. He liked the end results but not the means. For all I know, he thinks I am the only one who can keep you on the reservation."

"How do you think he will sell this?" said a now serious Adam.

"He said you are doing a great job and that your efforts to downplay SHOP have been effective while at the same time your accomplishments have far exceeded his expectations. On top of that, because SHOP is so unorthodox and at the same time so successful, he feels that this organization doesn't need to be hamstrung by the same rules that limit the usual government agency. For that reason, he is willing to give our working together a try, if you are willing."

"Erin, we both know what we want to do next, but the wedding always seems to take a backseat to what we are doing. What do you want?"

"Adam, all I want is our union to be legal, and soon. Maybe a small ceremony with some family and a few friends ... Let's do that first and then we will deal with the job. I'll tell Bob. Let's set two dates."

"Erin, you still haven't told me why we met here, instead of my office."

"Adam, this is where we had our first date. When I met you a year ago, I knew I had found the man I wanted to be with more than anything, and the last twelve months have only intensified that feeling. And, in case you hadn't noticed, I think I just proposed back to you."

# ABOUT THE AUTHOR

**Eugene M. Helveston, MD**, is emeritus professor of ophthalmology; founder of the section of Pediatric Ophthalmology; and former Chairman of the Department of Ophthalmology at Indiana University School of Medicine, where he provided patient care and teaching, and carried out clinical research.

After authoring hundreds of professional papers and several medical textbooks, he turned to writing for the public. To date, Gene has written and published a nonfiction book, *The Second Decade: Raising Kids to be Happy, Self-Sufficient Adults through WORK,* and several novels. He also gives presentations on writing and publishing.

Recently, Gene launched an online community for seniors called Your Good Life. Check it out and share your comments with Gene at www.yourgoodlife.org.

A native of Detroit, Michigan, Gene resides in Indianapolis. You may contact him directly at ehelveston@msn.com.